Judy Bruce

I0681921

Voices in the Wind

Editions Dedicaces

VOICES IN THE WIND

Front cover design: JOSEPH GENTZLER

Published by:
Editions Dedicaces LLC
12759 NE Whitaker Way, Suite D833
Portland, Oregon, 97230
www.dedicaces.us

Library of Congress Cataloging-in-Publication Data
Bruce, Judy
Voices in the Wind / by Judy Bruce.
p. cm.
ISBN-13: 978-1-77076-465-1 (alk. paper)
ISBN-10: 1-77076-465-8 (alk. paper)

Judy Bruce

Voices in the Wind

For Jenny and Tom

Chapter 1

I wasn't ready to go home. I needed more time to think about the decision that would set the course of my life. Yet I was forced to go now, for the funeral was tomorrow. So I let my Camry take me onto Interstate 80, out of the trees and green, rolling hills of Omaha, westward into the flat dullness of the Great Plains. Cornfields rolled by. Should I take a position at my father's law firm? Wheat. He'd been prepping me for years—maybe my whole life. Grain silos. Or should I accept the job offer in Omaha I'd received only yesterday? Soybeans. A job in my dinky hometown of Dexter, in the middle of nowhere, meant leaving David behind. Center pivot irrigation. But Uncle Bill and that big ole house I loved were west—just about as far west as you could go in Nebraska. Black Angus. I received the Omaha offer because of all that I already knew, all that my father had taught me. Scrub brush. Did I owe him? Did I belong there? Buffalo grass. Was I brave enough to deal with all that haunted me—the voices in the wind?

When the Rocky Mountains punched through the land in the west eons ago, it thrust the land to the east upward, creating the High Plains. My anxiety rose with the elevation. The commerce of the region changed from grain-reaping to hoof-bearing—I was getting close to home. What should I do? Dealing with my father was a must. And I needed to find out why my recent search yielded no official record of my mother's death. My stomach cart wheeled.

I looped off the interstate southward onto Highway 51, proceeding past the ditches of green weeds and crunchy brown grass interspersed with purple prairie clover, white

5

aster, and pink smartweed. Bluffs, the big chunks of land left after a bazillion years of wind and water, rose out of the ground on both sides of the roadway. Harney Street, located a half mile north of town, came much too quickly. And my father, Frank Docket, was much too eager to see me. He must have timed my trip, including my stop for a sandwich at a truck stop in Grand Island, then left work early.

I stopped my car in the double driveway of my home, a stately red-brick two-story with white trim, black shutters, and three attic dormers, and gazed at my father and my uncle who had joined him on the front steps. Juxtaposed, they created an amusing impression—Uncle Bill, age fifty-four, was the robust rancher, weather-hardened and built solid, with a Husker cap covering a thick head of brown-gray hair; next to him stood the equally tall but thin man of fifty-seven years, with the paunch of an office worker and receding brown hair, grayed at the temples, in a white shirt with his navy tie still tight against his neck, bearing a disruption of the face that was meant to be taken as a smile. Uncle Bill greeted me with a bear hug and a big grin. My father thanked me for coming home on short notice then patted my shoulder once as I ascended the front steps into the house. Uncle Bill followed me up the main staircase and plopped my suitcase and garment bag down on my denim comforter.

A strange, fleeting thought struck me—how different would my personality, my life be if Uncle Bill was my father?

"Megan, this has hit your dad real hard," he said. "Not that he would ever talk about what he's feeling. Be nice, okay?"

"C'mon, give me some credit."

"Well, get unpacked and come down. I'm glad you're here, Shortstuff."

Of course I would be kind. Neither of us possessed cranky dispositions, apart from those two days last summer

6

when our air conditioner died. Even then, we were fine once the new unit was installed. But my father possessed a distinct personality. As an attorney, he was so many things— respected, formidable, reserved, prudent, immutable, and successful. But as a father he disappointed me with his inadequate, unresponsive, grave, imperious demeanor. We rarely argued, but when we did, Uncle Bill made an effort to get a ringside seat. My uncle always said I could go toe-to-toe with his brother like nobody he ever met—including himself. I think he enjoyed watching his big brother get taken down a few notches.

The key was to never get drawn into an impulsive spat. When I knew we had a confrontation coming, I thought out my attack and planned my counterattack to the points he would raise. After my boyfriend moved in with me in my Omaha apartment, my father said he wouldn't "subsidize a slacker." My ready response was a check refunding part of my allowance for rent. I countered his bishop with my bishop, his queen with my queen. The result was usually a draw, though I was smart enough to remember his deft moves, his choice words, and his good advice. The dispute often ended with both of us promising "to think about it." But now, as I sat on the edge of my bed, I knew I wasn't ready for all that lay ahead.

I roused myself by checking my texts and phone messages. I left a quick message for David to let him know I'd arrived. Then I located a cleansing cloth in my bag to wipe the travel from my face. After I brushed my teeth, I descended the main staircase to find my father waiting with a large glass of foamy root beer.

"You got the good stuff," I said after I took a long draw.

"You bet. Beulah says to come by when you can. Now come sit down."

I followed my father into the family room. As if on cue, we both stopped then moved together to the window to marvel at the sudden dark clouds. The panhandle had been baking—unusually high temperatures and twenty-seven days without rain had everyone worrying about a drought. Together we looked over to Bill who was grilling steaks on the patio as he watched the sky. The plate stacked with corn on the cob made me wonder if I'd brought floss. My father's voice broke the silence.

"I put new carpet in your office."

I turned to my father. His eyes were softened and his face was slackened with expectation. I knew what he hoped I'd say.

"Father, I just can't think about that tonight. What time is the visitation?"

"Seven to nine."

"So, had he been sick?"

"No. It just happened."

I'd heard my father give cogent closing arguments worthy of Atticus Finch, but I would need to ask Uncle Bill for the details regarding the brain aneurysm. For a moment, I thought he was ready to say more, but he turned back to the window. Why was he so closed off with me?

"How's Mrs. Whitfield?"

"Not good."

Then we heard the rain. At first, the sparse drops just dislodged the dust from the windows in streaks, but then it came down with a whoosh. I ran into the mud room to help Uncle Bill. Before I dashed out into the rain, I stopped my father from following me.

"You'll need to take that suit to the cleaners. You should stay in."

I ran out onto the brick patio, certain my father wouldn't follow after I'd raised such a sensible point. Ever since I had arrived, he'd looked at me with big basset hound eyes—a man most people would liken to a Doberman pinscher. Would he play the good old family dog—obedient, patient, and hopeful—until I said yes?

At supper, we laughed at the moist steaks and the wet corn then became somber for the two hours at the funeral home. Were those soft eyes for me or for the loss of his good friend and law firm partner? I went to bed listening to the rain and wondering about my father.

I awoke early the next morning, my mind and body still on Central Standard Time. With my destination clear in my mind, I donned my watch and tied my brown hair into a pony tail. While I was eating a bowl of Life, Patty White Horse arrived. Patty was our Jane-of-all-trades—our housekeeper, cook, grocery-shopper, counselor, and confidante. At age forty-one, she no longer shot baskets with me, but had remained staunchly loyal to my family for the past thirteen years. Tall and knock-kneed, she was three-quarters Oglala Lakota Sioux, yet an "Apple" as she called herself—red on the outside, white on the inside. She'd spent the first half of her life denying her heritage, the last half embracing it, and the past ten years trying to forget the marriage my father and uncle helped her escape. My father drew up the divorce decree and Uncle Bill pounded her husband after Patty came to work with a black eye. The townspeople considered my uncle a genial man and a good storyteller, but he had a wicked right hook that made me proud.

"Hey, Megan! Glad to see ya. Whatcha doin' up so early?" Patty said as we embraced.

"Ah, just antsy, I guess."

"Congrats on passing the bar exam. Your dad says they're tough."

"Somehow I managed it." I loaded my bowl and spoon in the dishwasher.

"You're gonna be a good lawyer just like your dad."

I smiled at her then looked out the window.

"Well, I know you, so it's no surprise where you're headed. I won't keep you."

"Yeah, we'll talk later."

"Might be much later. I volunteered to help over at the church with the funeral luncheon."

I headed out to the plush green lawn my father worked hard to maintain. With one step, I went from dense green fescue to brown scrub grass, still damp from the night's rain. The south wind pushed at my back, urging me onward as it whipped around the house. I continued north onto the dense patches of the gray-green curly leaves of the buffalo grass. Once the main source of food for the great herds of bison from the frontier days, the hardy tufts still provided forage for white-tailed deer, rabbits, and prairie dogs. This was the rugged land I loved—too full of ravines, gullies, rocky hillcrests, and scrub brush for cattle, vehicles, or people, as my father always contended. But I knew every crag, cranny, and crevice in every hill, butte, and bluff within miles. Along with our concrete basketball court beyond our green ash, this had served as my playground since I was a toddler.

As my feet took me onward, I thought about Patty's compliment. I did want to be a good lawyer. The law was important—you determined the facts then you applied the law. Humans had always tried to make sense of the chaos of our world. God gave us meaning, laws gave us order. So people like my father, and soon me, sought to make right what accidents, criminals, and human weaknesses tore apart. Laws made justice on earth possible. Laws were rational, I was rational.

And yet.

As a toddler, I had been frightened by the jagged shadows the ditches and rocky mounds cast at twilight, though nothing scared me more than the wind. Ever in fear of blowing away, I stayed close to the house. Later when I ventured into the rough land, I imagined I heard sounds in the wind—a cry like that of a woman and moan like that of a child, one trapped in a barrel or a closet. As the voices weren't threatening, I grew up listening, waiting, wondering about what I heard. In time, I dismissed the sounds as

10

imaginary. I decided the child's voice was mine because it seemed to age as I did; later, the deepening of the voice confused me. The woman's voice was surely my longing for a mother. Never did I tell anyone about the sounds that didn't exist. Only on this land did I hear the voices—no other place was so forceful, so haunting.

After I crested a hill I had nicknamed Rufus, a voice stopped me so abruptly that I stumbled to my knees. This was a new voice, a woman's voice, calm and steady and powerful. I looked around for someone who could be speaking, but saw no one. I jumped to my feet and ran back toward the house in a panic. I stopped when I heard another voice, that of a young man, the one I'd heard since childhood. This utterance—never did the voices make words—seemed as if it came from inside a well. I staggered forward only to be halted by the sound of woman's voice that always accompanied the young man's.

Nope. I hadn't heard anything. Yet the memory of the new voice kept me walking at a quickened pace. I checked my watch and was shocked that my brief walk actually took an hour. My mind had traveled farther than my legs. Questions swirled around in my head, but I needed to set them aside and prepare for the funeral.

The next few hours passed slowly. I decided to forgo the pink goo Uncle Bill plopped on his plate in the buffet line of the church's social hall. Instead, I opted for a limp salad with a dollop of French dressing to go with my sandwich of cheap wheat bread, turkey, and a large slathering of mustard, the strong kind they serve at roadside burger joints. I took a glass of iced tea from Glenda Purvis, my former second grade teacher, now retired and sporting recently permed hair tinged with lavender. I sat down with my uncle, while my father stood erect, just behind the shell-shocked Kathy Whitfield and her sons, Zach and Zane, as they greeted the funeral guests entering the hall.

11

Although I needed to talk to my father about Zach, his inadequate junior associate, I felt bad that his father had died. That must feel terrible. I lost my mother when I was three years old, so I didn't remember her. She existed only in a few photos buried in a dresser drawer. The yearning to know her haunted me always.

Needing to think, I roamed the hallway outside the Sunday school classrooms. This trip home was different, but how? Did my sadness feel stronger? Was there something I needed to understand? No, discover. Wait, why did I think that? Was something hidden? The response to my longing had always been passive—was I now to act?

Chapter 2

After the funeral, Uncle Bill and I walked over to Custer's diner, a block and half east of the church. At the luncheon, Uncle Bill had told everyone within earshot that I brought last night's rain. People chuckled and thanked me for breaking the drought. I'd been amused, but now a sense of gloom had settled over me. Yet it wasn't my grief over the death of Mr. Whitfield that made me miserable, it was a larger, more personal feeling of loss that shrouded me like a stifling black mist. Uncle Bill knew better than to force me to talk. Surely, he thought a root beer float would start me talking, and he was probably right. I needed to keep our visit short, as I needed to go back to the cemetery if I was to feel any peace this day.

As we approached the diner, I heard my name called and the sound of sandals clip-clopping up the alley concrete steps. As soon as I caught sight of Beulah, I suggested to Uncle Bill that he get us a booth inside. I walked over to greet her, but she had retreated down the steps and stood waiting for me next to a pile of wood crates outside the restaurant door. I clicked down the steps in my high heels, in the funeral-appropriate height of two inches. Beulah Shuster, aunt of the diner owners Blaine and Dane Shuster, was a spinster often referred to as Bear Lake Beulah for her days brewing root beer in an island shack on the Canadian border waters. Her coarse gray hair was tied back with the last of her aging curls gathered at her neck. Hanging over a thin, veiny body were lime green shorts with a white sleeveless blouse over a white bra, a fashion transgression—though I doubted she cared. She smiled at me, flashing her silver eye tooth. I drew close for I sensed she wanted a confidential conversation.

"I see you're still dressed in your funeral garb," she said. "I had to get outta there. Can't breathe among all those people. I suppose your dad is still there."

"Oh, I'm sure. How are you, Miss Shuster?"

"Heh, fine. And call me Beulah. You're old enough. Though your father always taught you respectful like."

"That was probably Mrs. Crenshaw, but my father would have corrected me if I was out of line."

"No doubt. Say, it's a shame your studyin' for that bar exam took up your summer…you coulda done it for me."

"Done what?"

"Well, I finally heeded your dad's advice to get a will. That young Whitfield was supposed to have been workin' on it…but it's been a month for something so simple."

"A month? That's ridiculous. I'll check on it."

Beulah nodded then looked around. She leaned in close to me. "You know I live in that house across from your dad's firm on Benson Street?"

"Right. The brown brick with the mums."

"Uh, huh. Well, I was thinkin' it was strange for there to be a light on in the middle of the night. I got up to go to the biffy 'bout three last night and I could see a crack of light through one of the front shades."

"Which office?"

"It was the front right, um, west. Then that went off. I thought it wasn't right, so I kept watchin'. Then the light came on in the east window. I was about to call Deputy Bo when it went off. Pretty soon that fancy black pickup came out from the parking lot behind the building."

"That would be Zach's truck."

"Yeah, I thought so. So I didn't call anyone. Just seemed strange to me."

"It is. But keep this to yourself, if you would. I'll check it out."

14

"'Course."

"And you better give us two root beers to go."

She nodded and shuffled to the side screen door. I located Uncle Bill in a booth by the front window. The décor of the diner was best described as functional. Booths covered in forest green vinyl lined the front and left wall, with tables and wooden chairs in the center, and a white Formica counter and six bar stools that ran the length of the right side, all of it over a gray-flecked white linoleum floor. Uncle Bill was reading a copy of the morning's Omaha World-Herald as I slid into the booth.

"Man o man. Hard to tell what'll happen in Egypt. Always wanted to go there and—"

"We need to go. Beulah's bringing our drinks to go."

"What? Why?"

"I'll tell you later. Now don't act like you're rushing."

Uncle Bill studied me as he rose from the table. We met Beulah at the cash register. I took the cups from her as Uncle Bill paid. At the door, I turned back and asked about Thursday's lunch special.

"Trout," she said.

"Hmm. We're having salmon tonight," I said. "I don't think I can handle fish on consecutive days."

"Well, I can't be coordinatin' with your menu ever' day."

I smiled at her. "Thanks. See ya soon."

I told Uncle Bill of my conversation with Beulah. Once back at the funeral home, we climbed, well, I climbed, he stepped into his silver Ford pickup. I directed him to drive down a back street to approach the law office from the rear. Docket Law was at the edge of the commercial area, occupying a ranch-style house converted into law offices. White trim, including a peak at the center, surrounded a red-brown brick exterior, with a concrete, ground-level porch running the length of the building, complete with six white columns and double doors for an entrance.

Uncle Bill and I entered through the back door, which opened to the kitchen and break area at the center rear of the building. The front lobby included a huge desk for the receptionist, in front of a wall of maple with "Docket Law" in gold, to communicate success, and a waiting area with four padded chairs next to a table covered in Sports Illustrated and Better Homes and Gardens. At the front, facing the street, were the offices of the two partners, my father's office on the west side, Mr. Whitfield's office to the east. West of the kitchen was the conference room, and the two smaller offices on the east side were mine and Zach's, along with space for two desks for the staff and a row of maple file cabinets. Unlocking my door, I took a quick peek at my office, which now had the plush tan carpet like that of the two partners' offices. A speckled cream and light brown Berber carpet covered the rest of the flooring, including Zach's office. I wondered what he thought of my upgraded carpet.

My father had a large desk of cherry wood across from the door. Various legal books, including rows of the American Law Report 1st through 6th, manuals on estate planning and workers' compensation, the Nebraska Revised Statutes and their supplements, a collection of Creighton University Alumni Directories, and assorted books on dozens of subjects and areas of law that filled the cherry wood shelves along the entire interior wall. Ugly gold curtains covered a double window that faced the street. The shade was down, as the office had been closed for the day of the funeral. I found nothing amiss in his office, so I selected a key from my ring, and then opened the cherry wood cabinet that ran the length of the wall behind the desk. I pulled Beulah's file and checked to make sure it contained all the personal information for her will. I looked up at Uncle Bill, who was grinning at me.

"What?"

"Just looks like you belong there," he said.

"Yeah, right. This chair is huge... my feet are three inches off the ground. I feel like a Munchkin."

I locked the cabinet then took a last look around the room. I crossed the lobby and searched Mr. Whitfield's office. His office featured oak, in the same arrangement as my father's, with an equally large desk. His office was also tidy, but with the same putrid gold drapes.

"Find anything, Sherlock?" asked Uncle Bill.

"No, well maybe."

"Do all the attorneys have keys to the other offices?"

"No. Father and Mr. Whitfield had a full set, but Zach must have swiped his father's keys to get into these two offices."

"But you have a full set."

"Yeah. But I never took them with me to Omaha."

"Still, he must trust you. What's in the file you plan to swipe?"

"Beulah's personal info. I plan to finish this will today."

After locking the office, I returned to my office and started my computer. I leaned back in my chair to wait for the antiquated system to start. Once it did, I emailed a copy of our firm's will form to my laptop at home. I took a sheet of our law firm letterhead and several pages of our heavy-grade watermarked law firm paper and shoved them into Beulah's file.

"All right, let's get out of here," I said as I rose.

"What does Zach's office look like?" Uncle Bill asked with a grin.

"A disaster."

I locked my door then opened his to mayhem—stacks of paper covered his desk, a jumble of manila file folders were piled haphazardly on file cabinets, books on his bookshelves had fallen over. A bookend even lay on the floor.

"My brother, Mr. Neat-freak, probably hates this mess."

"I hope so."

"What do you mean by that?"

"Come around for supper. You'll find out then."

Uncle Bill was still grinning when he dropped me off at home. Meanwhile, I was plotting the evening's discussion and cringing at the prospect of leaving my father with Zach as the only other attorney in the firm, as if I suddenly felt protective of my father and the firm. And what happens if I leave and take that job in Omaha? Would I ever discover what my guts told me was hidden?

Back at home, I read through the standard Docket Law will. Then I extracted a will from a collection of documents packed tight in a thick, gold envelope I'd brought from my apartment in Omaha. Strange, I had brought those documents when I wasn't even sure I'd stay. I set to work on the will, finishing just in time for supper.

Sure enough, Uncle Bill was present at the meal. My father looked tired, having spent the day in the company of the Whitfield family. Supper consisted of salmon and small talk. After the meal, my father and Uncle Bill wandered off to the family room. I helped Patty clear the dishes; though my father never encouraged me to learn domestic tasks, as if he thought I'd always have a maid, I did help out Patty whenever I was home. Before I joined them, I poured two bourbons on the rocks and handed one to my father, who sat in his big recliner, and the other to Uncle Bill, who sat on the sofa. I settled myself cross-legged on the other end of the sofa from Uncle Bill so I could gauge his reactions. I could feel my father watching my every move. Patty leaned against the threshold of the doorway.

"Mr. Whitfield was a man I always respected," I began. "He's a great loss to you as a friend. He's an even bigger loss as a partner."

My father gave a slight nod.

"But Zach…he's a problem. Who's going to cover for him now?"

"I will concede that he has not lived up to my expectations," said my father.

"Oh, he only works at the firm because his dad brought him on. And you allowed it, just to be nice. Well, nice doesn't cut it. I had to draft Beulah's will because he failed to."

"I assigned that to him over three weeks ago."

"And Lindsey? She's an airhead."

"Make your point."

"I have an offer to work at an Omaha firm…Mabry and Holmes."

Patty gasped. My father's face tightened then he blinked hard several times. I reached over and took Uncle Bill's glass from his hand, noted his shock, then took a gulp and handed the glass back to him. Meanwhile, my father's face had reddened with emotion.

With my voice still raspy from the drink, I said, "So, things will be different—"

My father looked at me with those big basset hound eyes he'd recently acquired. "But you never…I mean I always assumed that you would want to work for me."

The room was so still that I was certain nobody was breathing but for me.

"That's why I said things will be different. For starters, you need to choose—Zach or me. And you need to dump Lindsey, too."

My father leaned back in his chair, nearly grinned, and then took a swig of his drink.

"Okay. But I can't fire him right after his father died."

"No, of course not. Let him clean up his work, but you need to review everything he does. Don't give him any new work, and don't let him know he's getting booted. But you might want to find out why he was in your office last night at about three. He was seen. I checked the office this afternoon, but nothing looked disturbed. He certainly didn't go there to clean up his desk. Oh, and I'd get his father's keys back, too."

My father held his gaze on me then said, "The day Rick died, I made you a partner."

Now it was my turn to be shocked. "How can you do that? I haven't even started work yet. I mean... that's something I would aspire to, but I wouldn't expect it till after several years of service to the firm. Why would you do that?"

Patty handed me a glass of bourbon. I took a sip, felt the burn in my throat, and then grinned at her. Excluding my first semester of law school, I'd never been much of a drinker. Patty must have thought it appropriate, an equalizer of sorts.

Uncle Bill slapped his leg then started laughing. "Well, hell. Aren't you two a pair. Frank, you made Megan a partner to make sure she stays and because it will piss off Zach. You were hopin' he'd leave so you wouldn't have to be the bad guy and fire him."

I smiled then said, "And—"

"What next?" said Uncle Bill, scratching his late-day whiskers.

"You must get rid of those ugly gold curtains. I'll pick out the new ones." I took another sip as Patty and Uncle Bill laughed. "I bet Zach denies being in the office last night. He might even say his dad's keys are lost. If that's the case, we need to change all the locks."

My father smiled at me. "Anything else?"

"Not tonight. Oh, wait." I slid a folder out from under my dad's most recent Time magazine on the coffee table. I handed Beulah's will to my father.

He started to read it then looked up at me. "This isn't the firm's will."

"No, it's better."

He started on the second page.

"It's from Professor Tremaine's estate planning class. Your will is cluttered with all that boilerplate. People can't understand all that garble."

My father grinned as he continued to read. When he finished he looked up at me.

"You can have Rick's office."

"Not yet. Better wait till Zach is gone. We don't want to tick him off. Who knows what he'd do. Trying to steal your clients would only be the start."

My father rose from his chair, handed me the will, and then said, "You better deliver that in the morning. Send her to the bank to get it witnessed and notarized. I don't want her coming to the office. That would only cause trouble."

He walked out of the room with his bourbon. A few moments later, the door to his study clicked shut.

"Well, hell!" said Uncle Bill as he gave me a head noogie. "Shortstuff, you nearly gave me a heart attack. Do you really have another job offer?"

Patty landed on me with a pillow. "What a drama queen. You shocked me good. But you shouldn't scare your dad like that."

I pulled my head out from under the pillow. "I had to make sure he would get rid of Zach. And yes, I did get an offer just this week." I rose.

"Patty, you stayin' for poker?" asked Uncle Bill. "Go get yourself a bourbon and drink it quick. We can do root beer floats when James gets here."

"Why does she need to drink it fast?" I asked.

"He doesn't drink anymore—not since the car accident."

"That's a shame. He loved his brandy."

Things were worse with him than I thought. James Wilson was a beloved neighbor and a rare African American in our county.

I wandered out of the room, concluding it was best to call David right away. I climbed the back stairs, located near the mud and laundry room at the back of the house. Our main staircase was situated near the front of the house, with the living room and my dad's study on one side and the dining room and kitchen on the other. We spent our time in the spacious family room at the back of the house. The living room was for guests and for Patty to dust and vacuum. Otherwise, it was a worthless room filled with stiff, old-fashioned furniture. The family room was its opposite in every way—comfortable and welcoming, with cushy leather furniture, oak wainscoting, a brick fireplace, and a big screen television. The main staircase doubled back, complete with a landing and flared at the base; I'd heard it called grand, I thought it was as ostentatious as the word ostentatious. So I generally used the back staircase—a creaking wood structure with two landings and three cramped flights, which gave me the feeling of climbing upward in a closet. It had scared me as a child, though not as badly as our wobbly basement steps. Maybe I just had a problem with staircases.

My conversation with David was as kind as I could make it, but to the point. He was surprised and angry. When I returned to the kitchen, my father was standing at the sink. I didn't want to see him. Ditching David was painful and it left me feeling sad and mean.

"Megan—"

"What? What more do you want from me?"

Taken aback by my bitchy tone, he shook his head and left the room.

Chapter 3

After my father left, my legs and my anger led me out to the buffalo grass. The plaintive rush of wind on the graying slopes gave the hills an eerie, fantastic quality. The wind proclaimed tragedy—wait, how did I know that? The clouds became denser and darker in the southwest. The descending sun struggled to peek around the clouds. I headed for the north side of the nearest of the Seven Dwarfs, five rocky mounds north of Rufus. There I found a relief from the howling wind and Mr. Wilson, twenty feet away. He didn't see me at first, which gave me time to wonder if I could sneak away rather than break into his thoughts. But he caught sight of me then smiled and approached.

"I confess I often wander deep onto your land," he said. "I knew I'd come across you one of these times."

"Oh, I've never felt like we owned this land. Doesn't feel like anyone does," I said.

"Right now, feels like the wind is trying to blow it away. Feel that, it just shifted…comin' from the west now."

"Patty told me an old Oglala saying: 'A people without history is like the wind on buffalo grass.'"

"We've got history here, no doubt about that."

The wind drove us to the east side of the hill. Overhead a bobolink hung and fluttered in the wind then was swept eastward. The sky darkened in the west, blotting out the day's hazy sun. Despite his company, I heard a woman's voice, the one from before. I gasped—it was Mrs. Wilson. As I turned to the west toward the voice, he did too. Then we stared at each other for a few moments. Mr. Wilson set off walking directly into the wind. I had to jog to keep up with his long stride. Suddenly, he stopped.

"Did you hear something?" he asked.

"Um… no… did you?"

He dropped his head. I plopped onto the ground and started tugging at the buffalo grass. We were quiet for several minutes. The sky continued to darken.

Then I said, "She's not angry."

"But she should be. I was at fault. I don't care what the jury said."

"She doesn't agree. Mr. Wilson, do you hear anyone else?"

"Don't know why, but I have from time to time."

"Tell me."

It's um…well, it must be my dad. I can't say I miss him 'cause I don't remember him. They told me he rotted away in some ditch in Korea."

I felt the wind in my open mouth. I swallowed hard. "I hear a young man at the bottom of a well and a woman."

He scratched his whiskers. "I used to wonder if you heard, all the time you spend out here."

"How could you see me?"

"I head over to the creek… the ground's not so hilly."

"Past Pooper's Canyon?"

He chuckled. "Derek told me about that years ago. Made me promise not to say anything to Vonny. Never did."

I began to feel uncomfortable under his intense gaze.

"Who is the woman?"

"She makes me think of my mother, but I don't really remember her voice, so I don't know, because I always wondered if I was nuts and maybe torturing myself…I don't know…but she haunts me, and sometimes I want her to go away and let me be at peace and other times I can't wait to get out here and listen to—"

Had I really just said all that out loud?

Mr. Wilson patted my shoulder. "And the young man?"

24

"I—I don't know. Years ago I thought it was me, but then he became a man."

"You're not nuts... or we both are. And Lew Eldritch, too."

"Mr. Eldritch comes out here?"

"Sometimes he wanders this way."

Lewis and Cecil "Salt" Eldritch were brothers that lived on the land a couple of miles northeast of our house. The auto accident that killed Mrs. Wilson involved their father, Bob Eldritch, who also died in the accident. Derek had nicknamed Salt "Boo Radley" because of his creepy, washed out look and his unpredictable nature. Uncle Bill told me Salt disappeared after his father's death, but returned recently. I was certain I didn't want to meet up with either brother.

"Strange thing," Mr. Wilson said, "but I work at a cemetery and never hear a thing. Now wouldn't you think that's where I'd hear them?"

"Maybe that's just the stuff of books and—" The look of the darkening sky alarmed me. "That doesn't look good."

Green diffused the western sky as the mud-gray clouds formed a straight horizontal line. Lightning flashed to the west of us, causing the air to tremble and lash at us. Thunder jolted the rocky earth underfoot.

"That's a wall cloud!" he yelled.

By the time a burst of dark cloud spiked downward, we were already running south to our homes. I could run faster, but the wind slashed at us so that I had trouble staying in a straight line. I grabbed his arm to steady myself and to pull him along. We zigzagged through prairie dog holes as we skirted Rufus to the east. The spike plunged to the ground, and became a deadly twister.

In the distance, I could see my father standing at the back door. Mr. Wilson was gasping for air. I steered him toward our house. Suddenly, the sky emptied hail the size of pennies down on us, pounding our heads and shoulders, numbing my brain. With one hand, I hung onto Mr. Wilson, with the other I shielded my face so I could see. My father and Patty ran out to meet us with umbrellas and to help us into the house.

Without a word, we dashed to the basement door. Patty flicked the light on and we descended the steps. Right before the door closed behind me, the hail stopped. I felt my father's hand on my forearm, as if he thought I might fall. Just then, the lights went out. We slowed but continued down the steps into the dark room; I expected to hear Bill clomping down the steps behind us.

At the bottom of the stairs, Patty said, "This way, James, under the stairs."

We all ducked under the stairwell, a structure dubbed the "Cave," reinforced with four by four wood beams and encased in drywall to shelter us from tornadoes and straight-line winds. Our panting broke into the ninety hours of unnerving silence as I scooted forward on the cold concrete. Feeling my way into the safety of blackness, I ran my hand along the drywall, my father's quick breaths behind me. I guess it was okay to be scared if he was.

With a whoosh, Mother Nature roared, blasting away the world above us, and making me feel small and powerless. My father wrapped his arms around my body from behind. I was condensed into a little ball, completely covered by his wet, warm body. I felt his hot breath on the top of my head. I froze—in fear of the charging tornado above us—and in shock from my father's embrace. If he had ever hugged me, it was beyond my recollection.

Suddenly, silence hit again, except for Mr. Wilson's recitation of Psalms 23. I hoped green pastures still existed somewhere. My puny brain failed to imagine still waters anywhere.

"I'm okay, Dad."

He maintained his grip. I was beginning to fight for air in my squished position.

26

"Dad! We're okay."

He loosened his hold, while I resumed normal breathing. Lord above, how he had held me. I felt giddy with emotion.

Mr. Wilson said, "I think we can check now."

"Okay," said my dad. "James, follow me. You two stay here."

In the darkness, the two men made their way to the base of the stairs then clambered upward shaking the wood structure above us.

Patty scooted next to me and said, "You called him, 'Dad.' It's about time you made that a habit."

I was stricken. Had I been the cold one?

Patty and I crawled out of the Cave and waited in the darkness. The door soon opened and light came down the steps. I prepared myself for bad news.

"It's a bit breezy up here," said Mr. Wilson. "You folks got some windows out."

He shone a flashlight down the steps for us. Patty and I ascended the stairs. Before we reached the top, my dad yelled for Bill.

I dashed up the remaining steps. Outside, I quickly ran past my dad and Mr. Wilson. Ahead of us was a ranch house without a roof or a west wall.

I yelled back to Patty, who always carried her cell phone in her jeans pocket, "Call the police!" I ran on then yelled over my shoulder, "And everybody else you can!"

I ran till I reached the edge of the house. I turned to my dad, who was several yards behind. "Was he here?"

"Yes. He left to bring Traddles in, but he called to say he couldn't find him. He's in there."

I climbed over the rubble of the west wall. I could see a gaping hole where the basement stairway had been.

"Bill!" My dad waited for an answer then yelled again.

"I'm okay," my uncle yelled back. "But I can't get out!"

He crawled into the light of the opening. His head and arms were bloody.

I turned to Mr. Wilson. "Do you have a first aid kit? And a rope?"

"I'm on it," he said and ran homeward.

"Patty, call for an ambulance!"

Meanwhile, my dad told Bill to rest and wait. We tried to climb over the crumbled debris of the west wall, but found it too dangerous. Mr. Wilson returned with Patty, who was still making calls.

"You need to lower me down to him," I said to Dad and Mr. Wilson.

"What?" said my dad.

"He needs help now." I took the rope from Mr. Wilson and hurried over to the front door, which I knew would be unlocked. The four of us went through the front door to the stairway hole. I wrapped the rope around me. Mr. Wilson took the rope from me and tied a fancy-looking knot.

"Megan, I don't know," said my dad.

"Listen."

Police sirens blared on Highway 51.

"Now just lower me down there. He's really bleeding."

I looped the rope under my butt then took the first aid kit from Patty. The three of them held onto the rope, releasing it bit by bit as I descended into the basement. I swung around more than I anticipated, which annoyed me. At last, I felt Uncle Bill's hands on my ankles then on my knees. He guided me to the floor.

"Okay!" I yelled as I climbed out of the loop.

I made Uncle Bill sit down as he looked unsteady. I opened the first aid kit and applied gauze to the areas that were bleeding. Rummaging through the box, I found antiseptic. As I squirted each of the bleeding areas with the antiseptic, my uncle hissed in pain. Then I applied a clean pad of gauze to each of the bleeding areas. He had a gash on the side of his head and a four inch laceration on his left forearm. He needed stitches ten minutes ago. I added more gauze then pressed down. I heard the sound of car doors slamming shut. I took out the adhesive tape and tightly secured the gauze pads to his multiple wounds.

"Hurry up!" I yelled to the voices and shadows above. "He needs to get to the hospital. I'm putting him on the rope." I looped the rope under his legs.

"That's the best ropin' you've ever done," he said with a weak smile.

"Don't forget that bison."

He smiled. I tugged twice on the rope. It had begun to drizzle, so I couldn't see well when I looked above.

"Ready?" I called to the people above.

"Yeah!" said a deep voice from above.

Slowly, he ascended. He looked down at me.

"Thanks, Shortstuff."

When his legs disappeared from sight, I scanned the room. It was mostly full of the discarded furniture of two discarded marriages. The wood and metal steps were in a heap next to metal shelves containing extra supplies—paper towels, trash bags, Kleenex boxes, a case of Miller Light, a couple of sleeping bags, and a twelve-pack of toilet paper. The rope dropped down for me. I stepped over to it, but paused when I heard a loud creaking sound. I looked at the floor above me and knew I was in trouble.

"Get back!" I yelled as I ran for the shelves.

I yanked the two sleeping bags from the bottom shelf and tossed them aside as I scrambled into the shelf. I covered my head with my arms and wedged myself tightly against the back of the shelf. A thunderous collision of wood, drywall, and brick erupted then smashed down. Sections of the collapsing floor slammed onto the shelf, which sent it and me crashing onto the concrete floor. I struggled to breathe for several moments. I worked at slowing my breathing to help me regain my senses and to quell the sense of panic that seized my chest. I was alive, but trapped on my left side with the shelf on top of me. Alive, thank you, God, and Uncle Bill safe, thanks again.

I gathered my legs under me and pushed the shelf upward. I got wacked in the head by a package of ultra soft toilet paper that fell from the adjacent shelf then dodged a hunk of flooring that slid off the shelf. I pushed hard on the shelf as I scooted my body, bit by bit, out from under it. I heard yelling above, but could no longer see daylight from where the staircase was and where I had descended. Most of the house had collapsed. I found a place where I could stand then realized I now stood in his bedroom. Sharp pains in my left hip and left arm stabbed me.

"I'm all right!" I yelled to the voices overhead.

"Megan!" my dad yelled.

"I'm fine, Dad. I just need to find a way out."

When I moved beyond the collapsed wall, I saw that light streamed in from several places. Poor Uncle Bill—he was injured and his house was a disaster. Once out of the corner of the basement, the drizzle hit me. I knew what I needed to do. I located the box of trash bags. I carefully stepped over the crumbled drywall, two by eight chunks of wood, and even a few bricks from the front of the house. I tread my way around the bedroom, ever mindful of another crash, but with the roof gone, nothing else could fall. The drizzle was annoying, but it helped to clear the air of drywall dust. After I climbed over the upside down bed, I found his dresser then started bagging his clothes.

Someone called to me then the rope dropped. I shoved the bag through the loop and tugged. The bag rose. Men started shouting down at me to get in the rope. I told them to relax, though I could see that my throbbing elbow was starting to swell. I sent up two more bags of clothes, including some unmentionables, for my uncle would surely mention them if he didn't have any. I pulled out a handful of socks from the dresser that lay on its side then I saw it—a photograph of my dad holding me as toddler on his right hip as my mom was pulling me to her face for a kiss. My dad's face looked strained, but I liked the image of my mom

30

kissing me. I wrapped the snapshot into an old handkerchief then shoved it into my sock on the inside of my jeans leg. Men continued to yell at me from above. I went to my uncle's roll-top desk and shoved all the contents into a bag then sent it up. More yelling. This time the rope came down with my dad inside it. It was time to go.

"I was just coming," I said.

He carefully walked across a hunk of carpeted floor to get to me. He hugged me hard.

"Not fast enough," he said. "You should be dead. The whole house came down."

I showed him the shelf where I hid. He scratched his head.

"Where does he keep his photo albums?" I asked.

"This looks to be his bedroom. Should've been on the shelf in there."

We pulled apart the closet doors. My dad pushed aside beige luggage. The albums were beat up, but we sent them up in the next load.

"Hey, you're bleeding."

I had so many bumps and bruises that I didn't even notice the blood rolling down my head onto my neck.

"That's it. You're going."

"But it's raining, this might be the last chance we have to save his stuff."

"I promise I'll look around."

He looped the rope over my head. I tucked it under my rump and tugged on the rope. I ascended into the rain. As I neared the top, I scrambled over the edge of a wood beam then strong hands pulled me up from under my shoulders. Before I could get my feet on the ground, rancher Big Joe McCready lifted me up in his arms and carried me several feet away from the house. He put me on the wet ground as I pulled the rope over my head. I looked up to see Patty pushing her way past several people. She dropped to her knees and hugged me then saw the blood. Soon she was dabbing at my neck with some cloth. Somebody else pressed a handkerchief to my head. The rope was lowered again, but another plastic bag came up. I smiled. People started asking me questions.

Dazed and achy, started to stand up, but my left hip stiffened and complained, so I sat back down. I grabbed my left arm. Mr. Wilson was now squatting next to me. Another plastic bag came up.

"How's Uncle Bill?"

"He's in the ambulance—waiting for you," said Mr. Wilson. "He'll be okay."

Once again, I was in the arms of Big Joe.

"Mr. McCready, I can walk."

"No need, young lady."

The scene around me was chaotic. A throng of people stood in the yard and street. Cars and trucks lined both sides of the street, with more approaching from both directions. Our insurance agent was busy snapping pictures. People waved at me, some even clapped.

"Mr. Wilson, make my dad get out of there. It's really dangerous."

"Will do. I'll watch over things," he said. "You just get taken care of." He gave my right hand a squeeze. "By the way, I think it's time you called me James."

Big Joe set me in the ambulance. Uncle Bill lay on the gurney. I sat down and Patty climbed in. Two medics were tending to Uncle Bill; one was waving a small flashlight in his eyes. My uncle turned to me and smiled. The rear doors slammed shut and the siren started wailing. One of the medics started tending to my bleeding head as the ambulance started down the road. At the Sidney emergency center, they let me lie down. Soon a doctor was shining the flashlight in my eyes—my headache made me want to smack him. A few minutes later, someone stitched up my head then x-rays of my arm followed. I wanted to go home. My dad finished talking to the doctor then turned to me.

"How's Uncle Bill?" I asked.

"He has a mild concussion. They're keeping him overnight as a precaution. You'll be going home in a few minutes. Nothing is broken."

"But someone has to stay with him, at least till he goes to sleep."

"I will," said my dad. "Patty said she'd stay the night with you. I'll be home later."

Soon, I was back at home, lying on the family room sofa in clean, dry clothes. Tonight I'd need to recover the photo from the cupboard in the laundry room, where I had changed out of my wet clothes, even though I memorized every bit of it—me smiling as my mom kissed me, my dad looking like he was in pain. The dark woman—my mother, my mystery, my loss. I went to sleep wondering how that kiss would feel.

Chapter 4

We moved Uncle Bill into the empty bedroom upstairs. The upper level contained four rooms, with two bedrooms of a larger size on the north side, occupied by me and my dad, each with an adjoining bathroom, both of which could be accessed from the hallway, but I selfishly kept my hall bathroom door locked; otherwise, I'd be forced to decorate the room in pink to repel males, especially the new resident who spent his days around cattle and manure. The third bedroom was used for storage, the fourth as a guest bedroom for the guests who never seemed to visit. At the back of the house on the upper floor were the landings for the back "closet" stairs from below, and the stairs to the attic, a place I'd enjoyed as a kid, but hadn't visited in years.

After Uncle Bill arrived home from the hospital, he spent most of the afternoon asleep on the sofa. My dad insisted I use his recliner, which I did all afternoon. My dad kept busy inspecting the plastic covers on our shattered east windows, walking down to Uncle Bill's house, and coming back to check on us. Patty showed up, even though it was her day off, claiming she was just there to "hang out" with us. Still, she attended to us and spent the day answering the door to visitors who came to bring food. She knew they wanted to check up on Uncle Bill and me, but she told everyone that we were sleeping and shouldn't be disturbed.

Uncle Bill's big oak had been decapitated, so the county folks were busy with chainsaws most of the day. From the patio, I could see that a couple dozen people gathered around Uncle Bill's house, salvaging wood planks from the ruins or sipping lemonade in support. His barn, which was located thirty yards to the north, was spared damage, apart from some loose boards and shingles. A stream of people stacked the planks in the barn. The few personal items the good hearts could recover were stacked in our mud room for later inspection. His Ford pickup was found upside down inside the roofless garage. My dad said the workers and onlookers had been debating that oddity since they arrived this morning. The town's damage was limited to a few downed trees and several broken windows. Even the power shortage was minimal—the county had our power back on before we came home from the hospital last night. It was as if an EF-2 tornado had set out to land directly on Uncle Bill's house then dissipate.

Uncle Bill was truly tired from his rough night at the hospital, but I was groggy because of the pain pills. I needed to get up and walk around on occasion to prevent my left hip from getting too stiff and to get a new supply of ice for my two ice packs. My bruised wrist and elbow along with a jammed shoulder proved painful without my drug, forcing me to use a sling. I wondered how I'd feel tomorrow. Still, I was glad that my arm had taken the blow and not my head.

Late in the afternoon, Uncle Bill's chocolate lab came home. The seventy pound pup, Traddles, was so excited to see Uncle Bill, he piddled on the kitchen linoleum. My dad and I banished him to the mud room after that. However, the poor creature preferred to spend the rest of the afternoon running back and forth from our house to the wreckage of his former house. On occasion, the adorable dimwit would stare at us through the family room window as if he was waiting for us to go and fix his house.

In my forced repose, I often thought of the photograph I'd taken from Uncle Bill's sock drawer. I should be honest about it and tell him I took it, but bringing up the subject of my mother made my guts churn. Maybe I didn't really want to know. No, I did. I was just chicken. Her absence left a void in me, as if a huge bite had been taken out of my body, leaving a hole the yowling wind blew through.

After a couple of days, I'd ditched the drugs and my sling and even regained some mobility in my shoulder. Trucks continued to haul away the debris of Uncle Bill's house from Harney Street. In truth, the street was Road 47, but Grandpa Al made a sign and posted it on the corner. When county officials objected, he told them Harney was the name of a Dexter resident who died in World War II. Cheyenne County's silent acceptance encouraged Grandpa, later my dad or my uncle, to repaint the black metal pole every three years since 1946.

Besides the "Pocket Docket," people seemed to enjoy inventing new names for me, such as the "Shelf Elf," "Lara Croft, House Raider," and the "Hero of Harney Street." The tornado had left the people of western Cheyenne County disturbed, so I never protested the names. Yet, I wished for their demise—I was trying to build respect in the community as an attorney—so the elf reference, in particular, annoyed me. It didn't help my cause that a couple of the monikers had made the local papers in the surrounding counties.

Yet, I was restless and eager to make the trip out to the cemetery as I'd planned. Late the next morning, I parked my car in the shade of an old bur oak. I limped along the rows, past family names I knew—Mulvey, Phillips, Wolf, Collins, Petersen, Schmidt—the immigrants of prior centuries remembered in granite, probably the fine-grained variety from the quarries of Vermont. A tractor started as a car exited the lot. James had waited to finish mowing until the mourners left. We exchanged waves then he started down a row. I could see the tracks left by his mowing, straight and neat, row after row.

At a plot I stopped. The name etched into the silver granite made me gulp. It had been a full year, but that didn't stop my tears. A gust of wind blew by and I gasped. The wildflowers slipped from my hand. It was if Mrs. Wilson was trying to comfort me. I dropped to my knees as emotion thickened in my throat.

In a flash, I was a young girl again and Mrs. Wilson was smiling at me, her skin soft and smooth, the color of milk chocolate. Over the years, her hands had become rougher from hot water and detergent, but she had always warmed me with a smile or a kind word. I had been the playmate and arbiter of her two children, Derek and Yvonne. Never did a snack time pass without me hoping for Mrs. Wilson's touch on my shoulder as she placed milk glasses or a plate of cookies on the table. I went to sleep thinking about that hand on my shoulder—warm, firm, never in a hurry to move. Though not a beauty, I loved her round face and coffee-brown eyes that squeezed to slits when she laughed or smiled. Now she was gone.

The Wilsons moved into an old family house my father and my uncle decided to sell a couple of years after my father and I moved from Omaha. Uncle Bill told me in later years that several buyers had been rejected till they found a family with playmates for me. It didn't matter to my father that the neighbors were African American, and nobody in town would ever question Mr. Frank Docket about it. James once told me that he and his wife had grown tired of all the violence and pollution in Denver. So the only black family in the area moved next door and James started his landscaping business. On the playground, I punched both of the Breeley brothers for insulting my friends. Once, a tall fifth-grader called Derek the N-word. I couldn't reach his nose so I kicked him in the balls instead. The victims knew they'd get in trouble, so they never tattled on me. No one challenged me because they knew Derek would protect me, and they were afraid of him simply because he was black.

By the time Vonny reached high school, she had become the class beauty—slender, graceful, and exotic to

38

the ranch and small town boys of our school. She had the high cheek bones of her dad and the smooth chocolate skin of her mom. They were even more scared of her. Unfortunately, we had lost touch after her mother's death. She had imposed a distance between herself and anybody from her youth. So my calls and emails went unanswered, which only amplified the pain I still felt over the death of Mrs. Wilson and the wound the family carried.

I wiped my eyes when James approached. How did he manage to drive by his wife's grave every week?

"Hello, Mr. Wilson, ah, James. Gotta get used to that."

"And hello to you. You're walking better today."

We both watched my flowers blowing past several graves.

"I'm sorry about the flowers. Took me a half hour to pick them...now they're making a mess."

"Don't worry about it. Maybe the plover will use it for nesting."

We settled into an uncomfortable silence. I wanted to hug him, but my legs had turned to lead, so I remained next to Mrs. Wilson's grave. I swept my hand over the dark green grass that covered the grave.

"I don't know where you could find better grass than this. Augusta National, maybe," I said.

"Thanks. I dug up that sandy clay we put down on all the sites and put in my own mix. Then I put down the best seed I could find. Nursed it every day from March to May. Now I just need to keep it watered. I'll make sure Mr. Whitfield's grave is tended to."

Silence struck again. I think we were afraid to say anything that might cause pain in the other. He pursed his lips together several times, a nervous tic I last saw as he lay in the hospital bed after the car accident.

"Derek feels bad he couldn't get here sooner. But he's coming tonight, kind of late."

"Good. Haven't seen him in a while. Say, why don't you come over for supper and poker tonight? Uncle Bill needs to perk up. He's still on drugs, so it's a good thing we don't use money."

James chuckled. "He can't bluff worth a darn…he'll be even worse."

I smiled as I rose from the ground. "Deuces wild. See ya later."

James waved over his shoulder as he headed to the tractor. I walked on till I passed a sign indicating the Whispering Pines section. Mrs. Ruth Crenshaw's marker was flat, so harder to find. She had been my nanny from the time my father and I moved from Omaha to the family homestead until I was twelve. Uncle Bill told me I couldn't master her name at age three, so she had become "Crenny" to me, "Miz Crenny" when my father was around. Mrs. Crenshaw decided the name was affectionately bestowed, so she permitted it; when Uncle Bill adopted its use she decided it was flirtatiously bestowed, so she permitted it. During this entire time she was "grandma age" and more supervisor than playmate. I fondly remembered her chocolate pudding, cinnamon rolls, and fresh-squeezed lemonade. She said things like "Jesus made crusts, too," and "Vegetables are not for liking, they're for eating," then scolded me when I would laugh in response. We worked our way through the Laura Ingalls Wilder's Little House on the Prairie books, with me listening at first, then in time reading to her. My father credited her with my ability to read at an early age. I don't know if that was true, but she made her mark—I diligently ate my crusts and veggies, and I loved to read.

One day, I returned from shooting baskets with Derek and Vonny to discover a woman who would never wake up from her nap. My father was convinced I had suffered great trauma in finding a dead person. But I thought otherwise— death was blue skin, glassy eyes, and permanent absence— therefore no mystery for me. I had been saddened by her

40

sudden absence, but pleased with the addition of Patty to my life.

Patty didn't make great desserts, but she taught me card games and provided friendship. She told me stories about the people on the reservation and often quoted the wise old men and women of the Lakota tribe, people who had seen much and suffered greatly. Whether they were proud, tragic, hostile, kind, or mysterious, I always sensed they understood what I never could—loss.

Chapter 5

Early the next morning, I hobbled through a slow two-mile run that made me wheeze like a smoker. Dexter's elevation was roughly 5000 feet, a sharp change from Omaha, a river city. I'd spent the summer with my butt glued to my desk chair, studying for the bar—my lungs and my legs felt it. As I walked around to the back of the house, I heard my father and Uncle Bill talking. The windows had been opened for a "Texas cool," the airing out of our house before we needed to shut windows and curtains and submit to air conditioning. I headed for the back door until the conversation made me stop.

"She's been going out to that wasteland since she was little. Why? It's just dirt and scraggily grass," my dad said.

"It's like she's looking for something," said Uncle Bill. "I asked Patty once and she thinks Megan 'feels' something when she's out there."

"What does that mean?"

"Don't know. She's got your brains, but she's also got some Docket ranching blood. Maybe she's got some connection to the land. Still…"

"What?"

"It's like she knows something."

Silence ensued. I debated whether to go ask what I knew, but that sounded absurd, and a question my father could easily dodge. I retreated across the patio and headed to the Wilson house where I knocked on the kitchen door. I pounded again then went around to the side of the brown brick two-story and threw pebbles at Derek's window. Eventually, Derek threw open the window.

"Miggy, could you be any more obnoxious?"

"Well, I'll try if you want me to," I said. "Now get up, lazy bones."

I went around to the kitchen door just as he was pulling on a T-shirt. I'd forgotten how buff he was. He had a pink lower lip and a head that was square as a block—it had taken all of his teen years to grow into it. When he hit six feet in eighth grade, people started thinking he would be the Michael Jordan of western Nebraska, but he wasn't. He was a good player and a good all-around athlete, but he wasn't special. I knew the truth early on—he was a nerd. He liked math games. Math games! He was a worthy opponent in chess, but I refused to ever consider math fun. He would play one-on-one with me, but I found no amusement in disassembling the family stereo. As I was all about rules, I pointed out that his tinkering would void the warranty. He didn't care, nor did his parents, who were content with a nerdy son and a bookworm daughter. After college, Derek took a job doing really techy computer work that I didn't understand enough to remember. The closest job to home he could get was in Scottsbluff, ninety miles to the north.

"You look like hell," I said as I stepped into the kitchen.

"I was hoping to sleep in, but I knew you'd be around to pester me," he said as he tied his basketball shoes. "You don't look too beat up. Come on."

In no time, we were out on the basketball court. My first few shots went off the front rim. He hit half of his initial shots.

"You stink. But I guess a big shot attorney doesn't need to play silly games anymore."

"Hey, I'm not a big shot anything. Though I have decided to work for my father."

"No, kidding? Last time we talked you said he was a hammer trying to pound you into a junior version of him. I thought you planned to stay away."

44

"Yeah…well."

"How are you gonna work with Zach, the Witless?"

"I'm not."

Derek stared at me for a moment then laughed. "Already having your way. I gotta eat something."

We went back to his house. While he ate seven waffles, I quizzed him on his girlfriend. Suddenly, he changed the subject.

"Did you know my dad doesn't drive anymore?"

"Yeah, I heard. And no brandy…he loved his brandy and Dickens. So, how does he get around?"

"Your dad or Bill takes him to work. He grabs groceries on his walk home."

"I'm sorry."

"But we're both really grateful for what your dad did for us."

"Hey, we both know that intersection. You can't see cars coming over that hill, especially if Bob Eldritch is doing sixty, like the witness said. So your dad pulls from the stop sign…he can't anticipate what's going to happen…you can't see what you can't see."

"That's not Vonny's take on it," he said.

"What do you mean?"

He rinsed off his plate and loaded it in the dishwasher in an illogical place. I smirked but held my tongue.

"She won't return his calls. Nothing. The way she sees it, Dad pulled from a stop sign and he'd been drinking and Mom died."

"Oh, that's crap and you know it. His blood alcohol reading was so low it wasn't even admissible in court. Damn, it pisses me off that she's acting this way. She won't return my calls either. Do you think your Aunt Thelma is behind it?"

"Maybe."

We were quiet for a few minutes. I needed to get out of that kitchen, for it reminded me too much of Mrs. Wilson. At my urging, we set out northward. We walked for several minutes in silence. We reached a bluff that reached two hundred feet high and about twice as long. As children, we had called it Big Leo, and the name stuck. At the base, we paused to eye each other then bolted up the first several yards. My long-legged buddy quickly gained the advantage that was lost as soon as we hit the lose footing among the small rocks. I used my hands to pull on the scrub weeds as I scrambled up the slope, wincing at the soreness in my hip and shoulder. I kept my body low as I moved over rock, weed, and grass to the rocky outcropping at the top. I plopped down on a flat boulder as the laboring Derek was forced to crawl the last several yards.

"C'mon, you bean-pole!" I said as I tried to catch my breath.

"Yeah, yeah, I'm coming. Whose idea was this?"

"Yours... the first time you tried to race me up here. You were always challenging me. Remember the first time I beat you at basketball?"

"The first, the many."

"Just till that summer when you grew a foot. I never won after that."

"Six inches."

"Still, I bet it kept your mom at the sewing machine all that—"

I think we both stopped breathing. For ten minutes we gazed out over rough land to the west, the wind whipping at our clothes. We watched shadows of clouds move across the valley below. I felt rotten that I'd brought up the subject of his mother. But it was done.

"I can't believe she's gone," I said.

"It's easier to be away—but it's a kick in the gut to come home."

I could hear the choke in his voice.

"You loved her, too," he said.

I started to speak, but nothing came out. Finally, I managed, "Did—"

"Of course she knew. Hell, you lit up every time you were near her. Then you'd get to talking to my dad… sometimes I didn't think we'd ever get rid of you."

I smiled. "Well, your dad is fun. Wanna swap?"

"Whaddya mean? Your dad is big stuff…he's a well-respected man. All my dad does is mow lawns and manage a cemetery."

"Who cares? He's great company. My father is a stone wall. Your dad's company builds them."

"Man, he always scared me."

"Really?" I asked.

"Well, maybe not scared, but wouldn't want to cross him."

"I always made a point of it."

"I know." He nudged me with his elbow. "And I do remember exactly when you first beat me at B-ball."

I grinned. "You sulked."

"Then I kissed you."

"Then I slugged you. And you never did that again."

In a flash, I felt that pink lip on mine. Our embrace was as physical as any of our one-on-one basketball games. Clutching hard, kissing hard, we toppled over into the scrub weeds. We paused long enough to suck in the thin high plains air. He rolled on top of me as we kissed again. Then I pulled back.

"We can't," I said.

"Why not?"

"Your mother. Geez, buddy. I wasn't even allowed in your room. What would she think?"

His head sunk into the dirt. I lifted it up. "This will have to do," I said as I brushed the dirt off his forehead. "I always wanted to kiss you…ever since that day you got in trouble for playing ball without your shirt."

"Mom gave me hell for that."

"Know what?"

"What?"

"You had dinosaur sheets and I've got about ten seconds left of air in my body. You're squishing the life out of me."

Derek rolled off to the side. "Sorry."

"Besides, it feels kind of…um…incestuous."

"Ooh, ick. Yeah, I guess so."

After a few moments of uncomfortable silence, we suddenly started to laugh.

"Listen, there's lots of stuff I need to deal with," I said. "But one thing I know—I don't want to mess up the best part of growing up."

"I get ya."

I broke the resulting silence with a question of great cultural import: "Why do blacks call whites 'crackers'?"

Derek laughed. "I have no idea."

"I mean, think about it. What about Ry Krisp? Isn't that dark?"

"Oh, Miggy, you think too much. Hey, are you still with your boyfriend?"

"Well, I guess not since I'm staying here. I need to drive back to Omaha over the weekend to get my stuff. I don't have any work clothes here."

"I get ya."

"What does that mean?"

"You don't like getting put in a corner. So this is your way out of the relationship."

"That's not fair—"

"Do you love him?"

"Isn't that personal?"

"Sure. Do ya?"

"Nah. Do you love Tina?"

"Yeah," he said and smiled. "C'mon, let's get off this giant boulder."

We scooted down the side of the bluff, kicking up a cloud of dust. At one point, Derek reached out to grab my arm. He must have thought I was going to fall. At the

48

bottom, we laughed at each other, covered in dust that stuck to our sweat. We headed south toward our homes. Suddenly, a sharp pain stabbed at my ribs. What the hell? I winced and bent over with pain then hid my reaction by pretending to dig pebbles out of my shoe. I gasped for air, but was able to straighten. I had to ask Derek to repeat his question.

"I said, what are you gonna do about David?" he asked.

"Oh, you remembered his name. Ah, hell. What can I do? He's a grad student…and will be for some time. And he's got two jobs in Omaha. Can't see how he could move."

"You're in a tough spot, shorty."

"Yeah, and I'm spending the afternoon sorting through a dead man's office."

"That'll be creepy."

"I suppose. Mostly it's gonna be a bitch finding out all the work he left undone."

As soon as Derek entered his back door, I stumbled back out to Rufus. By now, the pain felt more like it came from my chest, as my guts stirred. What was going on? I sat down on the north side of Rufus so nobody could see me. Was I sick? I didn't hear the woman or Mrs. Wilson, but the young man groaned. Wait, no he didn't because he's not there. Megan, listen to your brain—not there. Nobody's there. A blanket of sadness bound me tightly. Nobody's there.

Chapter 6

I met my dad at Custer's for an early lunch, where we settled on a general course of action for Rick's office and files, even though we couldn't talk freely with customers all around us. Once we were back at the firm, I began with the most essential task—I moved my fabric swivel chair into Mr. Whitfield's office. His chair, like my father's, was clearly meant for a tall person. It was a fine grade of leather, which I envied, but the chair didn't adjust down to my height. And I thought it smelled like him, but maybe that was my imagination. As people would be coming from lunch, I shut the door, seeking to be inconspicuous in my afternoon's task. I took the note from my purse with Mr. Whitfield's computer password then logged in. Thankfully, I could easily match the pending cases in the paper files with its corresponding Word Document entry.

I sorted the files by topic—I knew the basics of wills and trusts, workers' comp, family law, bankruptcy, and personal injury matters, but the bulk of his work involved taxation and accounting issues for corporations, small businesses, and individuals. I couldn't possibly do this work. Most of the people in our part of Cheyenne County were not well-educated, but they knew bullshit when it was flung at them. These cases exceeded my knowledge and interest, and I knew my dad wasn't well-versed in these matters. Mr. Whitfield handled accounting and taxation issues for this town and Kimball, to the west, and Sidney, to the east, and from surrounding counties. My father wouldn't want to give up these clients for that meant losing the wills, divorces, and auto accident claims that derived from pleased customers.

We'd need to hire other attorneys to work these cases. The spreadsheets on these files made my eyes glaze over.

While I was trying to refocus my eyes, a soft tap sounded on the door. It opened and closed before I could yank my brain out of some case involving dissolution of Personal Service Corporations. I looked up as Melanie Sundstrom set a cardboard box next to the desk. Melanie was the assistant for the firm. She was a college-educated hometown woman a few years older than me, who had come back home only to find limited options. She had the bright blonde hair, complete with the pink scalp, only a true Nordic possessed, as if her parents mated north of the Arctic Circle.

"I thought you might need a box for Mr. Whitfield's personal things," she said.

"Great, thanks," I said as I glanced down at the box. "Oh, wait, you've left papers—"

She raised her hand to silence me. "For later," she said.

"My father always undervalued you, I won't do the same," I said as I folded and placed the papers in my purse.

She smiled then slipped out of the room. The door closed with the soft click of the latch. I was tempted to look at the mystery papers, but I didn't want to get caught reading something I didn't want to explain. I moved on to a file concerning a claim of fraud in the retirement fund of a C Corporation. Shit.

It was nearly three o'clock before Zach figured out I was in the office. The door swung open without a knock. He walked in then stopped, folding his arms across his chest. Zach possessed extreme good-looks and the swagger of a hot-shot former jock, yet I could tell he was going soft around the middle. He'd only been an associate attorney in the firm for about six months, as it took him a second try to pass the bar.

"How come I'm not doing this?" he asked.

"You have your own work. This is my assigned work for now." Then I decided to soften my tone. "We thought it might…

make you sad. You've got a heavy enough dose right now. But it's smart of you to come right back to work, to get things normal. I'll box up his personal things for you to take home."

"Yeah, all right. Hey, I'm glad you're here."

Zach was a liar.

"Thanks. Looks like Lindsey's feeding you well."

He turned and walked out the door. That last shot was mean, but it just slipped out. I should feel bad about it, but I didn't.

Zach was my first lover.

Zach had dated Lindsey Schnitzel since middle school. I got along with him; we'd known each other since kindergarten. He oozed conceit, but he kept it in check whenever he was around my father. And as our fathers were law partners, the Whitfields socialized with us. I thought Kathy, his mother, was uppity, but she meant so little to me that I simply ignored her when I wasn't required to be polite.

Lindsey and I were adversaries from the time her family moved to town at age thirteen. An excellent athlete with long blonde hair and a pretty face, she was also a ditz and a complete bitch. As teammates and as classmates, she took every opportunity to criticize me. I conceded that she was the superior athlete; still, I was a good teammate, for I'd feed her great passes in basketball and soccer so she could score. But I had a mean streak. Her hair started to darken so she started coloring it. Once when I was in Sidney—you couldn't do anything in Dexter without someone seeing you—I bought a bottle of hair dye in her shade, pitched the contents, cut out the front of the box, and then used duct tape to stick it on the front of her locker at school. Her hair became a school joke after that. I'm sure she suspected me, but she had no proof and too many enemies to accuse me. I was the superior student—she was lazy—and that annoyed the hell out of me. But her biggest fault by far was not that she was white trash, which was a circumstance of her family's position in life that could be overlooked, but it was the fact that she made no effort to better herself. She sought to marry out of her predicament, which was pathetic. She used push-up bras, heavy makeup, and a sleazy motel off Highway 30 to snare Zach.

The summer after my junior year, I achieved my ultimate revenge by snatching Zach away from Lindsey when she was off at a summer basketball camp. Derek and Vonny were in Denver spending a few weeks with relatives and I was lonely. So Zach and I started playing ping pong in the afternoons at his house. We'd play a game or two then he'd feel the need to complain about Lindsey, so I'd sit and listen quietly. I never gave any advice, but one day I commented that he deserved to be treated better. We made out till his mother came home from cards at the Meyer house.

The next day, his mother left again. We played one game then he unrolled a sleeping bag and took a handful of condoms out of his pocket. Suddenly, things turned serious and fast-moving. I'd thought of sex as the thing that excluded me from what adults and the rest of the world knew—a club I wished to join. I wanted to crawl inside that sleeping bag and feel his warm body on mine; I wanted him to unzip the bag and remove my T-shirt and shorts; I wanted to feel that his excitement was caused by me; I wanted to go back every weekday afternoon for the next two weeks; I just didn't want him. I hadn't meant for it to go this far. And it went beyond any desire for revenge—it went beyond anything I sought to handle.

Thankfully, Patty guessed my predicament. She helped make clear what my muddled brain could not. With Lindsey's return only days away, I needed to act fast. Patty told me what I should do and I did it. First, I stood on Zach's front porch and told him that "it wasn't working" and we needed to "step back." His mouth was still open when I got into my car. Immediately after that quick conversation, I met several of my friends by arrangement at the Pizza Shoppe. I told them that I had been seeing Zach while Lindsey was away, but I ended it and told him to go back to Lindsey. It

54

became the hot news in our little town. I'm sure Zach heard about it, but he never made any effort to deny our relationship. Unless Zach squealed on me, nobody knew the extent of our fling. Of course, Lindsey heard about it. She broke up with Zach, though it didn't last. She was stuck. She followed him to Lincoln where he attended the University of Nebraska for undergrad and law school while she worked as a waitress, after flunking out her first semester.

The experience left me feeling dizzy and humiliated. It was if I had taken a huge step forward in life only to land on my head. I was pleased to get away from the situation, but I missed the sex. I acted nonchalant about it when Derek and Vonny returned. I'm sure they wondered about it, though they seemed to know not to press me. By the time school started, it was old news. Bear Lake Beulah told me that by Labor Day, the chatter had stopped. I think the start of the Nebraska football season provided a distraction. It only made me a bigger fan.

Later in my dad's office, I heard myself say, "I don't care what happens to Lindsey, but I do want Zach to land on his feet."

"For someone who was interviewing at other law firms, you're acting territorial, to put it nicely," my dad said. "Now you're telling me that we can't handle much of Rick's work."

"Neither of us have the tax and accounting background to do the work. I think we'll need to farm it out. And a good chunk of it doesn't really need a lawyer, it needs a tax specialist."

"You're telling me what to do."

I squirmed a bit. "Well, I'm just telling you my opinion."

He smiled just a pinch. "You sound like you've made this firm yours. Glad to hear it. By the way, I think you're right about needing help. But I think we might find a way to keep our clients and get the work done." He opened his top desk drawer, extracted a business card, and handed it to me.

"There's an accountant in Sidney that Rick consulted. Contact this man and talk with him about handling the substantive issues with these cases."

The name Brian Culhane seemed familiar. "Mr. Whitfield needed help?"

"Sure. In turn, Rick could handle the legal end of some of Mr. Culhane's taxation accounts. It worked pretty well. And you can call him Rick now."

"We're going to need a great deal of help. I know the estate taxation basics, but I haven't had an accounting class since my sophomore year in college."

"Then think how long it's been for me."

He smiled and I smiled back. I'd spent the afternoon feeling overwhelmed, but now I was feeling optimistic and pleased with my choice to stay at the firm with my father. I'd go see this accountant, who I pictured as some skeletal, middle-aged man with a pallid, austere countenance, bifocals, and a limp-fish handshake. Strange, I thought the big confrontation would be with my father, but the decision had become sudden and easy, though I was still wondering why. Now the battle would be to disconnect from Omaha and David. I sighed.

"But first you have an unpleasant task ahead this weekend."

"Yes." I was unable to elaborate on ending my relationship with David. I felt my father's eyes on me. "And I don't have any work clothes, just these chinos and a dress for a funeral. I've been putting together a wardrobe…that takes time… with lots of alterations, even on petite suits."

"I can't remember the last time I bought a suit or even a tie without your assistance."

"You would have done just fine. Well, I better go see what else I can do in Mr. Whitfield's—Ricks's office. I'll leave after breakfast."

In the late afternoon, I stopped outside my dad's closed door. His voice was sharp and he dominated the conversation. The jargon of the other man indicated he was an attorney.

"Lloyd, your arguments are weak to the point of absurdity…and you know it. I don't think we have anything to discuss until you and your client come to your senses."

Yeah, that was my father berating an adversary. Did he really need to be so harsh?

I ended up staying at the firm till long after everyone else had left. At home, I ate a warmed up supper then headed out to the hills. Like I did every night, I stood on Rufus and waited. Her voice, the new voice, no longer made me want to run—just as I'd never wanted to flee the voice of the young man in the well or the sad voice of the woman. I watched the sun descend into twilight as the nearest grassy mound grew rosy-gray, the distant ones blue. To the south, the prairie rolled out like a dusty blanket.

The land seemed to draw me onward, so I went. To the west, I walked through the five small buttes Vonny had dubbed the "Seven Dwarfs" before she could count. I climbed a rocky-crested mound then wandered among the others. I gazed north to the largest bluff in the area, "The Beast," but decided to forgo scaling it. I sat down in the crunchy-dry grass and thought of the games I had played with Derek and Vonny as kids—cowboys, Indians, pioneers, buffalo hunters, posse, train robbers. In the winter, we were stuck building forts in the Wilson basement and our attic. First, I played G.I. Joes with Derek then Barbies with Vonny when she was old enough. Vonny would get mad at me, claiming that all I wanted to do was build the house, I never wanted to play. She tried to make the Barbies date the G.I. Joes Derek had abandoned, but it never worked—the Barbies were always over-dressed and over-eager—at least that's what I always said. No, my imagination worked much better out in the rough, open land where the Wilson kids seemed pleased to follow along with the scenarios I concocted. I suppose most of those ideas came from the westerns and war movies we constantly watched, though I always created a twist at the end that delighted them.

As the sky began to streak a darker blue, I headed south toward home, where I discovered Derek waiting at the top of Rufus.

"Do you still have all your old G.I. Joes?" I asked.

He laughed. "No, don't you remember? I found that if I put the head in my dad's workbench clamp and pulled, all the appendages fell off."

"Oh, yeah. Vonny was ticked off."

"Mom and Dad boxed up all her old Barbies though. Why? Were you thinking of playing with them?"

"No, but it would be more fun than where I'm going tomorrow."

"This sucks. I get here and you leave."

We turned and headed homeward.

"Well, if I wasn't expecting a fight with David, I'd invite you. I could use the muscle. I don't think he'll be cooperative. He's really pissed. My dad's letting me take the Great White Shark and I'm going to borrow Uncle Bill's dolly."

"I didn't think you had any furniture out there."

"Nah, just a ton of law books. Those suckers are heavy."

"Well, I could make myself scarce for the arguing then pop in when you needed the brawn."

"Yeah, that would work. We could leave early and make the trip there and back in one day. It won't too tough if we take turns driving."

Derek and I were halfway to Omaha when we switched and he drove the SUV. I took the pages from my purse that Melanie had given me. I had been too tired last night when I first read them, but the meaning was now clear.

"Shit!"

A startled Derek jerked the wheel. "What?"

"I can't share firm business with you, but let's just say we've had a breach, and we need better security, and we need it fast."

"A breach. Hmm. Well, I don't know what that might mean, Miggy, but I can help with security. It's my specialty. You need to update your dinosaur computer system and give it better protection."

"We need to do a number of things pronto."

The first thing we needed to accomplish was to fire Zach; otherwise, he'd embezzle even more. He'd started small, but he'd get bolder. Lindsey may have helped him or even suggested it.

"While you're battling with David, I can work on some ideas."

"We definitely need levels of security. I'm grateful to the person who discovered this, but I had no idea she could access this information."

"Man, I'm so curious I could bust."

"Let it go for now. I need to be able to tell my father that I didn't tell anyone else."

Once in Omaha, I dropped Derek at a coffee shop with free Wi-Fi. Then I proceeded on to the rental house in an older part of town. Oaks and silver maples formed a canopy of shade over the street and the lawns, still a lush green in late August after a hot summer. I'd lived in the top level of the furnished house since my junior year in college, but it was never home to me. The tenant on the lower floor changed nearly every year; a new student or two from Creighton University or the University of Nebraska at Omaha would boisterously settle in, happy to be out of the dorm.

David's car wasn't parked out front, though I expected him anytime. He would need to shower after his lawn care job before he went to his Saturday night bartending job. I had boxed up nearly all of my books and covered my clothes in plastic bags before he arrived. Strange, but I hadn't felt any misgiving about my action. In fact, I enjoyed the space from him these last few days. We dated for less than a year before he got evicted and persuaded me to let him move in. I now realized that had been a huge mistake. At home, everyone gave me space; here, I felt confined and resentful. Looking back, I'd been unhappy and bitchy this summer. This was the right thing to do. In my next relationship, I would heed my desire for privacy.

David had dark brown hair, green eyes, and the deep tan and trim physique of an outdoor laborer, yet he lacked drive. He considered himself a scholar, but he couldn't seem to finish his Master's thesis. During the school year, he worked as a teaching assistant and tutor, but he was a long way from getting the doctoral degree he'd need to become a professor. He had been wonderful company, but he was slovenly, lazy, too fond of booze, and he never worked out. I never brought him home to Dexter, maybe because he was so unlike any of the men I had grown up with. They were all tough and hard working. I could never tell Uncle Bill that I dated a man who wrote poetry—even if I did think it was good.

I was nearly done packing when David walked through the door. So handsome, so soft.

"I can't believe you're doing this to me," he said.

"I'm sorry. I don't want to hurt you, but it's time." I truly felt bad about hurting him, but I sensed it would soon pass for me.

"We've been together for almost two years, and you go away and dump me in a day."

"I guess I needed the distance to see things clearly."

When he wandered into the kitchen, I called Derek. Then he came back to argue with me.

"My student loans are going to kick in soon. What am I going to do? I can't pay for this apartment on my own."

"I paid the rent through November."

"I'm not going to sponge off you...or actually, your father."

"Who cares who pays the landlord? You can send me a check for your half," I said, though I knew he wouldn't and soon couldn't.

"Yeah, well you just cut off my balls."

I groaned—such drama. I heard a knock at the door. I weaved through the stack of boxes then opened the door to Derek.

"Oh, I get it cowgirl. You've been riding a black stallion."

"David, it's not that way. Derek's mother was like—" My throat seemed to contract. "We played G.I. Joes when we were kids. I made snowmen with him and his sister."

"Derek, right. Sorry about your mom. Megan still makes snowmen."

"I know. There's one out in her yard every year when I come home from Christmas," said Derek. "Dude, you got it wrong. She's like my sister...it's always been that way. I've got a girlfriend—she's black and tall, not white and shrimpy."

"All right, my mistake."

We stood in silence for a few moments then Derek picked up a box and went out the door. David went to the bedroom and slammed the door shut. He either just gave up or didn't have the balls to fight for me. I grabbed a load of clothes and followed Derek. It was done.

The ride home was quiet initially. Then we began to discuss the new computer system and the security software the firm needed. I needed to stop Derek every time he started to get too technical.

"First, I need to tell my father about...what I've learned. I hope he's still up when I get home. You'll need to talk him through all of this tomorrow. Then we'll need to get moving on it. How soon could we get the system?"

"I can pick it up and bring it back in the same day. It takes several hours to transfer information from one hard drive to another."

"We're already running behind. My father won't want to lose a work day."

I began to work through the process in my mind. After Rick's death, this would make for the continuation of Docket Law Firm's transformation. And "transformation" was the word I used when I talked to my dad that night. The reason for the speed at which it must take place was clear to my father when I told him Zach had embezzled $995.00 from the firm's account. He hadn't even used much cunning in the theft, which probably indicated his lack of experience. Perhaps he hoped a small sum would go unnoticed in the midst of the firm's changes.

Dad was quiet for several minutes, but his face flushed red with anger.

"Bourbon?" I suggested.

He nodded. I came back with drinks for both of us.

"What do you think about it?" he asked.

"I'm angry and I'm hurt. I didn't think he'd do something like this. It seems a strange time to be deceitful."

He took a few swigs as I suggested a plan of action.

"Yes, good," he said, looking tired. "I guess I shouldn't have been so trusting."

"Well, soon he'll be gone and it will be just you and me."

He looked at me with those basset hound eyes.

"And new curtains."

He smiled at me then rose. "I hope they're not hot pink."

"Lime green."

He chuckled. "I'm going to bed." He picked up the pages of evidence and his drink then went into the kitchen. He poured the rest of his bourbon down the drain. I took a couple of sips then poured my drink down the drain. We wasted a great deal of bourbon.

The next morning, I went for a run then did my curl-ups, back sit-ups, and push-ups. While I showered, I bemoaned the fact that the town lacked a decent fitness center. I'd be working too many hours to take time for a drive to Kimball or Sidney. I took all the plastic off my clothes from Omaha then selected slacks and a blouse for church. The rest of my belongings remained in the boxes stacked in the foyer. Uncle Bill rode with my dad and me in the Shark. At the First Presbyterian Church of Dexter, Derek and Mr. Wilson, then later Patty joined us in the pew. Derek looked good in a suit and tie, though I wondered why he was so dressed up. The other men, including my father, wore slacks and a dress shirt.

After lunch, by appointment, Derek arrived, still in his suit, with his laptop and print outs of options for a new computer system. My father listened attentively, even though he didn't really understand techy lingo—he had no idea what a gigabyte was and probably didn't care as long as the system worked. I predicted which system he would pick, just by knowing my father so well. He would and did reject the most expensive hard drive, as well as the cheapest. He did like the idea of larger monitors. And he wanted the most advanced security software. My father handed over the company credit card then Derek placed the order. The transformation would take place on Monday night.

But first, I had to meet with the accountant in Sidney on Monday morning. I hoped he would have good breath at least, for it seemed likely that I would be working with this man in the foreseeable future. His office was located on the main drag of Sidney, in a red brick building with a limestone façade. The outside door opened to a lobby with a receptionist behind a desk and in front of some exotic-looking plant with a green trunk and drooping branchlets. On each side of the room were three offices with glass windows covered by vertical blinds to the right of each door. I was directed to the first office on the right. I knocked on a fine-grained maple wood door partially opened, and then heard the command to enter. As I pushed the door back, I spotted a large photo of the great sea of red at Memorial Stadium on a football Saturday. In an instant, I knew where I'd heard that name several years ago. Then I saw the man.

Oh, my.

Chapter 7

Instead of the limp-fish handshake I'd expected before I arrived, his warm, muscular hand slid into mine and held on a couple of seconds longer than was socially acceptable for strangers. What an excellent specimen of man.

"Megan Docket, it's nice to meet you," he said.

"Brian Culhane. Thank you for meeting with me. How's your leg?"

"Healed long ago."

We exchanged pleasantries while I politely examined the fine Homo sapien before me. He wore a well-made, navy blue suit, a white shirt, a red silk tie, and a light tan. His hair, cut short on the sides, was sandy blond except on the top where the longer strands were tinged blond. Surrounding his medium brown eyes were eye lashes I envied. Even as he exceeded my height by more than a foot, he didn't make me feel small, even though he was the experienced tax specialist and I was the rookie seeking aid.

I even liked his office. The outer office featured an oblong, wood veneer table. I accepted an apple juice, and then followed him into his private office, complete with an L-shaped oak desk and row of file cabinets on the left and a window with a view of the street on the right. Despite the stadium photo, the rooms lacked a photo of him in his playing days. I liked him better for its omission, though I would have enjoyed drooling over it, for I loved men in skin-tight football pants. Yet my attention was mostly focused on him as he removed his blazer then draped it over the back of his chair. Pecs, lats, and tight abs. Part of my mind continued the small talk—he'd been to our firm and knew my father as the man who had successfully defended his brother in an auto accident

65

case—the other part wanted him to continue removing his clothing. He had a smile that lit me up, a quick wit, and the kindness to laugh at my attempts at humor.

In time, we proceeded to business. Back at the oblong table, I laid my charcoal gray blazer over the back of a chair then began to remove files from my brand-new leather attaché case. By the reflection in the outer glass of the stadium photo, I could see that he was checking me out. Pleased, I felt my skin warm; I hoped I wasn't perspiring through my blouse. I quizzed him on issues pertaining to Rick's tax and accounting cases. He knew everything I needed him to know. Once we had covered my basic questions, he invited me to an early lunch. On the way back to Dexter, his baritone voice reverberated in my head.

In the afternoon, Kimball Draperies and Wallpaper arrived to install the new drapes. The curtains for both main offices were neutral, and appropriately dull, but at least they weren't ugly. Each was beige in a woven texture with pinstripes of navy for my dad's office and burgundy for my office, which I'd claim tomorrow.

Just after the installation was completed, I received a call from Derek telling me that he had arrived with the new system and would wait at home for my call. A few minutes later, my dad called me into his office. A rotund man in a tight gray suit with a thick matte of graying hair shook my hand.

"Mr. Don Talmadge owns Balmont Industries," said my dad.

"Oh, yes, good to meet you, sir," I said as I shook his hand. "I interviewed four witnesses from the accident last summer."

"I'm concerned this will go before a jury," Don said as we sat down in the client chairs.

"You should be," said my dad. "Don, the liability is clear, your company truck had not been maintained... opposing counsel will get into evidence that the truck had a loose wheel... and the injuries are severe."

"And the jury will assume your company has deep pockets," I added.

"But a jury award will be in the papers and I'm afraid of that kind of publicity," said Don. "What can we do? We must settle this."

My dad nodded. "So, what do we do, Megan?"

"We have an appointment with Bernie Pratt on Friday. We need to convince him that we are serious about settlement."

"Then do so."

I stared back at my dad for a couple of moments then reached across his desk and picked up the thick file, located the attorney's phone number, and then turned my dad's phone around on his desk and dialed. Well aware that I was being tested, I was fortunate to get connected to the attorney just when I needed to.

"Yes, Mr. Pratt, this is Megan Docket calling to confirm our appointment with you on Friday at eleven o'clock…yes, in your Scottsbluff office… Bernie, okay. Now we do have a few things to discuss, but it's important that you know Balmont Industries believes the injuries your client suffered are terrible…right, the surgery to insert the steel rod in her leg…and Mrs. Adkins also needed a halo cast on her head…true, the jury will see those photos and I bet you'll blow those up to poster size to increase jury sympathy…but you should know that Balmont Industries truly feels that the dementia caused by the closed head trauma for a woman of fifty-one is horrific, beyond comprehension really…yes, her family is devastated, that's understandable, so we need to find a settlement amount that satisfies your client and her family. After all, it would be best for them to receive the money as soon as possible so Elaine can begin her adult care program. This won't get to a jury for another four months."

I glanced at my dad, who gave me a wink—he'd never done that in my entire life. I concluded the call with the attorney then turned to Don.

"Bernie says he's looking forward to the appointment on Friday and he would call Tim, the husband, and advise him of my message."

Melanie knocked on the door and summoned me to a phone call from Brian. Don shook my hand as I rose to leave. Later my dad came to my office and I informed him that Mr. Culhane would be out to our office for a portion of each afternoon this week.

"Oh, and that White Spruce out front would make a great Christmas tree," I said.

"A Christmas tree?"

"Sure. We could string lights on it…give the firm a nice touch."

"Okay, but only if you promise not to do it yourself. It's probably thirty feet high."

"Deal. I'll get Uncle Bill to figure it out."

"Oh, by the way. Don wants us, mostly you, to visit his company office. He says he has two unmarried sons."

I was still laughing when he went out the door.

I continued sifting through Rick's client files, determining the ones I could work on or work on with my dad, from those that needed Brian Culhane's expertise. Every summer through college and law school I'd studied the firm's old and current cases and listened to my dad explain the nuts and bolts, the procedural—and the meaty parts, the substantive aspects of cases. So, now that I had graduated from law school, I possessed a decent knowledge of the areas of law my father practiced.

Meanwhile, my dad called all of Rick's clients to assure them that with the help of an experienced tax specialist we would continue to handle their cases if they wished. At five o'clock, he came to my office and told me we hadn't lost a single account. He also informed me that Zach and Lindsey were preparing to leave. I said we should do likewise to avoid arousing any suspicion—we'd soon be back.

After supper, I walked out to the hills, but didn't get beyond Rufus. Wispy clouds hung overhead as the wind hurried by, taunting me with doubts. I couldn't relax enough to hear anything clearly in my head, apart from snippets of my conversation with Brian. So I went back to the firm to wait for Sherman Locksmiths and Security from Sidney to arrive. The plan was for the locksmith to appear at twilight and begin changing the interior then the exterior locks. Perhaps I was over-cautious, but I wanted the transformation to proceed quietly, unnoticed if possible.

Jack Sherman arrived as planned; he and his assistant began changing the interior door locks and the cabinet locks in the four offices. While Sherman was changing the front door lock and installing the dead bolt, a maroon Chrysler pulled into the house across the street. The car stopped in the driveway instead of pulling into the garage. When Beulah exited her car, I stepped out onto the porch and waved at her. She waved back then drove into the garage. Every time I peeked out a front window that night, she was sitting in her chair by the front window peering over at us. I guess we were more interesting than any show on TV.

Once the locksmiths left, I made the necessary phone calls. Within minutes, the crew arrived. Derek, Uncle Bill, and Mr. Wilson carried in the computer components. My dad and Patty carried in tool boxes. Derek started the data transfer between the old and new hard drives, while Mr. Wilson set up the new monitors and keyboards at the three desks. Uncle Bill brought in his dolly and wheeled Zach's file cabinets into Dad's office. Meanwhile, Patty and I boxed up Zach and Lindsey's personal items, which were left in the kitchen. Then we moved everything of mine from my old office to my new office. Patty told me she was pleased to be part of our sneaky doings. Meanwhile, my dad removed Rick's old name plate from his door and attached a shiny new one with my name. He gave me a grin when he finished. Once all the hauling was finished, Uncle Bill and James undertook the important task of making root beer floats.

I summoned my dad and Derek into Zach's office then closed the door.

"We need to know what Zach was doing, with his cases and with… whatever else," I said. "But we don't know his password." I looked at Derek. "Do you know how to hack into a computer?"

"Yeah, but I don't do it."

"Even if it's hacking into our own system?"

"Mr. Docket?"

"He's not even an employee anymore… I've terminated him on our books, so to speak." said my dad. "I guess we need to see if he's done anything else. Derek, go ahead. By the way, what do we do with the old hard drives?"

"Send them home with my dad and me. We have a kick-ass sledgehammer."

I looked on while Derek started typing on Zach's keyboard; different screens flashed on and off the monitor till my eyes started to blur.

"Let's see what you can find," said my dad. "Then I'll need all his file information on each of his files transferred to my computer." He sighed. "I need a root beer. Let's go. Derek, we'll bring you one."

Once we left the room, I steered him to the front desk. "For the sake of security, we're not even going to connect the receptionist's laptop to the Internet and certainly not to our system. The only information it will have is a list of appointments. Melanie's computer will have only what she needs. Access to confidential information will be blocked."

"And what receptionist are you referring to? Ours is gone, or will be at eight o'clock in the morning. What a nightmare."

"Tomorrow, I'll call Mrs. Purvis. Maybe she'll fill in for a while," I said as we walked to the kitchen. "People say she makes good coffee."

We gulped down our root beer floats as I passed out the new keys to my dad. I demonstrated how the new floor bolt lock worked on the front and rear doors. Then Patty and I tidied up each room while Derek finished. Derek did discover that Zach had tried to make a late day theft, but my dad had already terminated Zach's access to our finances, so the attempt failed. After James stashed the computer boxes in the basement, we went home.

Despite the late hour, I felt wired. Early tomorrow we'd have our showdown with Zach. I slept fitfully in those few short hours, and even rose before dawn. I had been running before work each day, but I didn't feel like it today. The thought of Brian's appointment in the afternoon gave me a boost. I showered and breakfasted and was ready to leave when my dad shuffled down to the kitchen in his robe.

"I know, we both look like hell," I said.

"Lousy day ahead. I've never fired anyone in my life."

I nodded to him. "I might as well go in. I'll see you there."

At eight o'clock, Zach and Lindsey arrived. I summoned my dad then let Zach fumble at the back door lock till he grew angry. I opened the door when Dad entered the kitchen. As Zach and Lindsey entered the room, I handed each of them a box with their personal items. Too flabbergasted to speak, they looked at my dad then at me then back to him again.

He looked at Zach then Lindsey. "This is the end for both of you. You'll get your paychecks on Friday."

Lindsey's face reddened. "But why?"

"I'll give you 995 reasons," I said. "Do you think we're stupid?"

Zach's jaw dropped.

"By the way, the locks aren't the only things that have changed. We have a completely new computer system with loads of security and extra building security. Oh, and I'm a partner."

Zach clamped his mouth shut.

"Zach, why?" asked my dad.

I could hear the hurt in his voice. I fumed.

"I would have given you an advance or a loan... anything," he said.

For a few moments, Zach looked down then he turned and walked back to his pick up. Lindsey watched him go then looked back to me, unable to face her boss.

"You're behind this...I know it!" she hissed. "And you were one of my bridesmaids. You bitch!"

Delighted, I held my tongue and let her walk away. My dad departed for his office. I heard his door close. Both Melanie and Derek had discreetly stayed in their cars during the exchange. When Zach's pick up roared out of the parking lot, they emerged. I gave Melanie her keys and a quick rundown on the changes. I roused my dad and he attended Derek's tutorial on the new computer and security system.

In private, I thanked Melanie for the information that had exposed Zach. I asked her to mind the receptionist's desk and phone then apologized for the trouble. I told her of Mr. Culhane's arrival in the afternoon and his role. She and Derek then helped me move a short banquet table from the basement to my office. I stacked some of the tax files on it then expressed my gratitude to Derek and told him to send us a bill.

I called Glenda Purvis, who was absolutely thrilled by our request. She was in our office within the hour with a load of pastries from the bakery. My former second grade teacher apologized for not bringing homemade goods. I showed her how to work the phone and the laptop, though she was mostly eager to make us coffee. I followed her to the kitchen.

"I think you may find the office dull. The first appointment isn't until ten-thirty," I said.

"Oh, don't you worry, dear. And I've seen the television shows, so I know all about attorney-client privilege. I won't be prattling away like some women do. You can count on me.

Do you like scones? I make good cinnamon ones. Oh, dear Megan, I always knew you'd do well."

She thanked me three times for the job before I could make my escape. Obviously, she had been bored in her retirement. I gave my dad a quick report on our new employee. I enjoyed seeing his face brighten. Then I could tell his mind had reverted back to Zach. He ran his hand across his chin a few times, which meant he needed to think and I needed to leave.

Back in my office, I concocted a scheme. I told Mrs. Purvis, who now insisted I call her Glenda as she was working for me, that I needed to step out for a half hour or so. I drove over to Custer's and walked down the steps and knocked on the screen door. Beulah soon emerged.

"Why, Megan. Don't you look spiffy. That's a purty blouse... some would call it burgundy, I say wine. Now, what's up?"

"You'll soon be hearing that Zach and Lindsey were fired this morning. The whole town will be talking about it. And it looks callous on our part since his dad was buried just a few days ago. But we didn't do anything that didn't need to be done quickly."

Her eyebrows rose for an instant, and then she nodded. "He did something fishy...more than just ignoring an old lady's will."

"Yes. But I'm concerned that people will think badly of my dad for firing him."

She nodded. "So, I should say somethin', right?"

"'Fishy' is a good word. Don't act like you know much... just say that you overheard something."

"Gotcha. I'll wait till people start talkin' then I'll mutter somethin' vague, but insinuatin'. It'll spread faster than a grass fire."

"I knew you were the person I could count on."

She beamed so broadly her silver tooth glimmered. I'd made two elderly women very happy that morning.

When I returned to my office, two boxes sat on my desk. The first was a set of embossed business cards in my name; the second was an engraved silver business card holder. After my dad's appointment left, we walked the two blocks over to Custer's. From across the room, Beulah shook her head, which meant the news had not yet hit.

I arrived home with just enough time to change and clean up before supper. Patty and Uncle Bill seemed particularly animated.

"So, what're we going to do tonight?" asked Patty. "Rob the Wells Fargo?"

"Nah," I said. "It seems silly to steal from your own bank."

"I felt like a jewel thief…no a Bond Girl, and Megan you were M and the rest of you guys were James Bond," said Patty.

"Until I started scooping ice cream," said Uncle Bill. "That's not very Bond-like. But Megan, I gotta say, you took the bull by the horns. Your dad here says everything was working fine this morning and Zach is history. And you've hired a tax guy. Shortstuff, you've taken over."

Out of the corner of my eye, I saw Dad smile.

"Well, credit Derek for making the computers work without a glitch," I said. "I told Derek to send us a bill for his time, but I bet he won't."

"He'll get paid," my dad said.

After supper, Uncle Bill told me that he'd never seen his brother so pleased. As I walked out to Rufus, I considered the comment. It was true, my dad looked content tonight. I guess as long as we kept to business, he and I would get along fine. But I was still unable to ask him why I couldn't find any record of my mother's death. The desire to research her struck me suddenly, well, maybe not, as I often thought about her, or the lack of her. It seemed natural to be curious, though unnatural for me to be so cowardly about asking my father and my uncle about it. Why did I hesitate?

Chapter 8

The next morning, I began daily meetings with my dad to discuss the nitty-gritty of running a law firm—payroll, insurance for the staff and building, paying utilities and property taxes, setting retainer fees, strategies for serving papers, hiring experts, and even the best techniques for plunging the toilets. We also divvied up all the firm's files. I took over all of Zach's clients and some of the estate planning, personal injury, insurance, divorce, and bankruptcy cases— areas of law I'd previously worked on with my dad. He retained all of his cases and added Rick's taxation disputes.

Brian arrived early for his appointment. I had been studying the tiny print of an auto insurance policy on toiletpaper-thin pages when Glenda rang me. My hands had begun to sweat in anticipation of his arrival. I loved to see men in suits. It had been a huge distraction my first year in law school—all the seniors with clerking jobs strutting down the halls and through the library. After a month, I moved to a study carrel against the wall to avoid flunking. And here in front of me stood the tax stud, again shaking my hand, again holding on too long—or was it me?—in a fine, charcoal gray suit. We chatted about the hot weather, and the upcoming Husker football and volleyball seasons. We then turned our attention to the mounds of tax and accounting files.

"Look," I said. "These are yours, if you want them. I've separated out the files I can work with my father. But, I can't do this stuff. Some of it is just tax work. But Rick handled all that…even basic 1040 filings. Otherwise, Dexter people had to drive to Kimball or Sidney."

"Some of it looks complicated and may need legal action," he said.

"Then we can do that. But my father thinks he needs to hash out contracts for these files, like you did with Rick."

"That's fine. I bet you could do some of these simple tax forms."

"No, thanks. Columns of numbers make my head spin. Give me this stuff." I put my hand on a pile of manila folders. "I can understand auto accidents and divorces and wills, but I have no interest in your taxation issues."

"I see. You like the people work. Fair enough. I'll work through these files, sign the contracts, and record my time for each file."

"Can you spend that much time away from your office?"

"No," he said with a chuckle. "But my calls and emails will come to me anyway." He held up his smart phone.

He plugged in his laptop while I wheeled Rick's clunky chair up to the banquet table, which sat next to my desk. He started studying his new files, while I tried to concentrate on the insurance policy. On occasion he took a tax form out of his black leather brief case. We worked through the rest of the afternoon, occasionally taking phone calls the other tried not to hear. We also spent a good deal of time in chit chat. He was the third of four kids, all born in Chicago. When Brian was a high school freshman, his father took a management job at Cabela's in Sidney. His mother died of brain cancer his senior year. After he graduated from Nebraska and passed the C.P.A. test, he worked at one of the prestigious accounting firms in Omaha for six years before returning to Sidney to strike out on his own.

I was glad we were in one of our quiet times when my father came to visit before he departed for the day. We worked another hour then we decided to finish for the day. It hadn't been my most productive afternoon. I was distracted by him even when we weren't talking. I walked with him to the front door. He took my hand in both of his in a handshake that didn't feel much like one. We stood frozen for a few moments then he let go of my hand and went out the door. I wanted to go after him, but I didn't. When I did turn to go back to my office, my face flushed warm.

On Wednesday, the news hit, confirming my sense of disquietude as I entered the diner. I sat in a booth, waiting for my father and sipping a root beer. Tom Sedlacek, a boyhood chum of Zach's, approached me. I greeted him in a friendly manner.

"What's this about Zach getting fired?" Tom asked, as the diner became quiet.

"I will confirm that he has left the firm," I said loud enough so that anyone interested could hear my reply. "Beyond that, I will not comment."

"This sucks. I bet it was your doing."

"Zach was a good friend of mine. You know that. But this was business. Now if your family wants to take the handling of your grandfather's estate from Frank Docket and give it to Zach, they may do so at any time."

With a huff, Tom took a step back then turned around to find my father standing behind him. He dropped his head and skulked away. My father sat down, gave me a nod, and then picked up the menu. I looked over to the counter at Beulah. She returned my look with a grin—she knew it was her turn.

Brian arrived that afternoon, again early. We spent the afternoon hours in proximity. For Thursday, we decided to meet for lunch at the Pizza Shoppe—I didn't want Beulah's scrutiny at Custer's. Late in the day, Melanie brought in correspondence that had been sent to my father. Two letters belonged to my cases; the third pertained to one of Brian's tax files. I waved goodbye to my father as he walked across the lobby to the back door. The office was quiet. I rose from my chair to find the appropriate file for the letter.

He reached to his left just as I reached for a file on the center of the table. His shoulder and my waist met. We froze, even as his shoulder became warmer by the moment, or maybe that was me. I looked down at the point of contact, expecting it to glow. In a flash, I was in his arms and our lips were pressed together. He became so impassioned, my feet left the floor. His powerful arms drew me even closer. I made a sort of a moan, or maybe it was a whimper. Then his hands were on both sides of my hips, pulling them into his. We both groaned.

He backed away then pulled the window shade down and closed the curtains as I locked the door and turned off the overhead light. A flash of electricity arced between us, drawing us together again. I started working on his tie as he unbuttoned my blouse by the light of the desk lamp. He laid his shirt on the floor as I ogled his meaty pecs. Then we were two lean, hard bodies—my body fat was concentrated in ideal locations—melded together in heat and excitement. When we came up for air, I took the opportunity to explore his muscles. He was beyond buff—he was sculpted. I slid out from under him to nestle onto his back. I just had to see and feel it.

As I ran my fingers over his shoulder blades, he asked, "Taking inventory?"

I laughed. He tolerated my appreciation for as long as he could, then I was back on his shirt exploding again. Rick was found on this floor, dead. Now we were making love where a man possibly died. I didn't mention it, I was too busy. In time, we lay together, side-by-side.

"You know, we've made love without even going on a date," I said.

"Are you trying to make me feel cheap?" he asked. "First you ravage me then you call me easy."

I grinned. He traced his fingers along the contours of my six-pack. I giggled.

"Really, you lure me here, claiming you had work to give me then suddenly you're undoing my tie and popping buttons off my shirt."

"We better find those. I don't want to try to explain them."

As I nestled my face into his neck, two thoughts came to mind—one, we had made love without any protection, though I was on the Pill, and two, I was shocked that I had found someone so quickly who lit me up. I had expected a long drought in the love department. Now I was lying next to a man who'd made me whimper and giggle in the same day.

"So let's go on a date," he said, breaking into my thoughts.

"I dunno. I just met you on Monday."

"Tomorrow night."

"But what will your girlfriend think?"

"I'd like that to be you." He kissed me softly.

After supper, I went out to the hills. As I crested the first of the rocky-topped Seven Dwarfs, a woman's voice whispered then swirled around me. Was it the power of suggestion that I'd imagine a woman's voice just as I was thinking about my mother, the thin, dark woman in the wedding photograph? She would have been my age when they married. Full-blooded Lebanese, she gave off a mysterious aura, or was it my imagination at work again? It was even debatable whether she was Syrian or Lebanese as my great-grandparents left the Middle East fifty years before Lebanon became a country. But I didn't want to claim Syria, which was ruled by a family of murderous monarchs. In fact, I usually told people I was half Phoenician—it was less likely to conjure images of terrorists and bombed cities. Ancient Phoenicia was a country of great sea mariners—though it was just as likely that I was a descendant of pirates. Its greatest downside was that it lacked Jesus Christ—he didn't show up on earth for another thousand years—a huge bummer. My

Syrian-Phoenician people were forced to wait for St. Paul to learn of the Gospel.

Uncle Bill liked to muse over our ancestry deriving from two victim groups—Arab Christians on my mother's side and Celts on his family's side. He had a collection of books on Celtic history and even one devoted to the musings of Celtic bards that I had bought him last summer. Once my uncle admitted he thought Arab women were exotic. When I asked him if that made me exotic, he'd said I was as fascinating as a Number 2 pencil. Even my father had laughed. Clearly, Brian hadn't thought of me as a writing implement. I flushed warm thinking about our late afternoon romp. Perhaps that's all he thought it was—just playtime, though he did ask me out. I guess we'd both need to figure it out. For the time being, I enjoyed the memory of our love making.

A thought stopped me halfway down one of the dwarfs—had my father played matchmaker? I knew at least two other accountants contributed time to Rick's cases, but my father had sent me to the young stud. Maybe he felt guilty for taking me away from Omaha and David. Strange, while I was plotting how to secure the firm, he was planning my love life. That seemed haywire, though I wasn't ready to complain.

I walked onward; the western sky was streaked in lavender and yellow as the sun dipped toward the horizon. This beautiful, rugged land had proved too wild for most settlers from generations ago, when they roamed from the east, looking for open land, or fled from the Civil War, looking for peace. The cowboys, the herds, and my great-grandparents had stayed. The bison disappeared, only to be revived by a strong dose of nostalgia. Many who came here did find peace—my father seemed content. Uncle Bill loved the wide open land and his stinky cows. I loved the wild, untamed, unspoiled land, away from the glass and concrete of the city, with its Pepsi spills on the sidewalks and trash in the sewer grates. I was glad to be here.

And yet.

I wasn't at peace. One part of my life felt settled—I had come home to the shelter my father had always provided and the start of my career; but the other part of my life felt muddled—I came home to a sense of disquiet and yearning so powerful I imagined I heard the voices of dead people. And yet, this place beckoned to me as if I could someday find the nebulous answers I sought.

At the top of a hill, the three voices intermingled, yet remained subdued as they had been since I first crested Rufus. Perhaps the presence of Brian in my mind quieted them tonight. I headed home as the last swaths of orange lit the western sky.

The next afternoon, I looked up to find Brian standing in my office. I had been so absorbed in the Schumacher bankruptcy details that I only noticed him because I felt a disturbance in the Force.

"Have I been evicted?" he asked.

We moved behind the door and kissed.

"Yes, to my old office. But I gave you the big chair. I can't work with you sitting beside me. How am I supposed to concentrate when I'm busy thinking how much I want to pop your buttons? Oh, here." I took three shirt buttons from the pockets of my slacks and put them in his warm, strong hand.

He smiled and shoved the buttons in his pocket as I walked to my desk.

"Okay, now I have a serious question," he said. "What do I do about the files that Rick worked on with John Donaldson and Drew Mensching from Sidney?

"I don't know. I think you need to ask my dad. My objectivity has been compromised."

"Well, after our date, let's compromise ourselves again."

We planned to go to dinner and a movie, but we just kept talking till I thought the restaurant would claim rent. He was easy to talk to and we laughed at the same things. We went back to his Sidney apartment, where I knew we would stop talking long enough to compromise ourselves. It was beige and more beige, yet tidy.

"I know, it's dull. I've been here two years, but haven't felt like doing anything more than clean it. It's not even my furniture."

With a smirk, he agreed to show me a poster of him in his playing days. He crawled into his closet, then pulled out a rolled up two by three foot poster of him in his Nebraska uniform, red jersey, white pants, posed for a tackle.

"Hot stuff. Ever get a concussion?" I asked.

"Nope. It happens really easy though. But I never tackled with my head. I mean…why bust your butt in college just to bash your brains out?"

"Or blow out your ACL halfway through your senior season."

He chuckled. "That hurt like hell."

"Second team Big 12…did you ever think of playing past college?"

"Great times, but no. I was so dang pleased to get that scholarship money…but I knew it would be four years and done, time to get serious. Most sports are dressed-up kids games anyway."

"I suppose so."

"My mom was happy that I got the money. I know she was concerned about that." He rolled up the poster, set it on his dresser, and then sat on the edge of his bed. "One of the assistant coaches came to her funeral. I thought that was nice."

I sat down next to him. "Did she get to see you graduate from high school?"

"She was still alive, but no. The number of brain tumors doubled, so they stopped treating her. She was fighting headaches and seizures and sleeping a lot. You lose use of your muscles at the end and you even have to be fed. That was my job in the mornings before school. My brother and I carried her wherever she needed to go. She was very brave through it all, very trusting in God. In time, swallowing was hard and she could only drink through a straw. We'd crush her meds and put it in her juice. After graduation, she lost the ability to even smile. Everything was shutting down. But the pain stopped, too. At the end, she just slept all the time. Then she slipped into a coma and was gone in a day." He looked over at me. "Uh, sorry... got carried away."

"That's okay. I bet it was terrible for you. It's probably good to talk about it."

That has to be tough for a mother to leave behind her kids. I wondered if my mom had a chance to think about me before she died.

"She didn't even make it a year. I grew up fast— couldn't stay a young, stupid male after all that."

I had done something young and stupid at that age with a guy I recently helped fire.

"What... um... I've never heard your mother mentioned."

I felt closer to him—till now.

"She died when I was just a toddler. Car accident."

"Do you remember her?"

I rose and went back to the poster. "No."

"I thought you said it was good to talk about it."

"There isn't much to say about absence."

I really wanted to change the subject. I was pleased he could open up to me, but I was certain it shrunk his balls to recall something so painful. He wrapped his arms around my shoulders from behind and we stood in silence for a couple of minutes. I unrolled the poster, and then traced my finger down over his numbers to his groin. He kissed my neck. I moved my finger from one knee upward then from the other knee upward. He stepped to the bed to throw the covers back then scooped me off the floor and kissed me. I had never been scooped—I loved it—so Tarzan and Jane. He set me on the bed and I yanked my blouse over my head then threw it on the floor. He kissed me just below my belly button then unbuttoned my khakis. I decided I liked white sheets after all.

84

Chapter 9

The next afternoon, my dad asked me to come to his office. Brian was seated in one of the chairs in front of my dad's desk, with his laptop perched on the corner of the desk.

"Megan," my dad began, "Brian and I have been talking about renting out one of the offices to him. He could take on the taxation and accounting work for the Dexter folks, and help us with our tax and business lawsuits. In fact, we've added two more clients this week. What is your opinion?"

My opinion was that the matter had already been decided without my involvement. I didn't want to be a bitch about it, so I stuck to business.

"I do have a few questions. Have we settled on his fee for his consultation on our files? And, what is our split on the files we've given him that don't require legal action? Have you set his rent? And will it include use of Glenda and Melanie?"

The two men looked at each other. My dad cleared his throat.

I continued: "And most importantly, have you trained him on plunging the women's toilet—that sucker is always getting plugged."

Brian laughed. Even though my dad grinned, his eyes never left mine.

"Oh, I want that last part written out of my contract," said Brian.

"Ha! You plunge or you'll get none of Glenda's pastries."

"Okay, you win."

My dad gathered up the notes then closed file. "Here are the answers to your questions. Write up the contract." He reached across the desk to hand me the file.

"Not a chance. You two plotted this, you two can finish it." I rose and left the room. I knew I'd passed his test.

Later that night, I lay in the white sheets running my fingers through his sweaty chest hair. I sighed.

"Tell me, Miggy," he said.

I smirked. "Yeah, all I need is you giving me a nickname… or actually borrowing one."

"Well, I still think the Pocket Docket is clever."

"It is, but I hope it goes away soon."

"But you've got something on your mind. Is it about me staying on in your office? I know I didn't tell you about it. In fact, your dad suggested it then told me to go think about it. It may not even be every day."

"No, I think that's fine… excellent really. It's just that I've got my first court date next week."

"Really? That's a big deal."

"It's just a pre-trial hearing, but it's my first time…it does make me a bit nervous. I'm not a natural performer."

"With experience, you'll be fine. Even Thurgood Marshall had his first time. You don't have an imposing appearance, just an imposing manner."

"Hummph. Imposing? Is that a nice word for bitchy?"

"Not at all. You have a very professional manner. Just don't stand behind any tall exhibits and don't wear flat shoes."

"Very funny. But I've got a stack of cases higher than Mount Doom, so I'd better be ready to put on the bitch hat when I need to if I want to keep my clients. By the way, have I told you what great gluts you've got?"

"Obviously, you're smitten with my body. But do you care about my mind?"

"Oh, that takes much longer to learn."

"Good point. Now then. I haven't inspected your left hip in at least five minutes."

"The bruise is gone."

"I better check."

I giggled. I couldn't help it. I was bedazzled with the excitement of this beginning, this relationship with my brainy stud.

My dad had shrugged his shoulders and said I could handle it. And it was a simple matter—a motion to suppress evidence, a motion in limine, to preclude from trial evidence that the defendant had been drinking prior to the auto accident. Our defendant's Blood Alcohol Test indicated a .03 reading, well below the state limit of .08. I expected the motion to be granted as the plaintiff had no evidence to prove alcohol was a factor in the case, a simple rear-ender. Even though the motion could have been made in writing to the county judge, my dad decided I should present the argument at the pre-trial hearing. I think he wanted me to get the experience. Still, I was nervous. It wasn't as easy as it looked on TV, where professional actors recite lines written by someone else.

So, I drove to Sidney for the 10:45 hearing. The presiding county judge was the Honorable Dean Shelton, who favored Scotch, the Broncos, the Option offense, and aggressive tactics in chess. I'd played and beaten him on three or four occasions in my teens when I studied the game and even won a couple of small tournaments. I tended to start defensively, pick off key pieces, and then launch my attack, which worked well against the judge.

Mark "Gus" Gustafson, the plaintiff's attorney sat down in the row in front of me. He turned around and shook my hand. Gus, also a Dexter attorney, was well-respected by my dad. He was stout, with a paunch and thinning brown hair. Gus didn't play chess, but I babysat his daughters in my early teens. So, it was hardly an adversarial setting; still, I could hear my heart pounding in my ears. I'd rather be back at my desk, perusing a case in the ALR 5th, hunting for legal precedent or at least a damn good argument.

But here I was. When the people from the case ahead of us cleared out and the bailiff announced my case, I took my place at the defendant's table. Neither party to the case was present; it was a formality, though an important one to prevent the jury from becoming unduly prejudiced against my client for the boilermaker he drank before the accident. I placed directly in front of me the precise language of the motion, typed in large print, in case a moment of near blindness overtook me. On cue, I stood and clearly stated the language of the motion and the supporting argument. I didn't even need to read the paper, since the words had been bouncing around in my head all night.

When Judge Shelton asked Gus if he had any objection, he replied, "No, your honor."

Soon, I heard, "Motion granted," then the sound of the gavel, which the judge, a man who could never protect his queen, pounded with more enthusiasm than in the prior case. He gave me a little nod.

I tried not to look too relieved. Now that it was over, my brain began to function again. When Gus shook my hand, I suggested a chat in the hallway. As I started down the aisle, I discovered that I had my own cheering section—Patty, Uncle Bill, and Brian were seated in the back row. While I spoke with Gus, they waited for me down the hall.

He confirmed the well-being of his family then proceeded to talk about the tornado. He had been one of the men hauling up bodies and plastic bags from Uncle Bill's basement. I thanked him for his help then turned to business.

"Now, Gus," I began, "we're not that far apart. Your client has run up a tremendous amount of chiropractic bills for a moderate impact. And we both know your client won't make a good impression. He's been in this courthouse in an orange jumpsuit on three occasions. You can't live in this county without knowing about him. Now, what do you think we can settle this for?"

"I'll check with Len, but he's been pretty stubborn."

"You know this county—this jury will be tight with the buck. Now, this is a one-day trial with several expert witnesses. The jury's decision could keep us late. Correct me if I'm wrong, but isn't September tenth Katy's birthday?"

"Dang, what a memory. I'll call you early next week, Pocket Docket."

A family looking uncomfortable in their Sunday-Go-To-Meeting clothes stared at me. Oh, dang. I hastened to my cheering section.

While I was being congratulated, a man stopped next to our little group and scowled at us. Balding and beer-bellied, the whiskered, ashen-faced man of about sixty years walked on. He smelled as if he'd been hiding in a dank cave for a month. His denim overalls were too roomy and too short, as if they belonged to another person.

Uncle Bill called after him, "Hey, Salt, how are ya?"

After Salt went into the courtroom, Brian said, "I didn't know they let the Unabomber out of prison."

"That's our neighbor to the north," I said. "He looks so old... though I haven't seen him since I was a teen. Remember the car accident last summer that I told you about? The one that killed Mrs. Wilson? Well, it also killed Salt's father Bob. Lew is the brother. I bet that's Lew's trial... though it wouldn't be in—"

The courtroom door whipped open. Salt trudged across the hall to another courtroom, jerking that door open so hard, it smashed against the door stop.

"We called him Boo Radley when we were kids," I said.

"Yeah, I get that," said Brian.

"I wanna see this," said Uncle Bill.

We followed him to the courtroom. From my seat I could see Lew, younger than Salt, but tall and gangly. Looking tired and humbled, he wore an orange jumpsuit as he stood at the defendant's table. His attorney from Dexter was Stan Spurlock, thirty-five, with thin arms and legs, bad posture, and slicked-back red-brown hair that gave him an unctuous, Uriah Heep look. He handled most of the criminal cases in Dexter, an area of law our firm generally rejected. We heard the judge sentence Lew to two days in jail. Salt sprang from his seat.

"Damn you, Judge!" he bellowed. "He was provoked!"

Two police officers dashed down the sides of each outer aisle.

"Silence!" yelled the judge, who then pounded his gavel. "Or I'll hold you, Cecil Eldritch, in contempt."

"This is a crock o' shit!"

Both Lew and Stan Spurlock tried to hush him.

"Bailiff! Officers, arrest this man on contempt of court."

"Please, Mr. Judge," pled Lew, "he don't understand."

Salt struggled, but the bailiff and the officers contained then handcuffed him.

"You'll cool your jets in jail for two days." The gavel banged again.

"Damn Judge. Damn lawyers." Salt twisted to try and free himself. Now looking directly at me, he said, "And Frank Docket is the biggest son of a bitch of them all."

Patty jerked. I smiled coolly back at him. Then I felt an arm tugging at me.

"C'mon, let's go," said Uncle Bill.

We rose from our chairs as the judge addressed Salt. "By the way, your brother has already served his two days. So you'll be going to jail just as he's leaving it."

Once we got out of the courtroom, we all broke into laughter. We needed sustenance, so Brian led us to a Chinese restaurant, which we lacked in Dexter. Patty and Uncle Bill gorged themselves on the exotic food. Brian and I watched them and smiled with the knowledge that you could get Chinese food in most supermarkets in Omaha and towns of a reasonable size.

With Brian's urging, Uncle Bill gave an account of the Eldritch family.

"Well, I went to school with Salt…Lew is a couple of years younger. They were always dirt poor, never had a big enough herd to sustain themselves. Bob, the dad, was the only true rancher. Lew tries, but Salt likes to stay indoors. During the drought years, they had to sell most of the herd and much of their land to feed themselves. Then Lois, the mother, the one who held things together, got cancer. Lungs, it was. Went quick and painfully…had to be on Medicaid. We tried to help them out. Frank and I bought some land, worthless scrub acres up north of the Beast. We were even pallbearers at her funeral. She musta put up with a lot. I don't think Salt was ever right in his mind, but he got worse. Heavy drinkin' mostly. Lew's all right, been kicked around… kinda goofy, but more like his good-hearted mother." He stopped and stared at his egg roll.

"Then the accident happened," I inserted.

"Bob always drove like his butt was on fire. Anyway, Salt disappeared after that. Lew had to try and make it on his own. Me and Joe McCready have been helping him. He's not a rancher, but he'd been doing all right till Salt came back in June. Lew tried to get him to come out of the house then finally succeeded. They went to the Cowpoke where Salt drank himself into a stupor. Some of the guys started making fun of him. Lew took all he could then he punched Trent Maxwell and Junior Percival. The deputy came. Megan, you know Bo, he settled things down. Junior wasn't even mad. But then big shot Police Chief Ray Dobbs comes and arrests Lew. Even Trent protested. And Dobbs threw Salt in jail for public intoxication. Frank went up the next morning and argued…as he does so well. Dobbs was forced to release Salt. But Lew went to jail…they couldn't post bail."

"So why was Salt insulting your brother?" asked Brian.

"Because Frank represented James in the auto accicent trial and won. In Salt's mind, James was guilty."

"My dad also represented State Farm, James' insurance company," I said. "But it never went to civil court and James never pressed a case against the Eldritch estate."

"But you have some plaintiff cases," Brian said.

"We do both. State Farm, who insures about thirty percent of the people around here, got tired of losing to my dad. So now they try to jump in and try to hire him first. But we still get plaintiff cases from five counties."

"But he talks like he still hates your dad."

"Fine, let him. Maybe in taxation cases you can make people happy with bigger refunds, but an attorney always has people who hate his guts…or her guts."

Though that didn't mean people always held a grudge. Junior Percival, for instance, lost an auto accident case to my dad, but then came to him when he needed someone to fight with his medical insurance company over benefits for his son's disability. My dad prevailed then charged Junior a fee so low, Melanie came to me and asked if it was a typo.

I settled the case with Gus on Monday, after a half day of negotiating. My dad even told me to call State Farm, which I'd never done, to advise of the settlement. This was one of our best clients, so making a good impression was important to me.

Autumn brought cooling winds from the west and north. Brian and I always dated in Sidney, as I didn't like to be on display in Dexter. Sometimes we went out with old friends of his. Soon we'd covered all the restaurants and movie theaters in Kimball. Once we watched a movie from our DVD collection, but the thought of bringing him up to my bedroom—the room across the hall from my dad—stifled me. Then in October the solution appeared—the house two down from Beulah on Benson Street was converted into apartments after Emily Dewitt, who had lost her wits, was sent to live in a nursing home. Brian rented a room on the main floor at the rear of the house, a converted dining room with space enough for a double bed. However, I insisted on selecting the bed linens—a 600 thread count sheet set in gray sateen with a matching pillow sham and a black comforter. He painted the room a pale gray. I thought the room looked manly. He added a small closet, a dresser, a coffee-maker, and a small fridge. This worked well for us, though I truly wished I could wake up next to this man in my own bed, in my own house. But living together was a prospect I'd soured on. And as a matter of appearance, I thought it bad form to live with a man while I tried to hold myself out to the community as a woman of integrity—a Pocket Docket in the best sense.

Meanwhile, Glenda stayed on with the zeal of a new-born Christian. I also persuaded my dad to pay for some online paralegal classes for Melanie with the community college in Hastings. That fall I began tag-teaming trials with my dad. He did the opening and closing arguments while I interviewed the witnesses. I'd discovered years ago that I did well with people and could winkle out of them things they had never intended to say. Judge Shelton appointed me guardian ad litem in three custody cases, which meant I represented the children in the contentious divorce proceedings. That led to clients coming directly to me in divorce cases, which led to the need for wills to cover the new family and step-family arrangements. In January, I received my first solo bodily injury assignment from State Farm auto, which had commended my negotiation skills.

The winter, with its harsh cold and biting wind, kept me indoors and away from my land for most of December through February. Some days, I huddled against the bur oak in the backyard, straining to hear, hoping to hear the young man's voice. Other days, I braved the stinging wind and made it out to the Seven Dwarfs, convinced I'd hear better out there. Oddly enough, his was the voice I missed the most when sleet or snow drifts made it impossible to get clear of the house. Inside, even in the quiet of my room, I felt the yearning, but I could never hear anything. Three times over the course of the winter, I felt the stabbing pain in my chest. More than the pain, it was the distress and confusion that wounded me most. It always took several hours to shake off the despair the attacks brought. I wanted so badly to hear him, to know he was okay. The malady hurt like hell, but somehow I sensed it wasn't me, as if my yearning brought on psychosomatic pain. Maybe I really was nuts.

One night in late April, I awoke to horrible chest pain—ten times worse than I'd ever felt.

Chapter 10

I'd gone to bed early, feeling tired, dizzy, and achy. My fingers even tingled. It wasn't like any illness I'd known. Maybe I was working too hard. I think I fell asleep quickly, but then I was hit by the most terrible pain I'd ever experienced. In my confusion, I tried to push off my chest the thing that had crashed on it—but nothing was there. I clutched at my nightgown, writhing in pain, gasping for air.

I must have called out in pain because my door opened and a beam of light from the hallway shone into my room.

"Megan?" said Uncle Bill.

"Are you all right?" asked my dad.

I said, "Sorry, bad dream," then rolled over on my side.

The clock read 3:43 a.m. After a few minutes, the door closed and I rolled onto my back, still gasping for air, still feeling the crushing pain in my chest. I slid out of my bed and crawled to the window and opened it, sucking in the dry, cool air. My legs felt too weak to stand, so I sat down on the carpet under the window, bracing myself against the wall as I tried to withstand the stabbing pressure.

Then it was gone.

Still breathing hard, I collapsed to the floor. Without the pain, relief washed over me. I scooted over to my dresser then pulled out a T-shirt to wipe away the sweat that stung my eyes. What happened to me? And where did it go? It resembled some sort of cardiac incubus, yet a sense of trauma remained. I scrambled to my feet then dressed. I tiptoed down the main staircase; in a flash, I bolted out the back door to seek answers in the rough land.

I ran in the darkness with enough awareness to pick my way across the jagged earth. Did that pain really happen? It felt more real than any nightmare. I felt fine, so I kept running, now aware that my heart attack had turned to heart ache. What had I lost? Grief overwhelmed me. I stopped running. Realizing that I had passed through the Seven Dwarfs, I stared up at the stars so close I could've touched them. The massive bluff, Big Leo, blocked out the eastern sky. Unsatisfied, I ran again, my feet as sure in the darkness as they could be in the light. As soon as I had passed the edge of the gully, Pooper's Canyon, I struck out toward the Beast. But heaviness pushed down on my shoulders, making my legs give way. Sprawled in the buffalo grass, I wept.

In time, I wiped my sweatshirt across my eyes. I needed answers. I scrambled and clawed my way over buffalo grass and rocky soil till I reached the top of the Beast. Next to one of the several rocky mounds, I stood and listened. Nothing. I yelled something. Then I heard it—the wailing of a woman's voice. This voice of my earliest memories smashed into me, knocking me to my knees. I didn't hear the new woman's voice, as if she was listening and wondering as I was. Where was the young man's voice? It was gone, completely gone. His absence tore at me. The wailing changed to sobs. I cried, too.

I stayed till I saw the red streaks of sunrise form in the east. I scooted down the Beast and walked home. I didn't want anyone to come looking for me, asking questions I couldn't possibly answer. But Uncle Bill was waiting at the back door, drinking a cup of coffee. For the first time, I realized my sweatshirt was inside out and I wasn't wearing socks.

"Well?" he asked.

I shook my head and bounded up the back steps. I showered then dressed—triple checking my clothing and making sure my earrings matched. I grabbed a bagel then heard the phone ring just as I closed the door to the garage. Who would be calling at this hour?

At work, I tried to shut out the weird events of the night, yet I felt both sad and haunted. I hadn't seen my dad at home. When he failed to show up at his usual time, I began to worry. Did the night's pain foreshadow something?

Finally, he arrived a little after ten. He didn't respond to Glenda's greeting; instead, he shut the office door, failing to emerge for lunch. Brian worked at his Sidney office all day. I skipped lunch—I didn't want to go anywhere near anyone. Nobody could help me. Both Melanie and Glenda kept peeking in at me, but I ignored them. At two o'clock, maternal forces overwhelmed Glenda—she sailed into the office with a plate of scones and a mug of Earl Grey.

When I came home that evening, Uncle Bill was gone. That man never missed a meal, so what was up? Patty looked confused. I didn't know what to tell her.

"Did something happen?" she asked.

"Yeah," I said.

"What?"

"I don't know."

"Did...um...has something touched you?"

Walloped would me more accurate, but I just said, "Yes."

"And it's powerful."

I nodded.

Patty reheated the pork chops then we ate supper together in the kitchen with sparse conversation. She seemed deep in thought. Then we heard the garage door open. I stopped eating then waited. My dad walked through the garage door and stopped abruptly when he saw me. Did I see him flinch? He turned and went up the back stairs, something he rarely did. We listened to his footsteps on the rickety wood stairs echo in the stairwell.

"Were you concerned about your dad?"

"Yeah, but he seems all right. Do you know where Uncle Bill is?"

"Not a clue. Your dad probably knows, but he doesn't seem too...um...friendly right now."

In fact, I never did ask my dad where Uncle Bill went. I don't know why. The weight of mysterious grief still stalked me every hour, every minute. Uncle Bill showed up late at night, five days later. Surprised that I didn't know, he said he'd been in Omaha. He didn't say why and I didn't inquire.

Tuesday morning, I walked down the front stairs and entered the kitchen. Though I hadn't heard anything specific, my dad and my uncle stopped talking. What the hell?

That day, I had lunch with Brian at Custer's. He looked around to make sure nobody would hear. I waited for the questions I couldn't answer.

"So, what's going on? You hardly talk to me. Your dad does everything he can to avoid you."

I sighed. "If I could tell you, I would."

"Why can't you tell me?"

"Because I don't know... I don't understand...but it's as if something has happened or is going to happen and I can't see it."

Brian thought for a few moments then said, "Patty called me yesterday, asking me about you. I figure she must know you pretty well, so if she doesn't know then—" He sighed. "She's worried about something you're feeling."

I nodded.

"You and your dad can't go on like this."

"No, we can't."

For the first time in my life, I realized the burden of him—his expectations, his neediness. His life consisted of work and me.

We stopped talking while we were served our food. Soon Beulah shuffled out.

"Where's your pa been?"

"Just busy," I said. What could I say?

She studied me, shook her head. "I could send somethin' with you."

"Thank you. I'll…ah…think about it."

"Hmmm" She shuffled away.

Midway through our meal, a force slammed me back against the booth. I gasped.

"What?" asked an alarmed Brian.

I grabbed my purse and bolted from the booth and out the door. I'd crossed the street before Brian caught up to me.

"What? What's wrong?"

I ran onward to our office.

I knew.

I threw open the front door then dashed toward my dad's office. I called out to Melanie and Glenda, who were both at the front desk in the process of switching shifts for lunch.

"Call an ambulance!"

They both looked startled.

"Do it!"

I burst through his closed door.

My dad lay face down on the floor.

Chapter 11

I rushed to my dad's side. His face was still warm. Brian flipped him over on his back and started CPR. Melanie appeared at the door.

"Call the clinic," I said. "Tell them to bring the defibrillator."

Back at my dad's side, I saw his eyes flutter. Brian kept pumping on his chest.

"Do we blow in his mouth?" I asked.

"No, we just keep pumping," said Brian.

The color started to rise in my dad's face. He coughed, and then opened his eyes. He found mine.

He started to make a raspy noise. Brian stopped pumping.

"Megan, I love you. I'm—I'm sorry."

His eyes closed. Brian started pumping again. Both Melanie and Glenda were in the doorway.

"What can we do?" asked Melanie.

I shook my head. We needed to wait for help. It was an excruciating wait. Finally, I heard vehicles out front. Soon, paddles were pressed against his chest. "Clear!" His body jolted. His pulse was checked. "Again!" Another jolt. A pause. "Better."

The nurse from Sidney, on rotation at our clinic, looked at me and Brian. "We'll keep him monitored till the ambulance comes."

I nodded. Glenda waited by the window. After a thousand minutes, the ambulance arrived. As they placed him on the gurney, I sought out Melanie.

"Call Patty and tell her to find Uncle Bill. Then lock down the office."

I ran to the ambulance alongside my dad. Brian ran to retrieve his car at Custer's. Not soon enough, we arrived at the hospital. I was led away from him and the ER area, past the main waiting area to one near the adjoining ICU and surgery areas. The room was painted in well-meaning beige, with a dozen brown padded chairs. A clerical person came to obtain his health insurance information. I sat and waited and prayed.

Brian and Patty soon joined me. Later, I don't know when as my sense of time had disappeared, Uncle Bill came in, wearing his work clothes—a white cowboy hat he quickly removed and brown cowboy boots, ones I'd helped him pick out. Docket men were particularly indecisive in their clothing choices, so they often relied on me to help them make up their minds. I hugged him—he stank of sweat and cattle—I hugged him all the harder. Behind him stood James, who put his hand on my shoulder.

"That tubby nurse wasn't gonna let James in," said Bill. "She said he was supposed to be family. So I threatened to go get you, Shortstuff. I told her she didn't want to mess with you. You'd say she was being racist."

I nodded then we sat down. I stared at Bill's boots. I wondered if they'd need to send my dad to the University of Nebraska Medical Center. Brian sat with his hands on his knees, as if he was ready to pounce. Patty gripped the clasp of her purse so tight I could see her knuckles turning white. I sat completely still, in a trance of apprehension. My head snapped up. The door opened and an elderly woman, probably a volunteer, came in and flicked a switch on a coffeemaker that sat on a table near the door.

"It'll be just a few minutes," she said. She sat down in a chair next to the table. Soon the trickle of coffee cut through the stillness.

Uncle Bill broke the silence. "Megan, Bo says you knew. Says he saw you run out of Custer's... and Melanie told him the office door was closed, so nobody could've known."

102

I shrugged. I could feel Patty's eyes on me. I avoided her look and went back to staring at Uncle Bill's boots. The door opened, we all jerked then looked. A wizened oldster with a cane glanced at us then shuffled to the other end of the room. He sat down in a chair by a half-assembled jigsaw puzzle of some furry creature.

After a few minutes, the door opened again. The words cut the air like a knife: "Miss Docket, Mr. Docket?"

Brian grabbed my hand. My heart seized for a moment, but I stood and followed the physician out of the room. He led us to a quiet stretch of hallway. Soon I heard him say, "The enzyme damage is massive," and "I'm sorry."

I braced myself against the wall.

"We don't think it will be too long. But he could awaken. It sometimes happens, so...I need to know your wishes. Ah, the resuscitation, if it worked, would give him a few more hours, maybe days. I don't think he'll regain consciousness."

I looked at Uncle Bill, who was stunned open-mouthed, and then I looked at the doctor who appeared old enough to have held this conversation several times before.

I nodded. "He has a Living Will. Yes, to the DNR."

Uncle Bill opened his mouth then he slowly let it close.

"What would you want for yourself?"

He hugged me. We let the physician lead us back to the room. Before he opened the door, he asked. "Would you like me to tell them?"

Uncle Bill nodded.

"And the crowd in the lobby?" asked the doctor.

"Yes. Can we see him?" asked Uncle Bill.

"In a few minutes." He opened the door for me and Uncle Bill to enter. The doctor told Patty, Brian, and James the news. Patty broke out in sobs; James shook his head then dropped his chin into his chest; Brian rose and drew me close. I nestled my head into his chest and wept. The elderly lady managed to move my shock-still uncle to a chair. She scurried back to him with a cup of black coffee. The door closed behind the physician. The people in the lobby would know in about a minute, the entire town of Dexter would know within two minutes, for cell phones would be dialed, in disregard of the posted rules.

After a few minutes, Uncle Bill and I were escorted to his room in ICU. Machines with flashing red and green numbers. A convoluted mass of tubes. A room with dimmed lights. A man waiting to die. I felt a hand press on my shoulder, encouraging me to sit. I did. Uncle Bill was harder to convince, but he sat. As I stared at my dad's pale face, it struck me with profound sadness that we were it—two people. Uncle Bill would later call his son Kyle, from his first marriage, who lived in Houston. But I didn't know him well—he was a baby when my dad and I moved to Dexter. Two years later, after the divorce, he moved away with his mother. At eighteen, he went to work on the oil rigs in Texas, and had remained there.

Two, just two.

Uncle Bill and I sat in silence, looking from my dad's face to the monitor and back again. Time crawled. No, I didn't want to eat. Yes, I'd take some water. No, I couldn't believe this was happening. Then I thought about Patty, James, and Brian sitting in that waiting room, and Melanie, Glenda, and certainly Beulah, and the others sitting in the lobby. Waiting.

Suddenly, I was struck by a force that launched me out of my chair. I looked down at my dad then at the monitor, and then back to his face. An instant later, his eyes popped open and the green line on the monitor went flat.

"He's gone!" exclaimed my uncle as he stood.

Two nurses appeared in the room. One grabbed my dad's arm for a pulse, the other pushed buttons on two different machines. I saw the emptiness in my dad's eyes. He was gone. My trance broke—I pressed my dad's stiff hand to my face and wept.

My uncle turned my shoulders to him and we hugged hard. He broke away to close my dad's eyelids. I didn't like seeing them open like that—he seemed so exposed, so unable to control who looked in him. Uncle Bill pressed his fingers on the lids, but they didn't move.

"They won't close," he said to the busy nurses attending to their protocol. They didn't seem to hear him. "Nurse!" he snapped. "Close his eyes!"

The nurse pressed them closed. I suddenly hated all the movies where the eyelids closed with a sweep of the hand. The physician came in and led us into the hall. For the first time, I read his name tag—Dr. Cline. He said something apologetic and then he said something about organ donation.

"It was on his driver's license."

He looked from Uncle Bill to me. He must have been accustomed to the strange behavior of people in shock. He waited a few moments, looked back at me, and I nodded. Then like sheep, he herded us to a different room, one with stained glass, lots of boxes of tissues, and wastebaskets in each corner of the dimly-lit, small room. We sat down next to each other across from the door. Soon James and Patty walked in. We embraced each other, though few words were said. What was there to say that wasn't obvious? Then I saw Brian standing in the hall, stuck to his spot. He had been in this room before. I reached my hand out to him.

He said, "Should I go and tell the people in the lobby?"

I nodded. He turned away just as a middle-aged woman in a taupe polyester suit came in. She spoke to Uncle Bill, who mentioned Burton Funeral Home and our church. My legs suddenly felt like lead. Patty shuffled me to a chair. Uncle Bill now held a large gold envelope marked, "Frank Docket."

In a few minutes, Brian came through the door. I stood up and we hugged.

"They are taking it hard," he said.

"Death always comes out of season," said Patty.

I'm sure she was quoting a Lakota saying. I would have like to hear more of what the Sioux had to say about death. But she just stared at the stained glass.

"Glenda will be baking all night," I said. Smiles. "Can we get out of here? I want to go home…but not through that crowd out front."

Brian nodded. We followed him through the halls and exited through an outpatient entrance. The sun was just beginning to set. Though the ride to the hospital seemed to take forever, our arrival at home came in a flash. I felt unconnected to time. At home, our little clan filed in through the front door.

Uncle Bill chuckled.

What could be funny?

"Hey, Megan, you don't have a car. Both the Shark and your Camry are at your office."

I shrugged and dropped my purse on the foyer bench.

Then Bill grabbed me by the arms and pulled me to him. "You need to promise me that you won't go out there. We can't find you. You must promise me that."

"I promise I won't go out there…when it's dark."

He released me. "I guess that'll haveta do. I'm gonna shower." He trudged up the stairs, each loud footstep sounded the death knell.

Brian stepped forward, "James and I can go get the cars. Is that okay?"

I looked at James. He nodded. I gave my keys to James then gave him my dad's keys from the gold envelope. He turned and followed Brian out the front door. Patty and I exchanged looks; she gradually allowed her eyebrows to settle to their natural position.

"We need food," she said.

As she walked away, I discovered I was bolted to the floor. My legs had turned to lead. I looked down the hallway to my dad's study. After a few minutes, Patty came back, walked behind me then gave my shoulders a shove. Soon, she had me eating yogurt and drinking orange juice. Like a sheep, I ate whatever she put before me. She carved the leftover roast beef and made me a sandwich. Then she carved the rest for the men. Though she continued to make preparations for our meal, she turned from her cutting board to look at me.

"Brian says you knew. He says you jumped up from your lunch and ran to your dad. How did you know?"

"I—I don't know. It just struck me… not clear what… but something had happened to him." I didn't know how to finish.

"You feel things."

I sat thinking about that. Yes, I felt things. Did I feel his heart attack days before it even happened? Should I have guessed that and made him go to the doctor? He would have done it. He'd become putty in my hands. He acquiesced to my "transformation" plans, he'd lowered me into a collapsed building when I demanded it, he had even let me interview a couple of witnesses in our last case that he thought had no value—I still believed they did—we won the case. But he was gone. My brain knew it was a fact—the doctor said so, the line went straight, his hand had gone cold while I held it—but my heart, my guts, felt it was too incredible to believe.

I looked down at the tin of tuna Patty had set in front of me. I pushed it away. "Very funny."

"Just testing you," said Patty.

We heard the garage door go up. That would be the first car. We both scampered to door to the garage, opening it ever so slightly. We saw James walk back to Brian's Jeep Cherokee. I turned to find Uncle Bill standing over us peering out the door.

"I'll be damned," said Uncle Bill. "Good for him."

Uncle Bill sat down and started on a double meat sandwich. I had just started on an apple, when a thought struck me. I excused myself and went to my purse in the foyer. I made a call on my cell phone.

"Vonny, pick up, please." After a few rings, she did.

"My dad just died. I need you."

After Brian and James returned and ate, we all went to the family room. James, Brian, and I sat on the sofa, while Uncle Bill sat in the corner leather chair, leaving my dad's recliner empty. Patty gave us all glasses of bourbon on the rocks. Even James drank his. Then she brought in chips and French Onion dip—so we drank and ate and didn't make much attempt at conversation. After a bit, James stood and announced he was going home. We walked him to the front door. Just before he went out, he turned to Uncle Bill and me, thinking he should say something.

"I know," I said.

He nodded to me and left. Uncle Bill followed him with a flashlight to make sure he didn't fall in the darkness. Uncle Bill came back a couple of minutes later.

"We ought to have a sidewalk between these houses. I'm going to bed. Shortstuff, remember, you promised."

"I did. Goodnight."

He put his big hand on Brian's shoulder. "You make sure she doesn't bolt." Then he turned to Patty. "You ought to stay." He started up the stairs.

"I think I will," she said. "I'll tidy things up first." She turned and went off to the kitchen.

I took Brian's hand and led him up the back stairs that let out near my bedroom door. I left him standing in the middle of my room while I grabbed a nightgown from my dresser and toothbrush from the supply in my bathroom for Patty. I left a toothbrush out for Brian, too. Then I returned to him. I needed to be wrapped up in his arms. The poor guy had to keep wiping the tears from my face. I just couldn't stop them from coming.

Chapter 12

At dawn, I slipped out of bed and into a pair of jeans and a T-shirt. In the hall, I stopped and stared at the closed door in front of me. He's not there. I don't know how long I stood in my trance, but finally I roused myself. Uncle Bill's door was shut, as was the guest room where Patty slept. I crept down the front stairs to the kitchen. I smiled when I saw Vonny sipping coffee on our patio.

"I knew you'd be up early, Miggy."

Her long arms wrapped me up. I hugged her hard and long.

"Lord above, I can't believe this," she said, her eyes tearing up.

"I'm just numb... I can't think... can't feel... just... nothing. I figure the damn will break and I'll... I don't know what."

"Gush."

"I hope I'm not in public," I said.

We sat down. She grabbed my hand. Traddles came looking for affection.

"How's your dad? I'm supposed to call him James now. He looked walloped last night."

"He looks that way now." She let go of my hand then began to pet the dog.

I wanted to ask about her feelings toward her dad, but I didn't want to get into an argument with her. I was just so pleased she had come. Knowing her, the topic was on her mind, too. The chirping of a horned lark in our oak tree attracted our attention. With its black mask, yellow chin, and black tufts of hair that stood up on both sides of its head, I thought, that's how you got to be out here—tough enough to withstand the winters and the wind and the deaths.

"Derek tells me you dumped the guy in Omaha and you've got a new squeeze."

"He's upstairs."

"No, kidding. With—"

She caught herself. I knew she was about to say with your dad across the hall.

"Yeah, I know. It's gonna take a long time…but yeah, Brian is probably still sleeping."

She nodded. "Well, just a bit of a warning for you— don't be surprised if he wants to back off. Most guys don't want to deal with stuff this heavy."

We both turned back toward the house. I'd left the inside door open, so we now heard someone in the kitchen closing drawers then the doorbell rang.

"Could that really be someone this early?" I wondered out loud then realized I didn't know the time. I checked my top to make sure it wasn't inside out, though I'd forgotten socks again.

Vonny followed me inside. She stopped in the kitchen to greet and hug Patty, who then went to peek out the front window.

"It's some lady with purple hair and three cake pans," said Patty.

I opened the door to Glenda.

"Oh, hello, dear. How are you? Bad, I know. I know how people are—they'll be coming all day—so I baked these for you."

I took the pans from her and invited her in.

"Oh, I don't want to intrude." She stepped into the foyer, looking around. "Oh, this is just so lovely. Oh, Vonny! It's so good to see you, dear. How nice of you to come so quickly to be with your friend."

"Hello, Mrs. Purvis," said Vonny.

"Oh, call me Glenda, dear. Megan does. She's my boss now. Who could've guessed?"

I introduced Patty to Glenda.

"Oh, Patty, of course. I've heard so many wonderful things about you and it's so kind of you to look after Bill and Megan."

110

Of course, with such flattery, we had to invite her in. Patty went back to cooking breakfast while Glenda and Vonny sipped coffee. My stomach felt too touchy, too churning with emotional acid to drink anything strong. I thought about warning Brian not to come down, but then I realized Glenda had probably spotted his Jeep in the driveway. She wasn't one to miss the obvious.

In time, both Uncle Bill and Brian came down. Everyone was quiet as we ate our eggs and toast. Patty even cooked up a pile of bacon, which she rarely did—she called all breakfast meat "heart attack" food. Knowing her, she'd be agonizing over whether her cooking caused my dad's heart attack. Meanwhile, Glenda didn't eat, but seemed to enjoy the sight of people sitting around the table eating. Derek soon joined us, reporting that his dad had started work early, so he could be done and ready to do anything we needed. Next came Beulah with a load of root beer. Brian and Derek went to her giant Chrysler to haul it in. She cornered me in a tight hug with her bony arms and bony shoulders.

"Oh, sweetie!" she said. "Oh, sweetie! I don't know what to say."

I understood her difficulty with articulation. My brain was processing slowly. I did follow her gaze to Brian out at her car.

"You be careful now. Don't be surprised if that young man gets all serious on you. He may rush to proposin' if it's somethin' he's been thinking about. But here's my advice— don't do anything rash. That ain't like you, but these are strange times for you. Hold steady, Megan. Hold steady."

Over the course of the morning, our house bustled with mourners coming and going, bringing condolences and food. We had six bottles of Jim Beam Black by noon. I didn't realize we were known as a bourbon drinking family.

I watched Uncle Bill all morning. He looked as dumbfounded as I felt. Old cowboys don't cry—but they can become catatonic. He'd have periods where he sat rigid, staring out a window, and then other times he'd be up pacing the halls, scratching his head till his thick hair went catawampus. Patty and I kept smashing his hair down. At the hospital, I had agonized how it was just the two of us—now I was wishing for that feeling. Uncle Bill left, claiming that he needed to check the herds. Joe McCready told me he had sent some of his hands out to tend Bill's stock, but we both knew he needed to get away. Patty went up and hid in the guest room for an hour. I was aching to get away, too, but people kept coming and going—and I kept greeting, thanking, and saying goodbye.

Finally, at about three-thirty, I found my chance. I sneaked into the mud room, grabbed my shoes, and darted out the back door. In a flash, I was over Rufus and out of sight of the house, slowing to a walk and groaning in relief. Fifty yards from the Seven Dwarfs, the wind yowled and the buffalo grass beckoned. Skirting those crumbly rock hills, I drifted west toward the low grassy hills and a few scraggily conifers. After a quarter mile, I struck upon a path that dove into dells and hugged steeper banks, and then rolled onward to rows of cottonwoods lining Raccoon Creek. As I neared the trees, the wind began to whistle through the leaves. I stood and watched the branches bob in the wind, waiting. What would his voice sound like? Would he be in distress? The memory of his face contorted in pain made the chicken casserole in my stomach spin around. People had different conceptions of heaven; I didn't have a clear vision of it, yet I felt confident God wouldn't make us carry our physical woes with us—my dad's arthritic knee would be long gone.

I tried to think of him when he was younger, but he always seemed the same to me. One of my earliest memories was when we visited the Wilson house together for the first time. James had put little Vonny, just a year younger than me, on his shoulders. They spun around and Vonny giggled so hard she developed the hiccups. Later, when I walked home with my father, I asked if he would put me on his shoulders. He asked, "Why would I do that?" While Crenny was

112

instructing me on the necessary girlie things, it was Uncle Bill who taught me how to skim rocks and shoot a slingshot—not my dad. I would mourn him, but never idolize him.

He had said, "I love you. I'm sorry." What was he sorry for? Why did he wait till he was dying to tell me he loved me?

Suddenly, a southern blast of wind brought a howl that frightened me. I whirled around, looking for him, but found only a brilliant blue-sky afternoon. The heat drove me to the cottonwoods for shade where I sat down near the creek bank. For a few moments, the plashing of the water against the tree roots and pebble bank held my attention. I closed my eyes and listened to the sound of water trickling through the sockets of the tree roots. Then the low, mournful howl returned. He did sound in pain, or at least distress. Through my tears, I watched the sunlight filter through the branches and dance upon the surface of the creek. I laid back on the sand and rocks of the narrow bank and followed the trackless flight of the clouds. His lament was abruptly joined by the moaning of the woman— their discordant voices jolted my body. From my knees, dizziness overcame me and I collapsed back onto the bank. Feeling tired, I wished they would shut up.

I don't know how long I slept, but I was dismayed by my lack of enlightenment. It seemed like I was supposed to know something. Shouldering my melancholy, I trudged home. Just before I reached Rufus, I stopped. I lost my dad, my anchor. What was I to do now? I staggered forward in numbness. During the tornado, he had wrapped his arms around me tightly to protect me—I could almost feel that embrace. I stumbled to the ground sobbing. That's what I wanted—his love—not his howl of pain in the wind. But the voices wouldn't leave me alone. Why did I come out here to torture myself? I missed the young man, though he haunted me, too. If I was to hear someone, I wished it was Mrs. Wilson. Maybe she would tell me to call her Beverly now.

Her voice was always calming; nothing in her voice had that edge, that sharp sense of despair or pain.

Then I heard voices, ones that were coming from the house to find me. I leaned forward out of the shade to see the sun. It was later than I thought. Maybe the town had cleared out of our house. I hoped no one had wandered up to my room; I wondered if Brian made the bed. Three silhouettes crested the hill.

"Well, the posse has found me."

"Miggy, you've been gone for two hours," said Derek as he sat down next to me.

James and Vonny stood in the scrub grass. Traddles wandered over to us.

"Well, I fell asleep over by the creek. Isn't it nice to get out of there?"

"My God," said Vonny. "I thought they would never stop coming."

Derek stood then yanked me to my feet.

"Your uncle was wondering if you left the county," said James.

"He ran away first," I said as we walked toward the house. "Did they leave any food?"

They laughed—Patty was probably shoving containers of lasagna into the freezer as we spoke.

Uncle Bill sat at the kitchen table. He chuckled when he heard I'd been found just over the hill. Brian walked into the room. I gave him a smile. I tried to remember when he had gone back to his Benson Street apartment to change his clothes. The day seemed a whirl. I became aware of my need for a meal and a shower. I announced my intention for the latter and inquired about the former.

"Wait," said Uncle Bill. "I want to ask you something and these people might as well hear what you have to say."

I swallowed hard then sat down. I knew what was coming.

"How did you know he had his heart attack? People know how that went down. And then you jumped up at his

114

bedside a moment before he died. How could you know before it happened?"

I felt many eyes on me. From the looks on Brian and Patty's faces, I knew they hadn't heard about how I beat the flat line.

"I don't know...and that's the truth," I said. "It bothers me that I don't understand it. I wish I did." I drank the orange juice Patty put in front of me.

"And what about that night when you yelled in your sleep and then you were gone...out into the darkness? How is it you don't break a leg or get snake-bit out there?"

I was starting to feel defensive. "Why don't you tell me where you went? You disappeared for five days."

"I went to a funeral."

"Oh. Anybody I know?"

He paused. "No one you'd remember."

"Why didn't Dad go?"

Another pause. He looked down at his coffee cup and shook his head. An awkward silence ensued as the listeners processed the information. Then I asked a question that surprised even me.

"Why couldn't I find a record of my mother's death when I searched the Douglas County records?"

Patty gasped. She'd been doing that a lot lately. I wished she would stop. I wished my uncle would lift his head so I could see his face.

"She didn't die there." He rose and walked to the back stairs.

We listened to the heaviness in his feet as he trudged up the steps. The echo remained in the air. No one moved. I knew it was up to me. I rose.

"I stink, but I'll be back. You all must stay and have supper with us." I nodded at the counters, stacked with pans and boxes and Tupperware. "I promise we'll lighten up."

"Well, it sure as hell can't get any worse," said Patty.

"Amen," said Vonny.

I gave Patty's ponytail a tug then went up the front stairs.

And we did lighten up. After supper we watched the third period of an Avalanche game, which they lost, and then the start of a Cubs game in San Francisco, which they were sure to lose. I cornered Brian in the kitchen during the third inning and asked him to stay the night.

He gave me a passionate kiss. "Mmm. Chocolate cake and bourbon. It works." He smiled. "Yes. But would it be okay if I used my own toothbrush? Pink doesn't suit me."

I smiled. "And will you be okay when I tell you I need to be alone?"

"Sure. But give me that same promise that you won't go out there alone in the night."

"I promise. That only happened that once."

He studied me. He had questions, but he either wasn't sure what they were or was afraid he'd be rebuffed.

Very quietly I said, "I thought I was having a heart attack. It really felt that way. Then it suddenly stopped."

"Was it the night before your dad died?"

"No, it was several days before that—no, I don't get it either."

Uncle Bill walked into the kitchen. "Shortstuff, you know what we haveta do tomorrow."

"I do, but I hate thinking about it."

I awoke in the night. Although I didn't go anywhere, my mind raced. I didn't know why my dad apologized to me, but I felt certain Uncle Bill knew. Clearly, he wasn't going to be helpful—at least until I could pin him down with more concrete questions. Even though a number of important tasks awaited me, I was determined to solve this mystery.

Chapter 13

I opened the office the next day. Brian had several appointments, but all the firm's clients rescheduled. At nine o'clock, Uncle Bill came by and together we drove to the funeral home in Sidney. Our funeral home was so small that it only acted as a chapel and site for the visitation. So we went to the Sidney "showroom" to pick out a casket. We sat across the table from a woman of fifty or so in a navy pant suit. She expressed her condolences, blah, blah, blah. She possessed one of those caring industry voices, like the ones you hear on radio advertising for hospitals. The actual funeral home owners probably looked like the mad scientists in old horror flicks. In time, we were led into a side room, with a lineup of coffins. My first instinct was to scream and run. But Uncle Bill grabbed my hand and kept me close to him for mutual support.

We passed by the inexpensive, painted gray model. This was for Frank Docket, after all. At an oak one, I stepped forward. I had never really seen the inside of a coffin; the silver satin interior was padded and actually looked comfortable. I backed away when I saw Bela Lugosi standing in a dark corner.

"I think Mrs. Wilson was buried in one like this," I whispered so Dracula wouldn't hear. Mrs. Wilson's casket had been closed at her funeral due to her massive head injury. I shuddered.

Uncle Bill put his arm around my shoulder and moved me along to the fine-grain caskets. Looking over my shoulder, I saw Vincent Price standing in the doorway. Calm, be calm, I told myself—he only wants my MasterCard. I stopped at the cherry wood with a gold trim.

"Your dad always liked that cherry wood furniture you picked out. This would be a good one."

I nodded and we went back to ascertain the damage. Ouch, it was an expensive casket, but that would be expected. We got out of there as soon as we could then met James and Eldon Strumple, the retired Methodist minister who often helped with internments at the Dexter cemetery. They showed us a few samples of the good Barre, Vermont granite. I favored the copper-toned headstone, and my uncle agreed. Then James took us out to where he proposed the plot should be located. It was the next row over from Beverly. After James suggested a larger plot, Uncle Bill seemed more interested. James dropped golf balls in the grass to help us visualize the size of a two, three, and four person plot. Uncle Bill suggested the four-person plot. I was ready to bolt. James must have recognized my look of panic, for he slipped his arm through mine and led me back to the office.

Next we met with our pastor at the church. My only suggestion was to include "How Great Thou Art" into the service. I let Uncle Bill talk specifics with Pastor Ryder. I started to wander around the narthex. Three church members were fiddling with the cords for a stack of speakers. Yes, it would be a large gathering. Rick's funeral was substantial; yet my dad's reputation and reach extended across several counties. How could I ever live up to that?

We made a quick stop the shop of Carlos Hernandez. As I wanted to use Dexter services whenever possible to foster good will, I arranged for a wash and detail on the morning of the funeral, which would take place on Saturday. Carlos even offered to go get the SUV that morning and return it in time for the twelve o'clock service. I wanted to go back to the office, but Uncle Bill suggested an early lunch.

At Custer's, Beulah stepped in front of the waitress to wait on us herself. We were the first customers for the day's lunch; I appreciated the quiet.

"How are you two? Tired? You both look kinda puny." She took the root beers from the waitress and poured them into glasses for us.

"Been looking at caskets," Uncle Bill said.

"Heh. Done that a few times myself. Always want to run screamin' from the place. You go to Sidney? I been there. Got an owner that looks like Boris Karloff."

"I thought he looked like Vincent Price," I said, taking a long draw from the root beer.

"Nah, that's the father. He doesn't do much. Well, I'll give you two some peace." She shuffled off.

Peace? That didn't seem possible.

Back at my desk, I thought of three demands to make to Pastor Ryder. First, at the internment, I did not want to hear the old timey scripture that ran, "earth to earth, ashes to ashes, dust to dust." Oh, I hated that as much as I now hated phony, mushy eyelids on dead people in movies. My second request was to avoid any explanation for the death. At funeral for a Kimball resident, the minister had made a feeble attempt that annoyed me. I felt I had the right to limit the potential of annoyance at my dad's funeral. Third, I requested better food at the luncheon—hot food, not bologna and limp salad. Accordingly, I promised to make an appropriate donation to the church. My pastor agreed; I knew he'd be good to his word.

At three o'clock, after Brian's last appointment, I sent Glenda and Melanie home with full pay. It was time to proceed with Transformation Part Two. I was now the caretaker of Docket Law—I had no intention of letting it fail. Then I asked Brian for his help with the move. He raised his eyebrows, but didn't question me. Brian started moving books from my office to my dad's old office. I moved the chair and brought the contents of the desk and then the file cabinets to my new office. I forwarded my old phone so that all calls came to my new office. I made space on the bookshelves by moving the books on railroad law to the abandoned office. I began moving my dad's old desk contents to a cardboard box, just as I had for Rick. That gave me a queasy feeling. I looked down at the spot where my dad had laid. Patty had since vacuumed so the many foot prints and the gurney wheel tracks were no longer visible. Brian waved his hand in front of my face to get my attention.

"I said that you need a new chair. That one isn't right—it's a paralegal's chair in a partner's office."

He was right. I started to go online then stopped. I took out my dad's Rolodex and flipped through the cards. I gave Paul Ritter a call. Paul managed the hardware store that also stocked a limited selection of office furniture and supplies. Paul replied that he kept a few office chairs in stock. Brian and I drove over to the store. I liked the leather chair they had in stock, but the burgundy color wasn't right for the cherry wood of the office.

"Oh, I can get a black one in a jiffy," Paul said. "And if I may, I suggest this footrest. You'll sit up higher at your desk."

"I do sit low, probably too low. My neck and arms are stiff most days after work."

Brian bought some supplies I know he didn't need. He gave me a wink. We headed back to the office. Just before Brian turned off Elm Street, I saw the van for the hardware store turn down the street. He really did mean "in a jiffy," as he looked to be heading to Sidney to get my chair.

Back in my new office, I started arranging the desk drawers to suit me. As I was investigating one of the lower drawers, I took out a large, old cigar box. I was stunned at its content—an old fashioned handgun, with a silver barrel and a wood handle. Why did he have a gun? I handed the box to Brian.

"Wow! I'm no expert, but this Colt is really old… maybe even 1800s."

"But why would he have it?" I asked.

"Well, he didn't intend to use it. There aren't any bullets. I bet this is worth something. Maybe your dad took it in payment for some service."

"That's possible."

"He wasn't a gun collector or he'd have this wrapped up or stored in a case. I could take it to my dad. He'd know someone at Cabela's who knows old firearms."

"Yeah, that's fine." I had already returned to arranging my desk.

"So… um… what do you plan to do with your old office?"

I smiled at him, well aware he hoped to get it. "I'm going to put a partner in it."

"Oh, who?"

"Well, I plan to make an offer to Gus. If he turns me down I'll need to look around. But I need somebody. So many of my dad's cases are beyond me. I'm not even going to attempt to learn railroad law. I remember my dad spending so much time studying those books while I was growing up. And he was already established in his practice." I stood up. "Follow me."

We walked to Brian's office. I suggested that he expand his office to the two rooms formerly occupied by Zach and me. A door in between the rooms would give him an office-conference room arrangement like in his Sidney office.

"I like the idea," he said, "but how much more a month would it cost me?"

"Oh, who cares? We'll figure it out." I looked at my watch. "We better get home. Patty will be waiting to heat up tonight's supper."

I stood still for a few moments, thinking about the visitation that awaited me tomorrow night and the funeral the next day. Brian must have read my mind, for he came and wrapped me up in his arms. My mind drifted to the bourbon and brownies, in equal longing, that I planned to consume after supper.

We invited James over for supper, as Vonny and Derek had gone back home, with plans to return tomorrow. The proposal of bourbon and brownies was heartily accepted, as was my suggestion for a John Wayne movie. We narrowed it down to Rio Bravo for tonight, and then El Dorado for after the visitation.

The next day, I worked in the morning then went home for the afternoon. Paul Ritter delivered my new chair and footstool at eight o'clock, an hour before his store even opened. Glenda and Melanie just nodded when they learned of the office change. Melanie pointed out that I needed to change the gold name plates on the office doors, which I did before leaving for home. Brian remained at the office and Uncle Bill stayed with his cows. Though I needed to attend to burying my dad, I also knew I needed to take every opportunity to start my search.

The biggest problem I faced was to figure out what I was searching for. Maybe I should find the old photos of my mother. I didn't know if she was even a part of the mystery, but I knew she was at least a starting point. I didn't need to look in my dad's room because Uncle Bill and I planned to clean out his room together. Then another thought struck me—keys. I'd be finding locked drawers and cabinets, particularly in my dad's study. So I needed to find the keys. First, I went down to the kitchen to the gold envelope we'd brought home from the hospital. I took his key chain and removed all the keys for which I didn't know their purpose. I also went through his wallet, the only other item in the envelope. I cut up his two credit cards into thirds and discarded the pieces in different waste baskets. I stuck the seventy-four dollars in the cupboard for Patty to use when needed. Then I heard a car door slam. My search had ended for the day. I dashed up to my room, put the three keys in an envelope, slipped a note inside indicating their origin, and then shoved the envelope under my mattress.

The three-hour visitation lasted ninety hours. Uncle Bill and I arrived a half-hour early. Cars were already lined along the street on both sides. Most had Cheyenne and Kimball County license plates, but many had Banner, Morrill, and Scottsbluff plates. The small funeral home had a lobby with thick, forest green carpet, several flower arrangements, the guest book, several stiff-looking chairs, and the corpulent Burton brothers, Jim and Joe, dressed in black suits, each a size too small, with soft, warm hands. My uncle and I had met with them earlier in the week, so there wasn't much to say. But they kept nodding and grasping my hands, which was oddly soothing. They confirmed that obituaries had been sent to numerous newspapers. They led us into the main room which stunned me for more reasons than my head could comprehend. Several rows of brown, stiff-backed chairs filled the middle of the room, with an aisle down the middle, which was surrounded by flower arrangements crammed together along every inch of every wall. Joe or maybe it was Jim, led us along the right wall where people would walk till they came to the casket on its bier at the front of the room—a sight I had avoided.

Soon, we stood before it. I looked up and saw his face. I blurted a sob and Uncle Bill wrapped his arm around me. We stood together and looked at him. His face had just enough of a pinkish tint to make him look alive. I waited for him to sit up, but he wouldn't. It disturbed me that he looked that alive. He wore the fine, navy suit with a white shirt and a red silk tie I selected. He looked ready for his office, ready for court, ready for anything but to be lowered into a trench and covered in dirt.

One of the brothers stepped to my side and said, "We did just as you asked, Miss Megan."

"What's that?" asked Uncle Bill.

Though the ground was well-thawed and the days had been warm, I kept thinking about the cold ground. So I had called with a special request.

"He's wearing those black dress boots he liked," I said. "I didn't want his feet to get cold."

Uncle Bill squeezed my shoulder and we chuckled together over the absurdity of it. A Burton nodded beside me. It probably wasn't the strangest request he'd heard. The other Burton urged us forward to the corner of the room where we'd stand to receive condolences.

God help us.

As planned, Patty, Brian, James, Derek, and Vonny sat down in the chairs closest to where we stood. While we waited for six o'clock, I looked over the flowers near us. Some were small pots filled with flowers from the grocery store, others were elaborate arrangements. Just before six, Kyle, Uncle Bill's son, came down the center aisle, dropped his head for a moment over the casket then walked over to us. I wouldn't have recognized him, as it had been ten years since he and his mother visited. Tall, with light brown hair and his father's square jaw, he stepped up to me and hugged me hard. He said the first "I'm so sorry" of the evening. Kyle shook his father's hand, greeted him then added something in a low voice. He then took his place alongside his father as the only other kin. Just three of us. I braced myself for hours of other people's grief and sentiments.

At home, I quit the movie halfway through. I felt a tremendous sense of exhaustion and the need to escape. Brian and I had agreed that he'd return to Sidney for the night and travel back with his dad and brother. Bill asked Patty to stay the night and she accepted—they probably worried I'd bolt. I didn't, but I slept little, rising before dawn.

At eight o'clock, Carlos Hernandez came to get the Shark. He liked the nickname. He had it back at nine-thirty. He said he threw in an oil change in lieu of flowers. I paid

124

him, tipped him generously, and thanked him. Flowers we didn't need—we had some of the overflow in our living room. They provided the house with fragrance, but like my dad, they would begin to rot in a couple of days. I turned away from my morbid thoughts and went for one of Glenda's cinnamon rolls in the kitchen. Lord, please get me through this day.

When I wandered toward the family room, Uncle Bill dashed past the back windows, followed by Derek, and another tall African American, who I assumed would be Vonny's boyfriend, Damian. I joined Vonny and Patty, who stood in the laundry room so they could get a view from rear and side windows.

"What's going on?" I asked.

"Wasps," replied Patty. "Too bad they don't know there's another nest."

They ran by again, now carrying black Raid canisters. Together they sprayed at a location under the back door eave. They backed away then turned and ran toward the back of the yard, spraying the air behind them. Traddles ran after them, barking. We laughed.

"That must be Damian," I said.

"Yeah," said Vonny. "I'll introduce you. Oh! Uncle Bill just got stung."

Patty held up a little gold tube. "I got the Neosporin ready."

"Oh, I met your guy last night, Miggy. You got yourself a hottie, and blond to boot. So does he make love like a football player...lots of fumbles?"

I laughed. "Nah. He's more like a hockey player—power and finesse."

Both women laughed. Patty started pointing toward the garage. Uncle Bill stared at her for a moment. Then the men regrouped and started searching for the second colony.

"The Three Stooges kill wasps," said Vonny. "I wonder where my dad is. I'm surprised he's not in on this."

"So, how are you and your dad?" I asked.

"We're talking. I heard he's drinking and driving again."

"Hey! That's not fair—"

Vonny cut me off. "I was just checking to make sure you still had the fight in you. You looked pretty whipped last night."

I nodded. Patty went to open the front door. James and Tina, Derek's girlfriend, entered. Kyle followed a few minutes later. Vonny and I turned back just in time to watch the three men spray and dash. They sprinted around the garage toward the front of the house. Soon, our group, several tall people and me, were assembled in the living room. Uncle Bill was expected to be the tough old cowboy. I found out that I was expected to be the pampered, fragile Queen Bee. I would allow it—for one day.

Lovely organ music, lovely hymns, grand turnout, grand words—it all floated by me without ever connecting. I had gone into a trance. Uncle Bill wiped his eyes once; I did likewise, with a tissue that stayed dry. I would and had gushed, it just wasn't happening now. That entire day was a fog, with a dark cloud overhead, and the weight of loss ever pressing down on my shoulders. Later people said that I had borne it bravely, and I graciously accepted the compliments, but I really couldn't take credit for numbness.

The moment that tore at me occurred at the cemetery, when the time came for us to leave the tent and the pastor's kind words. But my legs turned to lead after I walked up to the casket, which would be lowered into the grave once we all left. But I couldn't move. I didn't gush; I just couldn't abandon him to that black solitude. Uncle Bill tried to gently budge me, but he wasn't a strong enough force to move me. Eleventy minutes later, my arms were bent then hands under my elbows cleared me just off the ground enough to turn me toward the cars and propel me forward. Derek and Brian escorted me, never letting go of my arms. They sat beside me in the car. Maybe they thought I would bolt.

At the luncheon, kind words abounded. As I stood near the doorway alongside Uncle Bill, I discovered that repeating the same gracious replies helped me to cope with the series of farmers, ranchers, and cowboys in out-dated suits, tugging at their shirt collars; middle-aged women in flower-print dresses, clutching their vinyl purses; and the town folk in suits of linen or worsted wool, cringing through their community duty.

Later I sat with a plate of unappetizing food in front of me—it even included chocolate pudding I neglected—which demonstrated the extent of my disturbance. Enduring the advice of wrinkled old and not-so-old ladies, I patiently listened to their warnings about eating too little, or staying out in the sun too long, or neglecting to take my Vitamin D. I smiled, nodded, and held my tongue. Uncle Bill and I sat and listened to what a great man Frank Docket had been for western Nebraska. I heard story after story of how my dad had helped people in their time of need.

Mr. Talmadge from Gering, stopped by, as did Police Chief Ray Dobbs, the local bully, and Deputy Bo Schnitzel, who had been helpful on the day of my dad's heart attack, and seemed to bear no ill will for the firing of his sister, Lindsey Whitfield. One particular visitor did revive me. Al Carlssen, the North Platte State Farm Superintendant, paid his respects then complimented me on a recent case we'd won. Al helped me remember that there was life after today. The lawsuit had been my first time handling a court case from start to finish, even though my dad had been alongside me at the defense table. Before he left, I leaned in for a confidential word.

"I'll be hiring an experienced partner for Docket Law. I'll keep you posted."

Al nodded then shook my hand again before he moved on. I kept looking around, hoping to see someone from the old country, a person who looked like a darker version of me. But I never saw anyone who could have been a relative from Omaha. That made me sad—we were only two. Kyle would leave and I wouldn't see him for another ten years. I felt the itch to bolt. Brian sat at a table adjacent to ours with his dad and brother, and the Wilson gang. I really wanted to leave and go crawl underneath that hot, muscular body, and hear his comforting words in his dulcet baritone voice.

I stirred out of my thoughts when a man, wearing a suit with creases as if it had just been taken out of a storage box, approached Uncle Bill and me. He looked around to see if anyone was listening. On cue, James turned in his chair a little then started examining the number of pineapple chunks suspended in his lime Jell-O.

"Mr. Docket did me a great service once...me and my family that is. I won't bore you with the particulars, but my folks was able to keep our farm, even if some of it was scratch dirt. It was ours. He helped us when we got in trouble with the bank. Those men were right tough with us, but they backed off quick-like when Mr. Docket walked through the door. Yes, ma'am, yessir, I just hope they keep on bein' nice to us."

The man, Max Zimmer, early forties and lean, tugged at the hem of his suit coat and looked around again. I pulled a pen and my card holder from my purse.

"Which bank was it Mr. Zimmer?" I asked.

"The county bank, Miz Docket."

I gave him my law firm card. "Next time they contact you, you tell them they need to call me." I wrote a quick note on a doily and shoved it in my purse. "And it's Megan. Thank you so much for coming today. It means a great deal to my uncle and me."

"What're you growing this year, Max?" asked Uncle Bill.

"Soybeans, mostly."

"Got any hay? I've been slow getting mine up."

"Well, sure thing, Bill. Just harvested some this week."

128

"I'll buy it off ya. Give me a call. I'm still at the big house."

Max brightened. "Will do, will do." He shook our hands. "I'm awful sorry 'bout Mr. Docket."

After Max left, I said to my uncle, "You big softie. You don't need the hay and if he cut it this early, it isn't ready."

"So I'll store it, Miss I'll Take Care of the Bank."

"All I want to know is when we can get the hell out of here."

We had a full family room for our viewing of Red River. When the house was quiet, I tip-toed down the front stairs. I planned to make a search in my dad's office while I could. I was surprised that the light was still on in the family room. Uncle Bill was sleeping in my dad's chair. I'd never seen him sit there. I didn't like it. Maybe I should buy a new chair and claim it as mine. But that felt spiteful; anyway, I liked sitting on the sofa where I could put my feet up on a pillow on the coffee table or snuggle in close to Brian. My uncle's glass of bourbon was on the end table next to him, nearly empty. I roused him and sent him up to his bed.

I opened the door to my dad's office. The room, in fact, the whole house felt heavy with memory. I went back to bed.

Chapter 14

Brian always slept soundly, but I took great care not to wake him as I slipped the envelope out from under the mattress. I left him a note where I'd be. Uncle Bill's door was still shut, as was the guest room door where Patty slept. I crept down the front stairs, the quieter of the two sets, and then headed for my dad's office. It contained a desk, an old brown leather chair in the corner by the window, bookshelves, and a cabinet. As expected, the cabinet held old National Geographic and NEBRASKAland magazines. A tray on the desk contained current house and credit card bills. The drawers to the desk were locked. I discovered that one of the three keys opened the top center drawer, which released the locks on the other drawers. Much of the contents were old bank statements and ledgers, as well as his tax records for the last twelve years. One drawer was devoted to insurance statements and photocopies of insurance policies.

Two things became clear—Uncle Bill and I were the equal beneficiaries of a life insurance policy totaling a million dollars. I had a half million dollars. Holy cow! That much money was beyond my comprehension. Yet, the second fact tempered my enthusiasm. Though I saw no evidence of another life insurance policy, the annual statement from March indicated a second policy. The statement listed only policy numbers, one of which matched the policy for Uncle Bill and me. Where was the other policy and who was the beneficiary? I searched the desk again, but found no other information.

Uncle Bill would be pleased; he'd been disappointed by the compensation he received for the damage to his house. He sheepishly admitted that he hadn't followed the advice of either the agent or me, for we'd recommended replacement cost plus an inflation index. Then I began to wonder what he'd think of my sneaking about. I decided to make copies of the keys and return the originals to the key ring. I knew just the man to do the deed. After breakfast, Brian set off for Kimball on a mission. I'd delay telling Uncle Bill about our life insurance proceeds until I had a duplicate set of keys.

Out of curiosity, I went out to the garage to check the registration on the Shark. Whoa—it was mine. The Acura MDX SUV was in the name of Frank Docket and Megan Docket, WROS—With Right Of Survivorship. The all-wheel drive would come in handy this winter. And it was all nice and clean, with kick-ass horsepower, all the bells and whistles, GPS, and an awesome BOSE audio system. The financial implications made my head spin and my stomach churn. But who benefited from the second insurance policy? Before I proceeded to my next course of action, I went inside and took four Rolaids.

"You better leave that bottle out," said Uncle Bill. He took a couple Rolaids. "What're you doin' today?"

"Oh, I think I'll just hang out," I said. "What about you?"

"I should go take a look at that northwest fence. May need to replace it."

We heard the sound of a basketball bouncing. I went to look out the back door. Uncle Bill followed with his coffee cup.

"Not much of a game," he said.

Derek and Vonny sat close together on the concrete basketball court. Vonny held her head in her hands. Like me, she wouldn't have any memory of life before Harney Street and the wild, dry country. Derek, a year older than me, remembered only that they lived in a white house and they had a refrigerator with the freezer on the bottom.

"Damian and Tina must be sleeping in," I said.

"Remember when you tattled on that Webster punk for sayin' somethin' to Derek?"

132

"Oh, yeah. Dad called the coach and Brett warmed the bench for two games," I said.

"And Frank also paid a visit to his parents. I bet they just about crapped their pants," said Uncle Bill with a chuckle. "You know the life of the Wilson family was so much better than it would of been without your dad."

"You would've helped them."

"Yeah, I would have tried. Frank succeeded."

We turned at the sound of Brian entering the kitchen.

"You should invite the Wilsons for lunch," I said to Uncle Bill. "They won't think they're imposing on us if you invite them. And we have a ton of food. Make sure James comes. He hates the circumstances, but you know he's loving all the company."

My uncle nodded and walked out to the court. Meanwhile, Brian dashed back to the living room. I followed him and saw that he'd hidden the sack with the keys under the cushion in the living room. I quickly returned the original keys to the ring and dropped them back in the gold envelope, just before Patty walked through the front door.

"Miss us?" I asked.

"Ah, hell, it's too bloody quiet at my place. And somebody has to operate the microwave."

"'Bloody?'" Brian remarked.

"She's been watching Harry Potter again," I said.

Actually, we'd all become big fans, especially after the third movie, the Prisoner of Azkaban. Surprisingly, my dad enjoyed the movies as much as the rest of us did. James, Patty, and Uncle Bill even read all the books.

"I've started reading that first book again," Patty said. "It helps to take my mind off things."

I studied her. "Patty, what's on your mind?"

"Well, um, Bill says the house is in your name."

"How's that?"

"Your dad put your name on the deed to the house. Uncle Bill had his own house then."

"So it's in my name? Bloody hell. I didn't even know. Oh, and you're wondering if I'm going to keep you on? Well, no. I've decided to run the law firm, clean it, cook and clean here, and just give up sleeping." I gave her shoulder a shove. "Of course, you're staying…if you want."

She chuckled. "Oh, one more thing. My Lakota sisters are planning a march on Whiteclay next month. I was thinking of going."

"If I wasn't so busy, I wouldn't mind going with you."

"Oh, no. Bad idea. They'd find out you're a lawyer and, damn, they might kidnap you for the cause."

Patty turned to Brian. "You know about Whiteclay, don't ya? Pine Ridge is a dry rez, but those scum sell four million cans of beer each year to my people. And we're tired of all the violence and alcoholism."

"Of course, I know about Whiteclay," Brian quickly said. "Everybody does. It's a damn shame the government can't shut them down."

"Damn right," said Patty then nodded effusively.

"Is your Chevy going to make it?" I asked. "Hey, take my Camry. You can let Carlos work on your car while you're gone."

Uncle Bill walked in. "They'll be coming for lunch."

"Hey, is the house really in my name?" I asked him.

"Yep. He got that changed, oh, years ago. Strange, he never told you."

"Yeah, strange. The Shark's in my name, too. I didn't know that either." I wondered what else I didn't know. "We need to go to the bank and take a look at the contents of his safety deposit box."

"Yeah, we'll do that," he said as he put down his coffee cup. "I better get goin'." He strode out of the room.

I put my hands on my hips and stared after him.

"Don't you be pushin' him, Megan," said Patty. "He can't separate business and personal like you can."

"Fine." I turned to Brian. "Hey, let me show you where we hid during the tornado. Remember, you wanted to see? There's some strange stuff down there."

It's all personal, I thought. The will, insurance policies, deeds to the house and the law firm building were in that box. But it was a box the brothers shared—I had no access to it. Though now I knew that Patty considered Uncle Bill the one who needed to be protected. She assumed I would cry yet push forward. I guess she was right. Yet it was now clear that my search would need to be disguised as acts of nostalgia and grief—at least for Uncle Bill and Patty. In time, I would take Brian into my confidence, but I didn't have enough concrete information right now.

Halfway down the basement stairs, I paused and said, "When I was little, I was afraid of these stairs. They didn't have a railing and the backs of the steps were open. Derek used to grab at Vonny's and my feet. We'd shriek and run back up the steps. Sometimes, he'd hide down here and jump out and scare us." We walked the rest of the way down to the concrete floor. "Once, I told Uncle Bill about being scared of those steps. He told my dad, who hired a carpenter to rebuild the whole staircase. Look under here. This is where we hid during the tornado. See how my dad had the stairs reinforced with these four by four beams? Uncle Bill should have done the same, but he doesn't like to spend money. I've selected everything he wears, except his Husker gear. He will buy that stuff himself. Come to think of it, I picked out my dad's clothes, too."

The room was cool and smelled of dusty furniture and musty books. Much of the basement was filled with the discarded tables, lamps, bookshelves, and chairs Uncle Bill had salvaged from his first marriage, as his second wife didn't want it in her house. It only took three years before he didn't want her in his house.

"I suppose Uncle Bill will use some of this old furniture, if he ever rebuilds," I said.

In the far corner of the room, three plastic bags hung from a metal rack. We kids had never bothered with the six-foot cabinet behind the clothes bags because it was locked. I swung the rack away from the cabinet, and then pulled the duplicate keys from my jeans pocket. One of the keys unlocked the desk in the study, so I tried the other two keys, one smaller in size. The small key worked. I glanced at Brian just before I swung the door open.

It was empty—nearly. A plastic bag contained a yellowed stuffed bunny. On the other shelf was a photo processing envelope dated 1986. The first photo caught my breath—it was me as a toddler with my mother kneeling behind me. The tears started. More photos of me and my mom and sometimes with my dad. He posed with us in a couple of photos, but smiled more candidly with just him and me in the photo. The tears continued. The bunny, then white, even showed up in a couple of shots.

I gushed.

Brian looked around for something to dry my eyes, and then just pulled off his T-shirt to wipe my eyes. I just couldn't stop. I was an orphan. Yeah, I was twenty-five years old, but still an "orfling" as Dickens would say. I tried not to wipe my nose on his shirt, but it ran. He wiped it for me.

In time, the crying stopped and exhaustion hit. I locked the cabinet as he put on his shirt. While we climbed the stairs, I worked at hiding the photos in my rear waistband. I urged Brian to have some lunch.

"Megan," said Vonny, "come sit down. I know you haven't heard the bison story enough times."

I smiled, though I knew everyone could tell I'd been crying. "Ever have those times when you just gotta have a nap?"

"Every day," said Patty.

I nodded and ascended the back stairs. The room had gone quiet. I didn't mean to make them sad. I hoped Uncle Bill would go on with the story. I put the photos under my mattress, pulled off my jeans, and then slid between my sheets.

I awoke a couple of hours later. Brian was asleep on top of the comforter. His T-shirt was dry but crumpled where I had cried on it. I stirred and he awoke. I climbed out of bed and pulled the photo package out from under the mattress. I laid out the photos on the bed. I set the photo I took from Uncle Bill's dresser and set it next to the Omaha photos.

"Does this look like the same time?" I asked Brian.

He examined the photos. "Possibly. Or maybe later?"

"We don't look happy." That made me feel sad.

"Well, maybe you were. Where'd you get this one?"

"From Uncle Bill's dresser after his bedroom collapsed on me."

I gathered up the photos and shoved them back under the mattress, though their absence didn't relieve my confused mind.

"Your mother was beautiful."

"I don't think kids care what their parents look like. I bet you didn't care about your mom's appearance—you just wanted her alive and healthy."

After Brian left, I went over to the Wilson's that afternoon to say goodbye to Derek and Vonny, who'd be leaving for their homes. I pulled the packet of photos out of my back pocket to show Derek and Vonny.

Vonny gasped and covered her mouth.

Derek studied them for a long time. "I wish I could have known her. Where'd you get these?"

"You know that cabinet in the basement we could never open? I found this stack of photos and an old bunny."

"All these years..." said Vonny shaking her head.

Tina and Damian had stood off to the side, respecting our personal moment. James shuffled in. I handed him the photos.

He went and sat at the kitchen table. "Oh, Lord. Megan, did you just now find these?"

"Yes."

"How?" asked Derek.

"A bit of sleuthing. And you three have just seen it in confidence. Right?"

They nodded.

"You were a little pork chop back then," James said with a smile.

Oh, how I wish I could've remembered those days.

Chapter 15

Although I expected Monday to be hectic with appointments and catching up on work, I started the day with a run in an eerie, misty fog. At the first opportunity, I called Steve Moore, my State Farm insurance agent. He confirmed the life insurance policy for Bill and me, and then assured me it was being processed. He was tight-lipped on the second insurance policy, though he said he wouldn't deny its existence. After some prodding, he said he couldn't divulge the name on the policy, but said it referred to a trust.

A trust? Did my dad have an illegitimate child? That would be information he wouldn't want made public. I hoped the will would make things clear, though it was hard to predict when Uncle Bill would cooperate. Then I realized some of the contents in the safe deposit box would be rightfully mine. When I had a break, I zipped over to the Cheyenne County Bank. Though our firm business, direct deposit payments, and my salary all went to the Wells Fargo bank next door, my dad also used the county bank, again, to maintain good will.

While I was filling out the paperwork for my own safety deposit box, Jeff Finch, an old classmate and now a personal banker at the branch, approached me and asked if I wanted to delete my dad's name on the account. Stunned, I agreed. At his desk, I learned I shared a money market account with my dad. I would need to find that checkbook, even though I'd be issued new checks. Before I left, I obtained a cashier's check, drawn on the account, for $10,000.00.

I hurried back to the firm for my next appointment. Gus was right on time. We chatted for a bit then confirmed the three cases we had in opposition. Then I asked him to follow me. Just as we opened the door, Glenda scurried up to us and gave Gus a cup of coffee and a cinnamon scone. We walked across to the empty oak-wood office.

"Do you like it?" I asked, knowing full well it was far nicer than his office on Elm Street, our main drag.

"It's very nice. The curtains are an improvement." He started on the scone.

"Then take it."

"What do you mean?"

"I want to hire you. In fact, I'll make you a partner. I need an experienced associate, and you need the office you deserve with full-time staff and great coffee."

"I can't possibly accept. I'd just be eating Glenda's pastries all day. In a month I wouldn't be able to fit through this door."

I smiled then handed him the cashier's check. "This is just to make it even more tempting. You don't need to give me an answer now."

"Your offer is indeed tempting. My office is musty, it needs new carpeting, and the landlord is jacking up the rent."

"My dad paid off this building, so we don't need to worry about a mortgage."

"I believe I am quite ready to accept your offer."

"Really? That's great." I said as I shook his hand.

"We'll need to resolve our adverse cases. Then we can work out the details."

"Of course. We'll make that a priority. My dad told me that he wished he had you in his firm, but he didn't want to deprive Dexter of its only other good trial attorney."

I'd seen Professor John Tremaine at the funeral. My dad's old classmate, now a Creighton Law School professor, gave me a call that morning, as I had requested. We discussed my plans for the firm. He agreed to be "Of Counsel"—a paid

140

consultant for the firm. He promised to make another trip out next month to work on files with me. Transformation Part Two was now complete. I hoped there would be no need for a part three. I gave Melanie the new names for the firm's letterhead. I kept the exact style to provide a sense of continuity. I listed my name at the top. Though I was the rookie, by strange circumstance, I was also the boss. I left for lunch feeling satisfied that I had done my best to shore up the experience and credentials for my family legacy. The one act I wasn't ready to carry out was to remove my dad's name from the front of the building.

As I walked to the Pizza Shoppe to meet Brian, I realized that I didn't want to be like my dad—not as a parent, and not even as an attorney. I didn't want his intimidating style. He even made his own clients nervous. He was oh, so smart, and I envied his experience, but I did much better with people. Judge Shelton said we made a good trial team. My dad took on the law and the adverse counsel; I dealt with the people, the witnesses, the characters whose lives were affected by this need for legal intervention. Even when we had met with new clients, I asked most of the questions, drawing out of people the secrets they hadn't wanted to admit. And people did have those bits of life or particulars of business they didn't want to come to light. First, I'd try to get people to relax then I'd work up to more probing questions, and then hit the crucial issues. Sometimes, they flat-out lied. Then we were forced to deal with that, hopefully before trial or settlement. It was one thing to argue or lie about business dealings; it was an entirely different matter to fudge the facts in a child custody case. I was tough on liars who faced bankruptcy; I was bloody tenacious when it came to protecting children.

I stopped outside the door to the Pizza Shoppe. Realization smacked me in the head—I would be doing all the questioning, all the exposing, all the secret-keeping, all the protecting from now on. True, I would be consulting Gus often, but he specialized in business matters, whereas I would specialize in personal matters—the broken bones, the broken homes, the broken spirits.

Just then, some handsome blond came up behind me, rested his hand on the small of my back and kissed me softly. He mentioned his hunger for pizza and for me then led me inside.

That evening, after Uncle Bill went to bed and Patty left for home, I conducted a more thorough search of my dad's office. First, I separated the bank statements from the two banks into two piles, and then I stacked insurance information into a third pile. The insurance pile gave me no additional information; however, the bank statements did. My father didn't have the cash reserve I thought he had—of course, paying tuition and room and board for seven years in a private college and law school depleted his assets considerably—yet his Wells Fargo account, which also included my name as an account holder—indicated a $3000 automatic withdrawal every month. The beneficiary of this payment was a trust. It frustrated me, but I wrote a note to call the bank to make sure these withdrawals continued. If my dad had a dependent somewhere, I certainly wasn't going to terminate these payments, at least until I discovered his or her identity and worthiness.

I locked up the desk, closed the door, and then crawled onto the sofa in the family room where Brian was watching a late Giants-Dodgers game. I laid my head on his leg and stretched out.

"You're the sofa elf. Except for small children, you're the only one in town who could lay lengthwise on this couch and not even use it all."

"I travel well, too."

"Hey, I was thinking we should go to the Cowpoke sometime."

"Really? I've never been there. Uncle Bill goes there. My dad didn't think it was a respectable place for him to go."

"But you're not your dad."

"So true. I've actually been curious about it. I'm sure there's some serious twang coming out of Dexter's only bar. That's not my favorite music. Hey, can you do the Two-Step?"

"Sure. I'm rusty, but I know how. I don't care for those line dances...make me feel silly, but I'd dance with you. We can invite your uncle and Patty, if it would make you feel better."

"Let's go Saturday night. I finally persuaded Uncle Bill to agree to go through my dad's room on Saturday. We'll need something fun that night."

We watched the game for another inning then an idea jabbed at me. I jumped up from the sofa and headed back to the study, fumbling with the keys in my pocket. Brian must have been concerned, for he followed on my heels. Remembering the large space underneath the lower drawers, I yanked out the right one—it held, then I pulled hard on the left drawer and it landed on the floor. I peered into the opening. Brian switched on the desk lamp. I reached in, extracting a small fire-proof safety box. I tried the third and final key—it did not fit. Shit. Then just as quickly, I was running my hand along the inside of each drawer opening and along the bottoms of the drawers, hoping I'd find a key, not leftover spider webs from last summer. I suddenly stopped.

"What?" asked Brian, who had leaned over my activities with anticipation.

I worked a key loose from the black electrician's tape that had held it in place along the back panel of a right side drawer. I tried the lock and it opened. Inside was a stack of several old envelopes. I opened the top one, read a couple of lines of the letter. Oh, shit. They were letters between my dad and my mom. I dropped the letter and lay back on the floor. Brian snatched up the letter, read a few lines then deduced the same conclusion.

"Whoa, Megan." He dropped the letter on the pile and sat next to me. "What do you plan to do?"

I shook my head. I wanted facts, just the facts. After several minutes of silence, Brian shoved the drawers back into the desk. He handed me the letters and the keys, but put the box back in its hiding place. He helped me to my feet. I locked the desk and we went up to my room. I shoved the letters underneath the mattress. I sat on the bed then Brian sat next to me, waiting for me to react.

"God above, I am tired," I said.

He kissed me on the cheek then went to brush his teeth. We prepared for bed. But as I lay next to him, I felt the need to burrow into his heat. It was a strange behavior he tolerated—he allowed me to slide underneath him and generally grab onto his lats or fold my arms into my body. Though he must've thought of me as part badger, he waited as he held his body above mine and tried not to squish me. His patience always paid off—for I'd next want to experience more and more of his heat. Heat was good. It was wet, passionate kisses, and removal of clothing and his lips all over me. He was extraordinarily kind in giving me time to change horses and move from an emotional mess after work to a woman hungry for soft, hard, hot comfort. He was stud, through and through, and I enjoyed the benefits.

The next day, business kept Brian in Sidney. He was wining and dining a client that evening, so I wouldn't see him till Friday. It wasn't impossible that he could have been meeting with someone else. Maybe I'd become too much of a burden. He probably liked getting free from the heaviness of the Docket saga. He'd been in a long relationship that had gone sour before he moved to Sidney. Perhaps he didn't have faith in forever. Did I? It was just too much to think about right now. But no, I didn't think he was cheating on

144

me. He'd kept his apartment in Sidney and the room in the Benson Street house, but he seemed to like being at our house and with me. I suppose I'd just need to trust in that.

Meanwhile, the letters remained under my mattress. I didn't work as late as I usually did that day, for the thought of those letters left me disquieted. Patty and Uncle Bill had adjusted our mealtime without complaint. I suspected my uncle snacked beforehand. Now I was home with a bit of time to kill. Though I hadn't gone out to the hills since the day after my dad's death, I felt something unusual stirred in the late afternoon.

I headed to the Seven Dwarfs, cutting northeast. Just as I rounded a butte, a figure loomed ahead of me. I gasped. At first, I thought it was Salt then I saw the dark hair and knew it was Lew. The last time I'd seen him he was in handcuffs at the courthouse.

"Hello, Miss Megan," Lew said. "I didn't mean to startle ya."

"Hello. I didn't know you liked these hills," I said. "I guess the last thing you expect to meet in nowhere is someone."

"I'm sorry, I know I'm trespassin' on your land. Just beyond that bluff over there used to be our land. Salt still thinks it is, but we done sold that to your pa long ago."

He meant the land northeast of the Beast. He twitched like a prairie dog away from his hole—he was more nervous of me than I was of him.

"And how is your brother?"

Lew shrugged. "Ah, crazy as ever. Once he got outta jail he just took off. Don't know where he goes. Came back today. I needed some air."

A gust whipped through the hills and wrapped itself around us. I turned to the voices for a moment then turned back, hoping I hadn't been seen. Lew was still turned toward the wind.

He glanced at me then dropped his head. "Nothin'."

"I didn't hear nothin' either," I said.

Now he looked directly at me for the first time. "You don't seem like most young gals."

"I suppose not," I said, wondering what he heard.

He scratched his stubble for a few moments. He wore dingy, ill-fitted overalls like his brother wore. I'd be careful not to stand downwind of him. He looked back at me—I saw loneliness in his eyes.

"Mr. Eldritch, why don't you come over for supper and poker?"

"Heh! Ain't no mister about me. Call me Lew. And supper? I ain't had a good woman-cooked meal in forever. I eat canned beans and polish sausage lots a nights."

"Patty is pretty good." It took us awhile, but we had finished off the food people cooked for us. "It'll be Uncle Bill, Patty, James Wilson, and me." I thought he might be opposed to being around James because of the car accident. But he didn't react to the name.

"And poker? Man o' man. Ain't played that in years." He snorted and gasped in his delight.

"Well, don't get too excited, we don't even use money, and it's not strip."

Lew snorted even more. I would wait till he fell over before I started CPR.

Once he settled into a chuckle, I said, "Seven o'clock."

"Thank you, Miss Megan."

"Just Megan." I turned and waved at him over my shoulder.

Uncle Bill laughed out loud when I told him who I'd invited to supper. Patty put another steak on the grill as she muttered.

"What's that, Patty?" I asked teasingly.

"Well, it's your house, but I'm expectin' him to be mighty stinky. Probably come here loaded, too."

"Nah, Salt's the drinker…he's a bad drinker really," said Uncle Bill. "The stuff makes him mean. Lew will be all right."

But Lew surprised us all. Intent on making a good impression, he was showered and shaved, with his hair slicked back. His cotton pants were so new and stiff they could have stood up on their own, and his striped oxford shirt still bore the fold wrinkles. I wondered if he remembered to remove the price tags. He handed both me and Patty a bunch of wildflowers as bouquets. None of us mocked his efforts; in fact, we did our best to make him feel at ease. A tense moment occurred when James walked in and the two men faced each other. I doubt they had seen each other since the trial that placed liability on Bob Eldritch. My dad won that trial on behalf of James, despite the efforts of our racist Police Chief Ray Dobbs. He'd given Derek plenty of grief during his adolescence, and then failed in his attempt to get James condemned to felony vehicular homicide. Still, both James and Lew had lost loved ones on that night. I guess I should have called James to warn him. The room sighed with relief when Lew's hand shot forward and they shook hands.

While we waited for supper, I showed Lew the rooms on the main floor. Lew took special interest in our bookshelves, scattered throughout various rooms. He ran his finger down the spines of our fancy books—the hardbound copies with the gold-tipped pages.

"Used to love to read as a kid. Probably nobody would think that. You got lots of Dickens. I like his stories plenty, but I haveta watch the movies 'cause he's so hard to read."

We owned every novel and short story Charles Dickens ever wrote. Over the years we'd managed to locate a good quality new or used hardbound copy of each novel. James had his own set that Derek, Vonny, and Beverly had enjoyed. We had formed our own Harney Street Dickens Club. As teens, Vonny and I quizzed the other club members with lines from the novels to see who could name the character. Vonny,

147

Derek, and I used a code name for my dad—Mr. Dombey—the hard-driving father who pampered his son as his heir in business, while he ignored his daughter, who he deemed inferior. I was jokingly referred to as "Paul Dombey," the son. The story didn't otherwise fit as Paul died young and I didn't have a sibling to be neglected.

"I love his books, but it's slow going the first time through," said James.

Lew seemed pleased that James was friendly to him. I pulled a thick book off the shelf and put it in his hands.

"Ever read this one?" I asked about the Larry McMurtry novel, Lonesome Dove.

"No, but I heard it was good."

"Take it," I said. "It'll take you awhile because it's a long one. But I bet you'll like it."

Lew stared at me. "Really? I've tried to get a library card, but they keep denying me."

"I'll call the library. Check with them later in the week."

He seemed dumbstruck. Uncle Bill walked into the room.

"Time to eat," said Uncle Bill. "Lew, you'll like that. Here, let me put it by the front door so you won't forget it." He took the book from Lew then guided him out of the room.

In the dining room, Uncle Bill showed him a window the tornado shattered. "Frank had to replace four other windows on this side."

"That tornado headed our way after it hit your house, Bill," Lew said. "We lost windows and two trees. Still got plastic up."

"I never heard that. Why didn't you tell anyone?"

Lew shrugged. Patty encouraged us to sit down. Lew pulled out my chair for me. He tried to race over to Patty, but she'd already sat down. Uncle Bill sat on one end of the table. The chair at the other end remained empty. Lew ate an incredible amount of food. Later in the evening, Patty filled several containers with food she claimed we'd never eat and left them by the front door for Lew to take home. In truth, she skipped the poker game to cook for Lew.

Lew proved to be a lousy poker player. He relished his bourbon, sipping it slowly. Uncle Bill grinned at me across the kitchen table. My bourbon tasted better than ever. Lew was a good reminder not to take for granted the comforts of life, especially companionship. It sounded like Salt was in and out of the house and rotten company when he was home. I imagined Lew spent a great deal of time alone and miserable.

Before I left the game to go to bed, I invited the group to go to the Cowpoke on Saturday night with Brian and me. Lew became embarrassed and twitchy; yet I had a feeling that Uncle Bill would convince him to come. The events of the next day convinced me otherwise.

Chapter 16

As I entered Custer's for lunch the next day, Friday, I spotted Brian in a booth at the far side of the room. Salt Eldritch sat at a table in the center of the room with three other men. I paused behind the girth of Marva Gush as she fumbled with her purse. Although the room was full, I picked out Salt's voice, which he made loud for everyone to hear:

"Ah, Joe, forget that. Frank Docket ran around with an Injun and some niggers. I say, let him rot in hell!"

The diner shushed. My anger had no words. I stepped around Marva. I had just enough time to think about my execution. Salt turned his face toward me just in time for my punch to hit him square in the nose, snapping his head back. His nose immediately spouted blood. It was as hard as I could hit someone—my fist had been tight and I drove it from my shoulder, with my right foot firmly planted. As he covered his face with his hands, I walked around his chair and headed to the booth. The room was hushed in shock. Salt held a napkin over his face for a moment then threw it down. He rose from his chair and started toward my booth. Brian must have known he'd come for me, for he was out of the booth and standing in front of Salt in a flash.

"Now, what are you planning to do, Mr. Eldritch?" asked Brian.

Salt paused and looked up at Brian. He backed up and headed for the door, blood dripping off his chin onto his shirt. This time Beulah stopped him. I'd never seen her so mad.

"You disrespected Mr. Frank Docket. And nobody says Injun or the N-word in my restaurant. Then you get beat up by a pipsqueak. Get your sorry bones out of here and never come back!"

The diner erupted in laughter and applause as Salt yanked the door open and left.

Brian sat back down in the booth. "Da-amn, you busted him good. Where'd you learn to punch like that?"

"The playground," I said.

My heart was racing. I buried my head in a menu I had memorized years ago. I wondered at my act of violence. Salt hadn't seen me, so he didn't say anything to challenge me. I felt ashamed that I hadn't just given him a tongue-lashing. I always mocked professional athletes who got into fights. Now I deserved the same reproach. Yet, it turned out I was the only one who thought as I did. Brian grinned at me. When I looked around the restaurant, people waved or toasted me with their root beer.

Beulah shuffled over with two root beers. She wasn't even the owner, but she was the face of Custer's. Blaine often worked the cash register, but both he and Dane preferred to stay in back, working the books, or stocking the storeroom. Eldon Strumple's son, EJ, did most of the cooking.

"Young lady, that was a mighty fine punch," she said. "Now, you two order somethin' good, 'cause five different folks have offered to pay your bill. Oh, and Megan, don't be surprised if you pick up some new names. I heard Big Joe calling you Rambo just while I was walkin' past. Sorry 'bout the pipsqueak name. That one won't be stickin'." She chuckled as she shuffled away.

"Actually, I'm embarrassed," I said to Brian. "No way could I have let it go, but I should've just said something and left it at that."

"Don't worry about it. It was probably therapeutic for you. And people, especially around here, like to see strength, and they want to see it in you. They know you're

152

hurting, so they like seeing the fight in you. Plus, they may need you some day, and they'll want Docket fortitude when they do."

"Thanks."

It was all I said, partly because I sensed people were trying to eavesdrop. I marveled at this wonderful man. I've never been a romantic, head in the clouds type, but I truly valued him. I appreciated his brains, his brawn, his lovin', but as much as anything, I enjoyed just talking. He was five years older than me, but we had a great deal in common. We enjoyed just chatting about books, or movies, or sports, or sharing stories about growing up. I had even taken him to see the Seven Dwarves, Pooper's Canyon, the Raccoon Creek, and Big Leo. I suppose I had drawn him into my family mystery to bring him closer to me. And I never doubted his discretion. Maybe Vonny was right, maybe he would find it more than he wanted to deal with. So far, he hadn't shown any signs of bolting. But I hadn't told him how much I cared about him. I needed to do that. Otherwise, he might think I kept him around just for kicks.

Back at the office, Melanie and Glenda already knew about the punch. I just waved at their applause. I shut the door and called Jeff Finch at the county bank. I asked him if my father's safety deposit box had been accessed since his death. Then I quickly said, "Oh, by the way, do you know a personal banker who could help me invest fifty grand?"

It worked. My uncle hadn't gained admittance to the box. Jeff assured me he would let me know if he did. Then we made an appointment to discuss my money. Later, I called our puny library—Lois Demkowski promised to issue a card to Lew this week. Steve Moore came by to deliver the two life insurance benefit drafts. Then I called Uncle Bill to let him know we'd received the money. We agreed to get the drafts deposited in our bank accounts as quickly as we could. He came by an hour later to get his check. I'd already deposited mine in my Wells Fargo account. He laughed about the incident with Salt, but warned me not to cross him again.

The numbness I felt after my dad's death had turned to a biting, raw feeling. It was fully evident as Uncle Bill and I began to sort through my dad's clothing the next morning. The sight of his wool slippers made me sit down hard on the floor. Uncle Bill clutched a black Husker sweatshirt to his chest. It was going to be a long day.

And what were we to do with all of it? He had several expensive suits that wouldn't fit anyone I knew. Uncle Bill was too thick to wear the polo shirts my dad put on after work. Uncle Bill did claim three oversized sweatshirts and an armload of T-shirts. We decided James could fit into some of his nice sweaters; it wouldn't bother us to see him in my dad's clothes. Then I suggested James could fit into the suits with some tailoring. Uncle Bill got busy sorting a wide range of clothes into a pile.

"I think Lew would fit into all of this," he said. "He'd probably fit into one of those suits too."

I agreed. "He could cinch up these pants with a belt. You know he wouldn't get anything tailored. In fact, we really could give most all of this to Lew. Salt could wear some of the shirts, but he's too short for the pants. Otherwise, I guess we take it to the Goodwill."

As I opened the dresser drawer, Uncle Bill said, "You aren't going to mention those are you?"

I laughed. "Unmentionables" were a silly family joke Patty had started years ago.

"Hey, look at these. He kept my old report cards." I looked at a few of my elementary school marks. "I never could get perfect grades—not when they were still grading handwriting."

"He used to pass your report cards around the office," said Uncle Bill.

"Really? It would have been nice to have heard a compliment from him once and awhile."

"Ah, you know that wasn't his way. You got to think about what he did, not what he didn't say. Did you know he often rescheduled hearings so he could see your softball games?"

"Really?"

I stood next to my uncle and we sorted through some random pieces of his life—old wristwatches, an autographed baseball from the College World Series, an old pocketknife, an unopened package of combs, some ticket stubs from Nebraska football games, a few pens. Uncle Bill found my middle school grades in the sock drawer.

"Hey, do you remember when your dad got called down to school because you'd gotten into a fight?"

"Ha! He was so confused. I had to explain to him that a ho wasn't a garden implement."

We laughed ourselves silly—fueled by the erratic emotions of profound loss. After that, everything that started with "remember when..." was funny. I laughed though sometimes I needed to wipe away my tears, then the laughter would hit again. By the time we finished, I felt giddy and light-headed when I stood. We went down to the kitchen for a sugar fix of juice and brownies to revive ourselves. Patty stopped vacuuming long enough to scold us for our poor nutritional choices. We switched to making sandwiches and warming up some leftover potato soup. She joined us.

After we finished eating, I took the old pocketknife from my dad's dresser and slid it across the kitchen table to Patty. She stared at it for a few moments then picked it up.

"Not much up there for you and me," I said.

Her face flushed red. She muttered a "thank you," then took her plate and bowl over to the sink. "Gotta finish vacuuming," she said as she hurried from the room.

"So, who's going to take those clothes over to James?" I asked.

"Oh, I guess we haveta," said Uncle Bill. "Can we just leave it on the porch and run?"

"No."

"Then you do it," he said. "I'll drive over to the Eldritch place. I'll say it's a peace offering."

I didn't leave the bag on James' porch, but I handed it to him without replying to his greeting then hurried away. I ate two more brownies then downed a large glass of milk. Feeling emotional and stuffed with food, I went to my room for a nap.

Later, I found Uncle Bill sitting in my dad's chair. He looked upset.

"That place is worse than I thought. Damn. Lew was pleased with the clothes. Salt told me what I could do with my charity, but Lew held tight to the bags. Then Salt threw Lonesome Dove at me. Luckily it missed me, but it busted the spine and bent some pages back. I wanted to slug Salt, but you beat me to it. His face looks pretty bad. It's all swollen and purple. I'm sure you busted his nose. Bet he never went to the doctor. Anyway, I told Lew to keep the book. I knew you wouldn't want it back. I know you like your books just so."

I hardly knew what to say. Finally, I said, "I guess we won't be seeing Lew tonight."

He shrugged and dropped his chin into his chest.

Certain that my uncle had entered a bout of silence, I went and sat on the back porch steps. I looked out at the rough land, but didn't go out there. I wouldn't find answers, just a wailing woman and a groaning man, but no young man and maybe no Beverly. The sun cast the western sky in a luminous yellow as black thunderheads swept in from the south. Just as swiftly they passed by us without a drop of rain, and then proceeded northward. I went in to shower

156

when the sunlight came around the house and shone on the patio.

We decided to eat at the Cowpoke, as Uncle Bill raved about Johnny Two River's smoker. The bar was nearly empty when we first arrived. Johnny enforced the state's no smoking ban; otherwise, I never would have gone—I hated the stink of cigarettes. I'd been to bars in Omaha, but I expected a small town bar to be rougher, dirtier, more reflective of the Old West. Obviously, I'd watched too many old westerns. The walls were white but colorfully lit by neon beer brand signs. The floors were dark wood, with nary a spittoon in sight. The décor was primarily Huskers, Broncos, and Avalanche in nature; on the walls hung banners, caps, and Rozier, Rodgers, and Elway jerseys, along with a Roy sweater, encased in plastic frames. On the whole, it looked clean. Johnny Two Rivers even made an effort to please his female customers by hanging posters of shirtless models dressed as cowboys in the women's restroom. I didn't want to know what hung in the men's.

My biggest complaint involved the wooden chairs that left my short legs dangling. After we ate our burgers, mine was a whiskey cheeseburger with mushrooms, and the denizens rolled in and the music started, dancing relieved the ache in the back of my legs. We received a visit from Johnny, a displaced Nez Perce, who had once dated Patty. He was about forty years, medium height, with an ugly tattoo on his right arm. I despised tattoos. One of the best things about the NHL was its lack of visible tattoos—and it was the worst thing about the NBA.

"Bill, I see you brought the boxer elf," he said.

Yeah, very funny. I ignored him. Brian and I danced a couple of dances then visited the juke box. The selection was heavy on the twang, but we found a couple of Bonnie Raitt tunes and even "The Twist" by Chubby Checker, which proved to be popular with the crowd that continued to grow. When we returned to our table, Lew was hearing the bison story from Uncle Bill, who never seemed to tire of telling it.

When I was eleven, Uncle Bill taught me how to ride. He even fashioned a special saddle for me with notches up high to raise the height of the stirrups to reflect my lack of leg length. However, the kids of the ranchers never really thought of me as one of them. I often helped with the April branding season, though I had been caught reading in the saddle a few times, earning me the nickname, the Bookworm. I also hated the unnatural fit of cowboy boots, so my dad bought European equestrian boots for me, which invited more scorn. I didn't care. Still, I developed into a good rider. I convinced Uncle Bill to add a higher notch to raise the stirrups even higher. My horse, FloJo, named after the great American sprinter, Florence Griffith Joyner, knew what it meant when I rose off the saddle. FloJo, a black and white quarter horse, could really fly—outrunning any other horse. People kidded with me, telling me that I should be a jockey. But they knew who to call on to run down wayward cattle. So during my teen years, I helped at the various ranches, herding the calves so they could be branded.

Once, during a branding at a ranch in northern Cheyenne County, a bison from a neighboring ranch broke through a damaged fence. Uncle Bill and I set off on horseback to run down the bison so it wouldn't spook the cattle. Uncle Bill and I caught up with it; my uncle was a bona fide cowboy—though he'd mostly given up horses for pickup trucks decades ago. He was able to lasso the bison at a dead run and slow him to a walk. From about four feet away, I added my lasso to help secure the beast. As we headed to the break in the fence, my uncle decided we should switch ropes—so that it would look like I was the one who caught the big shaggy. Several cowboys caught up with us before we made it back to the fence the rancher was repairing. Neither Uncle Bill nor I said anything about the capture, but everyone noticed that I controlled the rope that hauled it in. When pressed about it at the campfire, I simply said that I was surprised how fast a bison ran. Ten years later, those rancher families still thought Frank Docket's daughter, the Bookworm, roped a bison.

Lew laughed so hard he began to slap his knees. Like some of the others in the bar, he was truly a hick. And being a hick is fine—but not for me, and it wasn't for my dad. It was an angle I used successfully on him when I wanted to spend a semester in Amsterdam. I went over in the second semester of my junior year with a Creighton professor and a group of classmates. Every Friday afternoon, I'd visit the Rijksmuseum Vincent van Gogh. He was my favorite artist and the reason a print of his Starry Night hung in my office instead of the elk photograph my dad favored. I loved the emotion he put into each stroke of the brush. That semester in Amsterdam also provided great opportunities to visit other European cities. I even persuaded a couple of my classmates to travel with me across the Channel to England.

No, I wasn't a hick—I didn't possess a simplistic world perspective, I was well educated, I had traveled, and I took the time to study current events from more than one perspective. I scanned the crowd of local folks, some of whom worked up the courage to obtain an autograph from my Husker stud. I didn't spot a single soul who hadn't attended my dad's funeral. These were good people. However, we ought not to stay too long—booze could turn harmless hayseed into its bigoted, violent form called redneck. No wonder James refused to come here with us.

At the next table, I heard men arguing politics; I knew not to turn my head toward them, lest I became pulled into the debate. I'd observed my dad get drawn into a few heated disputes. He played the diplomat. First, he would tell one person "you have a point," then he'd follow that with, "but some would say…and that's hard to dismiss," then conclude by saying, "it's a very difficult and complicated problem." I don't think my dad ever tried to persuade anyone to accept his opinion; he told me he thought it was important for people to consider other points of view and think beyond the popular opinion at Custer's. I thought his method was a prudent one, and a good example to follow. Still, their distorted perspective and mistaken information did make me want to straighten them out. I stopped eavesdropping when Lew caught my attention.

"Megan, I'm awful sorry about what Salt said. He was plain wrong." He ran his hand over his chin and he began to twitch. "He just has to vent his spleen sometimes, you know?"

"Oh, I've put it behind me. How's your burger?" I asked, pleased he came.

"Good, good. Your uncle says he started construction on his house."

"Yeah, they had to dig out the old cracked concrete and pour a new basement."

"I feel sorry for all them folks in the South who get the twisters and can't have basements 'cause of the soil. Bill already asked me to build him a good basement stairwell like you got."

"I've heard you're a good carpenter."

Lew twitched and writhed in his chair. He wore the same clothes he had hastily purchased to come to our house. Lew may not have been Einstein in the making, but he knew not to wear my dad's clothes in our presence. The compliment overwhelmed him and made him turn away. I'd remember to be more careful next time.

Brian stood and shook hands with someone behind me. Paul Ritter from the hardware store asked to talk to me. As it was so loud in the bar, we stepped out the front doors.

"I don't know if you heard, but my wife's filed for divorce," he said.

"No, I didn't know," I said, "but I'm sorry to hear about it."

160

He sighed and leaned against the brick front of the bar. "I'll be all right, but I'm worried about Kayla...she's stopped talking. Just won't say a thing."

"Taking care of your girl is important. You give me a call tomorrow. We'll just take it step by step."

He nodded and wandered down the street. I had other pending divorce cases, but this was my first Dexter divorce, and it saddened me. After a couple of minutes, I went back inside to ask Brian for a dance.

It was a slow, heartbreaker tune and our first slow dance. We made an awkward couple given our height difference, so we just rocked back and forth, with my arms around his midsection.

He said, "I'm not very good at these slow ones,"

"Oh, who cares?" I gulped then said, "I'm crazy about you. You know that don't you?"

"No, I didn't know. But I hoped so."

Chapter 17

After church the next day, I stopped outside the guest bedroom. Pushing back the door, I scanned the room, diffused with gold from the early afternoon sun. The room was much as it had been when I played there as a child—a light blue blanket covered the daybed I had often napped on; a nightstand with a white lamp sat next to the bed; a dresser drawer contained a few loose photographs; and a small closet was jammed with black luggage. Wait. Something wasn't right about the bed. Patty slept here a couple of nights after my dad died; when she remade the bed she left an edge of another blanket barely visible. I yanked back the blanket and discovered a blue and yellow four-square quilt. Had I seen this before? Why did it send chills up from my back to my scalp? I walked over to the closet door which I slid open. The black fabric luggage transformed to hard-sided beige Samsonite luggage, and then back to black again. This was my dad's black luggage. Why did I keep seeing beige Samsonite?

I opened the top dresser drawer and lifted out the wedding photo of my mom and dad. They looked happy. My dad had the broad grin of a man in love. My mother was harder to read. Then I stared at a photo of her as a young girl. The photo wasn't dated, though I thought she looked about ten with shoulder-length black hair and bangs, olive skin, and big, dark brown eyes that were as dark as James or Derek's. The third photo included several people sitting or standing around a long kitchen table with a huge chocolate birthday cake in the center of the table. I couldn't read the cursive writing on the cake. The back of the photo read:

163

Peter Paul Stephanie Liz Sophie Simon. Everyone in the photo was an adult, yet there were nine in the photo and obviously not listed in order, as the closest person on each side was a female. Were those six names listed all siblings? It looked likely. But the three others looked Arabic as well. I felt so bloody confused.

Who were these people? What was bothering me about beige luggage? Did I remember this quilt from this house or from Omaha? Luggage. Luggage meant leaving. Did my mother leave me? Was that the mystery my dad and uncle tried to protect me from? Did I seem so fragile at age twenty-six that my uncle couldn't tell me?

I wandered out to the hills. I wanted to hear the young man, but he was still absent. I heard Beverly and was overjoyed. I sat down on the shady north side of Rufus. I didn't want to hear any wailing or groaning from anybody else—and I didn't. I just listened to Beverly. She calmed me. Still, I resolved to press on till I knew everything.

Back at the house, Uncle Bill sat on the back porch, knocking the dirt off his cowboy boots.

"I'm gonna find out everything," I said.

"I know, I'm just not ready," he said.

I walked by him into the house, trying to recall the soothing voice of Beverly.

Patty was loading the dryer.

"What are you doing here on Sunday?" I asked.

"What are you going to find out?" she asked.

"I promise I'll let you know. You're so wrapped up in this family you can't even stay away on your days off."

"What if it's bad?"

"I expect it may be—but I deserve to know."

I heard a knock on my door. I'd been sitting on the edge of my bed, my feet dangling over the side. Who knows how long I'd been there? I looked up and saw Brian standing in the doorway.

"Oh, my gosh! I'm sorry! I've been thinking…ah, but I need to take a bath."

He smiled. "Never mind. Let's go to the Beast."

"Really? Well, that's getting a bit close to Salt. How about Big Leo?"

Soon, we were climbing the side of the bluff. As with Derek, I quickly passed Brian.

"What is it with you guys? Are you proud or just tall?"

He laughed. "Just stupid." He started crawling up the bluff like me.

We caught our breath at the top. He followed me around to the southern side. Looking out over our house to the field on the other side of Harney Street, we admired the beauty of the sun on the bobbing, golden tall grass, waving to the east. The wind made me feel unsteady.

"Megan Anne Docket."

I turned and looked at Brian, who was on one knee holding a blue velvet box. My stomach flipped over.

"I love you. Will you marry me?"

I went to my knees, fearful that my legs would turn to lead and I'd topple down the slope. I swallowed hard. I started to speak, but nothing came out. I could feel the blood pounding in my ears. I stared at the diamond ring in the box. Beulah was right.

"I-I don't know…I can't…it's not that…" I took a deep breath. "I've just got so much…"

He looked dejected.

"I'm not saying no."

"You're not?"

"You make the dark clouds go away."

"I remember those clouds."

"And that weight that's always pressing down?"

He nodded. We sat down next to each other.

"I need to figure some things out. Then you must decide if you still want me."

"Why wouldn't I want you?"

I told him about hearing the voices in the wind and the absence of the young man.

"Now, I figure I'm projecting myself into these voices somehow. But why did one stop when I didn't want it to? And why do others seem to hear voices, too?"

"Others? Who?"

"Well, I'll not violate their confidence in me."

After a few moments, he said, "You sense things. I've seen it. Do you... um... have anything else—?"

I laughed. "No, that's the extent of my oddness. And you're still interested in someone so weird?"

"Yep. I'm so interested that I'm willing to wait. I don't like it, but I'll let you see this through. But no chickening out. You must press your uncle."

"Oh, I can't stop now. You see, I think my mother is alive...or was when my dad and me came out here."

"Whoa, shit. Is it something you feel?"

"Yeah, I've always been bothered by some feeling... though it may just have been a yearning. But I'm starting to get the evidence I need, but fearing things won't give me anything but heartache."

We sat in silence for a few minutes, and then we climbed down the slope. Back inside, we took turns lathering each other in my bathtub. It was nearly eight o'clock by the time we made it to Theresa's Tex Mex, a dive south of town on Highway 51. Afterwards, we joined Uncle Bill in the family room. He had taken over my dad's chair. I told myself not to let it bother me, but it did. The frame work on his house was proceeding, so I'd only have him around for a couple more months.

Brian brought in the hand gun we'd found in my dad's work desk. The gun was identified as a Colt Model 1851 Navy Revolver, .36 caliber six-shooter, used by the Union

Army and Navy. It had been cleaned till the silver barrel shone. Brian's source said bullets could be bought online. It had been a commonly used weapon, so many have been recovered, but it was still a worthy piece of history.

Uncle Bill rose from the recliner and said, "Follow me."

We walked across our lawn to the Wilson house. The front window drapes were open. James was watching a baseball game on TV. As I walked past, I was struck by the brownness of it all—the brown sofa and chairs, the beige walls, the brown man in a brown shirt. Without Beverly, it was as if life had been sucked out of the house, leaving only brown behind. Uncle Bill rang the doorbell. James snapped out of his lonely stupor and looked out the window. I waved and he bust out a big smile. Inside, we showed him the revolver. He admired it then excused himself. He had been drinking hot chocolate—more brown. After a few minutes, he ascended the basement stairs carrying a long box, which he set on the coffee table and opened it. He untied a burlap bag, and then slid out an old rifle.

"It's a Sharps carbine, the 1859...the most famous of the single-shot carbines the Federal cavalry used."

Uncle Bill studied the rifle and then handed it to Brian.

"My great-grandfather fought in a tag-a-long unit of runaway slaves that hooked up with a Pennsylvania infantry company."

By the time Brian handed me the gun, I knew I was holding a special piece of history.

"But like many rifles of that time, it would malfunction. I'd never try to use it... maybe it would backfire on me."

"Can't beat a good shotgun, right?" asked Uncle Bill.

James chuckled and went to his coat closet where he withdrew a shotgun.

"Is that loaded?" I asked.

"Oh, it's got one shell in it. Been in that closet since we first moved here. Now how 'bout some brandy?"

We watched the rest of the game with James. During the seventh inning stretch, I suggested James give the room some color.

"How do I do that and what color?"

"Blue would jazz things up—pillows to start. Oh, and maybe some different curtains."

"Would you help me? I'm no good at that stuff."

"Sure, we could do it all online. Oh, and have you ever thought of a dog? One that would give you a bit of trouble— like kids do. It's too calm and quiet around here."

"Huh. A dog. I like big ones... little ones are too yippee. Beverly was allergic to dog dander, so we never could have one. I like 'em, though. Can't see putting in a fence."

"Oh, just get a long cord and tie him, just make sure he can't reach the street."

"Yeah," said Uncle Bill. "Tie him up to your oak and he'll make it halfway to Rufus. Traddles will enjoy the company."

We left James as he mused over blue pillows and a big dog.

Back at home, I begged Brian to stay the night with me, even though he'd need to drive to Sidney in the morning. I wanted to remind him that I hadn't said no. I woke up next to him and thought what a wonderful feeling it was to be loved. In spite of the mess of my personal life, he still wanted me.

Meanwhile, things were proceeding well at work, though I put in many hours and worked nearly all day on Saturday. Along with my cases, I studied old files my dad worked on, hoping to learn some of the things he would have taught me if he'd lived. Gus moved in to Docket Law, and the door was installed between Brian's two offices. Even though he still spent time at his Sidney office, he was picking up accounting and tax work in Dexter, Kimball, and the small towns and villages nearby. My big win for the month of May came by way of a Declaratory Judgment on behalf of State Farm. Although Judge Shelton grilled me for fifty-five minutes, I convinced him to dismiss the cause of action against the defendant, the State Farm insured and owner of a car that had been taken without permission by a former boyfriend. Declaratory Judgments were rare, so to win one and avoid a large payout by the insurer to two injured pedestrians resulted in praise from my client and two new cases, both involving questionable liability and broken bones.

Yes, everything was going fine—on the surface.

Chapter 18

At 9:05 a.m. on Friday morning, Jeff Finch called me. Bill was seeking access to the safe deposit box. He promised to try and stall my uncle to give me a chance to get to the bank. Bill was still chatting with Jeff when I arrived. I went to a teller to deposit a check from my Wells Fargo account to the Cheyenne County Bank, a completely worthless act, except to avoid making Jeff look like a snitch. I also signed in to access my safety deposit box.

"Oh, there's your niece," said Jeff.

I finished my transaction and approached them. Bill was holding a small envelope that held a safe deposit box key.

"I see you plan to get into the safety deposit box," I said. "Let's go then."

My uncle was stuck and he knew it. Another teller, a young woman whom I didn't recognize, led us down the hall, unlocked a door then led us into the room with the safety deposit boxes. The teller took Bill's key and turned the lock, and then used the bank key to open the door to the box. She pulled the key out and handed it to Bill, the sneak. After she retrieved my box, I asked for a room and she led us to a small alcove with a curtain and a counter. She set the boxes down and pulled the curtain shut as she left.

I looked at him. He looked down.

"This room is hardly sound proof, so we'll limit our remarks," I said. "Open it."

He lifted the lid. I slid the box in front of me. I removed the contents document by document. In one pile, I set my birth certificate, Social Security card, and the titles to the Camry and the Acura. I added the deed to the house and to the law firm building, both of which listed me as joint owner. Next, I opened an envelope that held the will. It was dated January 11, 1984. It gave all of his personal goods and his property to his wife, Elizabeth Docket. Children of the marriage became the beneficiaries if both spouses died. No child was listed, as I wasn't born till February 1984, nor was Bill indicated as a beneficiary. Death or divorce nullified the benefits to a spouse, in this case, Elizabeth, my mother. The language of the will gave all assets to any children equally. Bill was listed as the executor, known as the "personal representative" in Nebraska.

The will contained nothing helpful, though it irked me that Bill was the personal rep for the will, which meant he was supposed to pay any debts then distribute any assets of my dad's estate in the way he deemed appropriate. Anything that had my name on it—such as the two bank accounts, the house, the law firm building, and the Shark—wasn't controlled by the will.

Next I opened the wills of Albert and Anna Docket, my grandparents. They essentially gave all assets to the surviving spouse, with beneficiaries, in case they both died, to "all living direct descendants." Though it was duly attested, and therefore legal, the vague language made it suck, in terms of good will drafting.

"Now, I've always wondered what that meant," said Bill, pointing to the "direct descendants" language.

"It simply means, blood family members are the rightful owners of all the Docket land. So, you and my dad, now me, own the land. Strange thing, Bill, you use all the valuable land, yet you only own half of it. Did my dad ever lease any land or did he sell any of it to you? I sure as hell haven't."

"I'll start."

"Oh, I don't want that."

"Why are you mad at me?" he asked.

"Because you're the damn executor."

"I don't want it. You do it."

"Well, you're named, so you need to do a few things… like pay any debts."

"Just tell me what and I'll do it."

"Well, I'm not going to tell you how to run your business, but I want you to move your heifers farther east, at least in the summer. I don't want to smell their stink. You can move them back in the winter, though I don't want any cattle in the pasture across the street from the big house."

He smirked and said, "Aye, aye. No problem."

Though, I'd missed it the first time through, the will was dated June of 1985. I was alive when this will was made. How strange. My grandparents both died of cancer not long after my dad and I moved from Omaha to the house now owned by James. When my grandpa died, we moved to the big house. Bill was living with his first wife and Kyle in the house the tornado destroyed.

My head began to throb. This much was clear—Bill and I owned all the Docket land equally. Anything my dad put in my name was mine. Anything else was mine, unless my mother was alive and not divorced, then she owned those assets.

"I think we're done here," I said. "I'll photocopy both these wills then you can put them back in here."

"What about that other stuff?"

"I'm putting these in my own safe deposit box." I double checked the box for any other pertinent documents, but it contained only the deed to Bill's destroyed house and his Social Security card.

Bill reached into the corner of the box and pulled out a gold wedding band. "This was his. You might as well take it. I have my own collection."

I shoved the ring in an inside compartment of my purse, while Bill went to get the teller. She put his box away. Bill left as I placed my own documents inside my safety deposit box then decided to add the ring. When I was sure he was gone, I slipped an envelope out from under my documents. Inside was the marriage license of my parents, Frank Albert Docket and Elizabeth Jean Simon—Simon! That was her maiden name. How could I not know that? Had I forgotten it? Well, at least I learned something useful.

I struggled through the rest of the day. I was thankful Brian was working in Sidney all day—I didn't want to explain my mood to anyone. I left the office at four, which surprised everyone. I said I had a headache—and I did, one that no medicine could cure.

I lay in bed for a few minutes, and then fell asleep, my brain exhausted. I awoke knowing that I had ignored one area of evidence. I lifted my mattress and pulled out the letters. The first was dated in spring of 1984. It was a sweet, mushy letter from my mom to my dad. The next two letters were from my dad when he was out of town. The first was written on yellow, narrow-ruled legal notepaper, the second on Holiday Inn stationery. I suppose it was as sentimental as my dad could get. The next was from my mom, though it wasn't as warm in tone as her first. Then the last letter was in a standard envelope on white notebook paper. It stated her new address. Then I saw that the date was from 1991. The envelope indicated the letter originated in Omaha and was sent to this house.

Shit! 1991! This proved it. I had been lied to for twenty-three years.

I grabbed the letters, my pulse now in overdrive, and dashed down the back stairs. I overheard James in the family room say that his great-grandfather got a job on the railroad, laying ties. He worked for a while in North Platte at Union Pacific's Bailey Yard, moved to Denver in—.

I stormed into the room. The rage I felt for Salt was nothing compared to what now boiled within me for Bill.

Brian, Patty, Bill, and James stood around the coffee table examining photos. I shoved the letters into Bill's chest.

"You lied to me! My father lied to me! My mother was alive—I was taken from her and you knew it."

Patty gasped then sat down hard on the floor where she'd been standing. Bill picked up the letters from the floor then sat down in my father's chair.

"That's not your damn chair!"

"No," said Bill, who stood up, but avoided my eyes.

"Tell me!"

"She was alive."

"Is she still?"

"Yes."

I could feel my heart hammering against my chest. A sense of lightheadedness came over me, but I held my ground.

"Go on."

Bill dropped his chin into his chest.

Patty said, "It does not require many words to speak the truth."

Bill nodded at the wise words of some Indian chief.

"They had always fought. But they married anyway. Then they split, but Liz discovered she was pregnant. They tried to make it work, but it didn't."

"So my father took me away and she let me go."

"Shouldn't we talk alone?"

"Why? These people have been like family to me—maybe better because none of them have lied to me like you and my father." I took a few deep breaths. "Why hasn't my mother ever contacted me?"

Bill ran his hands over his face. Brian and James stood rooted to the ground.

"And you kept this from me all these years. Why? How could the truth be so difficult? What could possibly make this so complicated?"

All eyes were on Bill.

"Your brother."

I went to lead. I felt arms and hands and smelled the shaving lotion I loved and then I was on the sofa.

"He died in April," I said to the ceiling.

"Wait, how could you know about the death of someone you didn't know existed?" asked Patty.

"I felt it."

The room went silent. After a few minutes, Brian got up from the sofa and started pacing the hall. I continued to stare at the ceiling. James whispered to Patty that they needed to watch the back door. He knew I'd bolt.

Brian burst back into the room.

"This is madness. All these secrets. I want to marry Megan, but how can she when she has to deal with all this?" Looking directly at Bill he said, "This is all so screwed up. How could you let this happen?"

Brian stormed out of the room. He plopped down hard at a kitchen chair. I felt pleased that someone else knew how messed up this all was. I rose and asked Patty about supper. She promised to call me when it was ready. I climbed the back stairs to my room. Quick as I could I donned my sneakers and changed into a black T-shirt. I wanted to be alone. And I would be. I tip-toed down the cushy, carpeted front stairs. Screaming inside, I slipped out the front door and dashed east across the driveway then for a half block before I turned north toward the hills in the approaching dusk, now pricked by the biggest stars.

I ran and I cried. Traddles ran with me for a half a mile then grew bored and chased a slower shadow. I zigzagged through the rocky ridges then kept running till I passed Big Leo. I headed northeast to avoid getting too close to the Eldritch land. I hurdled Pooper's Canyon but kept going. I slowed as I neared the Beast and approached a large gully Derek had nicknamed "Miss Gulch" from The Wizard of Oz, because it was scary—deep, dangerous, and jagged. I didn't want to deal with Miss Gulch, I had so much, too much, to handle. I backed away from it and dropped into the buffalo grass. The slight rustle in the grass told me some creature, probably a snake, was making its departure.

My mother was alive. My brother was dead.

I had been deceived all these years. Did Bill know more than he was telling? What didn't I know? What do I do now? I wanted to kick Bill out of my house, he deserved it, but it would be noticed and I didn't want any of this crap to be known outside of my house. My father was dead, so I couldn't even give him the rebuke he deserved. Oh, the scathing remarks I could use to level my mother, no matter her personality—she let me go. What mother did that?

Oh, sweet Jesus, help me. I really need you now. Though I doubted I deserved much mercy with all the anger roiling and festering inside me. I felt meaner than any snake or creature I could meet out here. I heard no voices, maybe I never would again.

I looked up at the densely-packed stars glinting in the blackening sky and the tears began to roll again. I had a brother. He died. If I ever knew him I would have been an infant, a toddler at best. I wondered how old he was. I felt certain he had died of something like a heart attack. He had suffered, I felt his pain, and his absence stung me. I sobbed for my brother and his pain, and I wiped my eyes with my shirt and my nose with buffalo grass. Handy stuff.

My stomach was queasy with hunger. I didn't normally miss meals. Brian stood up for me and said what everyone was thinking—it was all so screwy. It didn't really make sense. It didn't fit with my idea of how two parents and an uncle would act.

There was more.

Chapter 19

I walked back to the house. They were searching for me—three flashlights darted back and forth through the hills. I walked past them without detection—as if they could find me. Once back at the house, I suggested Patty call their cell phones. I reheated the meatloaf, mashed potatoes, and broccoli. By the time James, Brian, and Bill returned, I'd finished my cantaloupe and was opening a bottle of Jim Beam Black.

Brian entered first.

"Sorry about our date. Thanks for standing up for me. By the way, where'd my father's chair go?"

For a moment, he just stared at me. "Don't do that again. You scared me."

"I'm surprised James even went out there." I handed him a bourbon. "He knows you can't find anything out there in the dark. Even where it's flat, there are places to hide."

"How about a compromise then. I can't stop you from going out there, so would you take a cell phone, so you could call if you needed help?"

"I guess that's reasonable. So where's the chair?"

"Bill hauled it out of the family room and slid it down the basement steps."

"Huh. Well, he won't enjoy the folding chair he put in its place. C'mon. I don't want to see anymore of him tonight."

We passed a quiet week. Bill and I generally avoided each other except for meals. One evening, Patty cornered me after Bill had left the kitchen.

"This has been a tough time for all of us," she said. "And I understand you being mad at your uncle, but can't you cut him a break? He confessed about your mom."

"Patty, do you really think we know everything? I think there's a whole lot more. So I'm trying to be patient and wait him out."

"A'right. But be nice. Listen, my dad was hardly around when I was growing up. My husband was a first-class bastard. Now, Bill is fun, but your dad was the most solid man I ever knew."

I nodded. "I did order a new chair from the Nebraska Furniture Mart."

"Good. It's better without that chair. It was so much your dad."

"I guess that's why I didn't like Bill sitting in it. He can sit in the new one."

"'Do not grieve, misfortunes will happen to the wisest and best of men…. Misfortunes do not flourish particularly in our lives—they grow everywhere.'"

"Who said that?" I asked.

"Big Elk, an Omaha Chief."

"And who knows more about suffering than the American Indian?"

On Thursday, Brian and I drove to the Pizza Shoppe for lunch. I'd been quiet about the news of last weekend, but I'd spent a great deal of time thinking about it.

Once he parked and we exited his Jeep Cherokee, I said, "You're right that my family is screwed up…but wrong that I can't see clearly enough to accept you. I love you. You're the best thing in my life."

"Then you agree to marry me?"

"Yes."

He wrapped me in his arms, right in the middle of the crosswalk. We stopped traffic in both directions, yet the mellow Nebraskans simply waited for me to drag him to the curb.

180

"When can we go tell my dad? Hey, want to come to the game with us on Saturday?"

Brian, his dad, and his brother were going to watch the Nebraska baseball team play Texas at Haymarket Park in Lincoln. I predicted a sound thumping and unhappy Husker fans, but I didn't want to say so.

"I better stick around. Patty's going to march on Whiteclay Saturday. Somebody may need to post bail. Johnny Two Rivers won't think to bring enough money."

My only objection to Johnny was that he had broken Patty's heart and would probably do it again if given the chance.

"Hey, let's go to Custer's. My dad has wanted to see where you punched Salt. He's heard of him...he's caused some trouble in Sidney bars. I bet my brother would come. He loves telling that story."

"You're kidding."

"Nope. People knew your dad and you've become quite popular."

"Hmmm! I thought my Sidney clients were coming to me because of my legal work."

"Don't worry, they are."

The next afternoon, I stopped home after lunch. Johnny Two Rivers was loading Patty's suitcase in his pickup. I walked out to the where he was standing with the Colt revolver in my hand. Johnny froze. I kept walking toward him.

"Hey, Johnny, wanna see something cool?" I said now smiling. I held up the gun.

"Damn you, Megan!" he said. "I nearly wet my pants. Let me see that."

I told him what I knew about the revolver.

"History, Megan, history is what counts. Now this gun might have been used against the Confederates, or might've been used against us."

"The Nez Perce don't come from around here, you're a northwest people."

"Well, against the Lakota Sioux then."

"Maybe both. The Nebraska Territory sent as many soldiers per capita to fight for the Union as most northern states—of course, that wasn't many men in comparison. But they fought and won at the Battle of Shiloh, and received the praise of General Sherman."

Johnny smiled. "And then they converted to cavalry and came home to fight Indians."

"Right, like I said, could've been used both places. Now my father's ancestors came here in the 1840s, but you can only blame half of me because the people on my mother's side were still in Syria."

"Fightin' a different battle," said Patty as she walked to the driveway. "Christians... Muslims, white men... Indians, it'll never get settled. Glad you two are getting along."

I gave Patty the seventy-four dollars from the kitchen cabinet.

"What's this for?" she asked.

"Get a decent hotel. The cheap ones probably have bed bugs. It's the money that was in my dad's wallet. Take it. By the way, I've accepted Brian."

"About time. Don't know why you left him hangin'."

But she did. She shoved the money in her purse.

About noon the next day, Bill called me. Patty had been arrested. I called Gus for guidance, went to the bank, and then met Bill at home. We headed north in the Shark to rescue our loyal friend. According to Bill, Patty was standing with some women who threw rocks through the windows of a liquor store. The police arrested the seven women closest to the liquor store. I let him drive while I slept or pretended to.

A crowd was gathered outside the Rushville police station. Though the town had nothing to do with the march or

182

the arrests, it was the closest jail to Whiteclay, a village on the northernmost edge of Nebraska, a stone's throw from the South Dakota Pine Ridge Indian Reservation. The crowd from the reservation cast unfriendly stares at Bill and me as we entered the police station. When we emerged with the seven jailed women, after paying each of their $500 bail fines, we were treated as heroes. Patty hugged and thanked us both.

"But why did you pay all the fines?" Patty asked.

"The police need to know you have friends," I said. "And that people are watching what goes on up here."

An elderly man stepped forward. He stared into my eyes, it made me want to squirm, but I returned his gaze. He had a wiry build, thinning silver hair, and deep set, brooding eyes.

Patty said, "She hears voices in the wind. And she knows death before it happens. She has the blood of the ancient ones of the Christian Holy Land, who had to flee from the Muslims."

Patty was really pouring it on. I wondered what she'd say next. People stepped in closer to me. I felt a little panicked.

"And this is her uncle, a Celtic, outcasts from the Gauls and the Saxons."

I hoped no one would suggest getting shovels for all her bullshit. Although some of it did ring partially true. I looked back at the elderly man, who had long life and hard times etched into his face. His eyes softened and he nodded. He reached out his hand and I shook it. He seemed unimpressed with Bill, for he didn't even look at him. I felt a few taps on my shoulder. Then Patty plunged her hand into my purse, which hung from my shoulder. She pulled out my engraved silver business card holder and began handing my card to the other formerly jailed women.

"When the police contact you, you tell them that you will be silent and they must contact Megan Docket. She can be your attorney in Nebraska, but only in Nebraska."

Oh, Lord. What has she gotten me into? Curious faces turned to smiling faces, and then more tapping on my shoulders. I nodded. One thick-set woman nudged in close to me.

"Do you believe the Great Spirit sends you the voices?"

Now it was my turn. "The Great Spirit and God are one. Jesus sends us love. God the Father brings me voices of those who are near to me."

More shoulder taps. I became afraid that they would grant me a Sun Dance and insist that I come. But the old man nodded once more and backed away. The crowd eased back. I felt a hand on my upper arm and knew it was Bill. He slowly pulled me backward. I nodded as I shuffled backward. I saw Johnny Two Rivers for the first time, he was smiling at me. Two police officers were also watching the scene. We made it to the Shark, which was parked across the street.

At the car, Johnny stopped me.

"Do you really hear voices?" he asked.

"Outside, north of our house," I answered.

"No kidding?" said Patty. "I thought I was making that up."

"And I don't know death beforehand...um...only when it happens...or maybe just a smidgen before."

Bill opened the door and scooted me in. As Johnny planned to stay, Patty rode home with us. The crowd had broken up, but several loitered outside, watching us leave.

Bill said, "For a while there, I thought they were gonna try and adopt you."

"Who was the old man?" I asked.

"Jackson, one of the Lakota elders. He senses something about you."

"He would be interesting to talk to," I said.

"Yeah, and now that they know where you work they're gonna come steal you," said Bill.

Patty laughed. "Nah, even with a tan, she's still too pale."

184

We were quiet for several miles. After a quick stop for supper, I asked a question that had bothered me.

"So, Bill, my dad died awfully young from a heart attack. I guess he had some defect. Did my brother have the same problem?"

"No, Scott had many problems. Heart, lungs…just a lot of stuff."

Scott.

"But why? He couldn't have been that old."

"He had cerebral palsy."

Patty gasped.

My brother! Oh, God!

I took a deep breath and said, "I don't know much about that. Ah… no muscle control, right?" I said.

"Yeah… problem with the central nervous system. His brain just never developed."

"Was he always that way?"

Bill was quiet for several minutes. I quietly waited—I wanted Patty to know I could be kind and patient with him, even though she chided me for not calling him Uncle anymore.

"Yeah."

"I don't remember him at all. Was he older or younger than me?"

In the time it took for Bill to take a deep breath, I knew.

"He was my twin."

Chapter 20

Patty and I sat in stunned silence. Bill drove, occasionally checking my face in the rear view mirror.

The questions bombarded me, so before I could let them haunt me, I decided to get the answers. Then I could suffer.

"Was I normal?" I asked.

"Yeah," he said.

"Did you see us after we were born?"

"Yeah."

Patty turned to Bill and huffed, but otherwise remained silent.

"Go on," I said.

"You were a pretty good size, over six pounds. But Scott was little...scrawny really. He went into baby ICU right away. You got to go to your mom and into one of those baby roasters, to keep you warm. Big shock of black hair with big brown eyes. Scott had dark hair and eyes, too. You both looked like little Arabs." He chuckled. "My goodness, you were cute, not right away of course, babies all come out lookin' like they've gone through a battle. We didn't think Scott was gonna make it, but he did and after a while went home. With all his problems, he wasn't supposed to live past five, maybe ten years. But he was a fighter, in his quiet way."

He took a deep breath, and then sipped his Coke. "You were a fighter in a different way. Your pediatrician said you were willful, but your folks already knew that. You crawled and walked months before my Kyle ever did. You were a climber, too. Always climbing into Scott's crib and snuggling in to him. He was so fragile; he was supposed to sleep alone.

But Megan, hon, you just wouldn't part with him. You were his entertainment. His eyes were always on you."

"When did my brother walk?"

"Never. Never talked. Just never anything…" Bill sighed and was quiet for a few minutes. "It was so tough because your folks were ready to split, now they had you two. One time I remember your folks staring daggers at each other—they never yelled or had fits, just a quiet, festering disgust for each other. I couldn't understand it. I mean, your mom, was wow, lovely, kind, funny. Then I found out that your dad wanted to put Scott in an institution. Your mom refused."

"Was my brother that much trouble?"

"Well, your dad just couldn't relate. But yeah, Scott was a lot of work. Liz got some state services, but he was still a load to handle. Just so much care was needed. I tried to come as much as I could, but my life was here. Had one of those trach tubes, and a feeding tube. Always going to the ER, especially for the seizures. Those were tough. Your dad did badly with all of that. He wanted a son really bad, but not one like Scott. He loved that you were athletic—did any sport you wanted to. He loved when you played basketball and you'd take a charge and pop right back up. He'd spend the next ten minutes elbowing me in the ribs, saying 'Did you see that? She jumps back up.' He always thought you shoulda scored more, but then he'd brag at how unselfish you were."

Bill shook his head and just drove for a while. Patty stared forward, her mouth agape. She would be thinking that her image of my dad as a hero was crushed. I stared out the window, trying to process all the information. Then a thought made my body jerk.

"What had I taken from him?" Did I say that out loud?

"What do you mean?" asked Bill. "You didn't take anything. Sometimes birth defects just happen."

188

Yes, I did. In the womb, I must have sucked every bit of strength out of him—to the point that he lived a miserable life, a soul trapped in a body that couldn't keep him alive past age twenty-six. He was the boy in the well. And I put him there.

"My father didn't even go to the funeral."

"Megan, I could see he was suffering. He was sick in his mind, his body, his soul. The heart attack didn't really surprise me."

"He died of guilt," I said.

Patty gasped.

"I suppose," said Bill. "Your dad saw strength in you. He bullied Liz, hell, he's always bullied me. But you fought him, you loved him, you never let him get the better of you, even as a kid. He loved you more than he's ever loved anyone. He certainly loved you more than he loved himself. That night you said you got that other job offer you scared him more than he's ever been scared in his life. But he admired that you stood up to him. You leveled the score right then, forever."

"But my father couldn't deal with Scott—wasn't that weakness?"

"It was, yeah."

"But why did it all need to be hidden from me?"

"Your dad was scared you'd go back to your mom."

"He was right."

"They never shoulda split you two up," said Patty. "We adults mostly get what we deserve, but that boy must have missed you awful bad."

"Well, thank you for going to his funeral—but you should have taken me."

"You were already hurting, I could tell. Your dad begged me not to take you. He said he needed you."

My father was a selfish bastard.

Back home, I returned Brian's call. I think I sputtered something incoherent. He was in my room in less than a half hour. Even in his presence, I couldn't get out what I had learned, except that Scott was my twin. I drank a full glass of bourbon, which made my brain slog even more. The next morning, I slept through church, as did Bill and Patty. Brian went to church in Sidney with his dad and was back in my room before I awoke. Patty must have alerted James last night because he, Derek, and Vonny were on our patio when I went down for whatever meal it is when you don't have breakfast but it's already noon.

"Patty, don't you ever go home?" teased Vonny.

"Lord above, I wouldn't want to leave Bill and this one alone right now," Patty said. "Don't you."

Vonny stared at me. I drank my chocolate milk. My eyes rested on the edge of the counter near the door to the garage. Patty had thrown away the envelope from the hospital, but his wallet and keys still sat in that spot, as if she designated a sacred resting place for them. I wouldn't confront her, but in time I'd move them so I didn't need to see them anymore.

They waited for me to finish my meal then we walked out to sit in the shade of Rufus. Patty had already described our adventures with the Lakotas, so it was time to tell them all that I knew. But where was I to begin? In time I did, and didn't shut up till I told them everything. When I finished, James dropped his head in his hands, while Derek, Vonny, and Brian sat stiffly, with their mouths open.

Finally, Vonny spoke. "I've read about the special connection between twins."

Derek nodded in support.

"He really was Mr. Dombey," I said. "He neglected one child for the other. One child was meant to carry on his business. But unlike him, my father never made amends with the wronged child. He couldn't even go to the funeral because guilt was eating away at him till it killed him."

190

"He died apologizing to you…I heard him," said Brian.

"Are you defending him?" I asked.

"Only that he knew he had wronged you. But no, I can't justify what he did."

James said, "Those last days, knowing his son was dead…knowing you'd discover the truth…that must of been hell. And your poor mother…all these years."

"She let me go."

"She has lost both her children. I expect Bill has called her. So now she's thinking you will never forgive her." James was quiet for a moment then said, "Yeah, I see how you're thinking Frank was Mr. Dombey and you were his Paul. Now you gotta be Florence and forgive despite years of being wronged by your father."

"Forgiveness comes easier in fiction," I said. "I have three people who let me live in a lie."

We were quiet for a few minutes. Then it was Beverly's turn to speak. Both James and I sat up and looked southeast toward the wind. We'd been caught—Derek, Vonny, and Brian stared from one of us to the other. James dropped his head. I lay back in the grass to listen to her reassuring hum.

"What's up?" asked Derek.

"I just told you my whole wretched life story," I said. "I don't need to tell you every dang thing."

"Is it your brother?" asked Derek, not to be put off.

"Nope. I don't hear him anymore." I closed my eyes, not wanting anymore questions. Why didn't I hear him?

"Son, it's your mom," said James. "She's just trying to calm Megan."

It was working—to an extent. I still felt as if a piece was missing from the puzzle. Things still nagged at me—beige luggage, the third key, the quilt. And I wasn't satisfied with the explanation of why the truth had been concealed.

There was more.

After lunch, Derek and Brian went out to shoot baskets while Vonny and I visited the attic. I don't know why I suddenly needed to go there, but Vonny was willing, so we climbed the steep, creaking wood stairs, holding onto the railings on each side as we had done as kids. Two bare bulbs illuminated the musty, dusty room. Vonny opened the heavy curtains that covered the windows in the three dormers then slid the windows open. The June sunlight spilled into the room, brightening the dark wood floors, as well as the abandoned rocking chairs, lamps, and trunks.

"How long do you think it's been since anyone was up here?" asked Vonny as she pulled open the top drawer of my small, white, childhood dresser.

"No idea," I said. "It would have been us."

"A long time, anyway," she said as she pulled two Barbies, one African American, out of the drawer, followed by a G.I. Joe.

We laughed at the dolls and at the fact Derek had missed an opportunity to amuse himself by destroying another G.I. Joe. I opened a trunk and inspected each blanket for memories—they all had them, but only in their usefulness for building forts in this attic and to hide from the Giant Pumpkin Head Man, also known as Derek wearing an orange Denver Broncos blanket.

"I'm glad we were kids when we were," I said. "We made stuff up, we talked to people face to face, we played outside. We weren't warped by electronics."

"Even with books we had to use our imagination to envision what the authors created." Vonny set aside a couple of old curtains from a trunk and said, "Hey, come here. Look at these."

We pulled out a few Nancy Drew mysteries, and then found my Little House on the Prairie books. Those had led to Little Women, then to Mari Sandoz and Agatha Christie books, and eventually Jane Austen novels. I was drawn to the orphan and absent parent stories—Jane Eyre, Wuthering Heights,

David Copperfield, and Oliver Twist. Of course, all those books were on bookshelves in the study, the family room, or in one of the bedrooms, each one in a fancy hardbound version. Vonny mostly skipped young adult books, like me, and went for the more mature stories, reading all our books then developing her own Toni Morrison and Maya Angelou collection, which I also read then passed on to Patty.

Vonny thumbed through the Little House in the Big Woods.

"Those are books I should have read with my mother," I said, feeling both sad and bitter.

"She knows it."

"Vonny, it still doesn't make sense to me. This big lie."

"I agree. It just doesn't seem how people act. Do you think you're still being lied to?"

"Maybe. Bill could be lying to me. Your dad says I should forgive, but how do I forgive stuff I don't know?"

"I guess you need to wait till your uncle is willing to talk again."

"That's another thing—why is he still hiding stuff from me?"

My hands tightened into fists. I looked down at my white knuckles. People hired me to resolve their disputes and keep their secrets. And I kept those secrets diligently. I'd learned a great deal of information about the people of the area from reviewing some of my father's old cases. But that was different—I was paid to be discreet. And when people kept secrets that should be told, I tried to make them come clean. Last month, I dropped one of my divorce clients because he was a scumbag who refused to confess. I sensed he was lying, even though I didn't have any evidence. I just knew. Although I didn't divulge any information, I told opposing counsel that I was backing out of the case because I couldn't trust my client to be truthful to me. The attorney hired a private detective to uncover the lies—no doubt he would.

"What are you thinking?" asked Vonny.

I just shook my head and moved over to the final trunk. It contained a bunch of old albums. When we were little kids investigating this old stuff, we didn't know about Carole King or Carly Simon or the Rolling Stones, and we didn't really care. Now I looked at these albums and their dates, with Lizzie S. written in black pen on the backside, and knew they were my mother's coming of age music. The Beatles, Stevie Wonder, Creedence Clearwater Revival, Aretha Franklin, Simon and Garfunkel, James Taylor, Fleetwood Mac—music I now knew. I wondered if she liked my coming of age artists—Alanis Morrisette, U2, Nirvana, Sheryl Crow, Tracey Chapman, Tom Petty, Michael Jackson. I didn't even know if she liked to read and watch movies and sports. She would be about fifty-two, and all I knew was that she was trim and dark. A question made me jerk.

"What?"

"I don't even know if my parents divorced. Bill didn't say. Shit. She could have remarried and had other kids."

"Shit is right. Maybe you should kick Bill out of the house—till he's willing to tell all."

"Nah. I don't want any of this to become town gossip."

"Well, I think we should listen to some of this music. My dad still has that old record player. I'm pretty sure it works. And it's getting hot up here."

I collected the albums while Vonny closed the windows and drapes. We brushed the dust off our jeans, and then slowly descended the stairs. We had a chance to listen to some of the music before Vonny and Derek needed to leave for their homes.

I was angry with my mother, but I was curious about her, too. Still, she let me go—maybe I should just drop the whole matter, let her live her own life; meanwhile, I'd continue as a lawyer, marry Brian, and never keep secrets from our kids. But would I be content with that?

Chapter 21

"It has to be something else. We can't call this a Tea Party—people will think we're all Republicans," I said.

Glenda smirked and Melanie laughed like a good Democrat.

"How about Tea and Crumpets?" I said. "It sounds very British. Glenda, your scones will be perfect."

So, it was settled. We'd have an open house for two days, a Thursday and Friday to formally introduce Gus as a member of the law firm. We posted invitations around Dexter and in the Kimball and Sidney courthouses. Invitations were sent to all clients, including my Lakota clients and Jackson, the elder, from the Pine Ridge rez.

But first, I had an important person to meet. After conspiring with Glenda and her blender, I left the office wearing jeans, with a strawberry shake in one hand and a chocolate one in the other. I drove to the Ritter house to talk to Paul Ritter's daughter, who had gone silent once she learned that her parents planned to divorce.

Kayla opened the door with a look of surprise at the attorney who requested to talk to her. I led her around the house to an old swing set.

"Chocolate or strawberry?" I asked.

She chose the strawberry. I sat on a swing.

"Parents can be such screw-ups," I said.

She stared at me, her long blonde hair blowing across her face. I pretended to be interested in my shake, while I checked her over—no signs of wrist cutting, no rebellious body or facial piercings, jean shorts and a white top with a pink dove on the front indicated this pre-teen hadn't gone emo or goth.

She sat down on the swing beside me.

"Did you hear my uncle's house got hit by a tornado?" Of course she'd heard, but I just wanted to get her talking.

"I heard it fell on you," Kayla said.

"It was weird. I was in his basement and all of a sudden, Kaboom! I'm in his bedroom. It was like I was in some freaky movie."

She smiled.

"Hey, tomorrow or Friday you should come by my law office. We're partying those afternoons. Do you know where my law office is?"

"Yeah. I walk by it on the way home from school. What's a crumpet?"

"It's a fancy British word for snacks. And Mrs. Purvis, my old second grade teacher, is now the receptionist and she makes some really good stuff."

"She was your teacher?"

"Yeah, now I'm her boss. Funny how things work out. She made these shakes."

"This is good."

We sipped our shakes for a while. Then I said, "I come from a broken family. It sucks. But I'm gonna try and do what's best, especially for you. You're the innocent one."

I set my shake on the ground and pulled one of my business cards and a pen out of my back pocket. I wrote on the back of the card.

"Is it for sure that my parents will split, like, forever?"

"Nothing is for sure except death, taxes, and God. And that's the truth."

She looked down at her feet, probably wondering, fearing, maybe praying.

"Here's my card. On the back are my cell phone and my home phone numbers. Call me anytime. If you call me in the middle of the night you might need to talk for a while before I remember who I am and who you are."

She laughed. I was succeeding. Then the screen door slammed shut. Sheila, the mother, still in her blue supermarket cashier's uniform came stomping out. I immediately ruled out adultery as a cause for the split. She was a thick-waisted, thin-lipped, dishwater blonde with kinky frizz on her ends from an old perm.

"Who do you think you are?" she asked.

"I'm Megan Docket. We had an appointment, as you know."

"Listen, girly. You ain't up to this. You ain't Frank Docket."

I rose. "I sure hope not, he's dead."

She huffed, Kayla grinned. I picked up my shake from the ground then stepped up to look Sheila in the eye.

"One bit of advice. Keep all of this to yourself. The county loves this kind of gossip, but they don't need to know your family business. If you've got some complaint, keep it to yourself or tell your attorney. People talk, and it'll all come back down on your daughter's head. I've seen it happen."

Sheila stared at me, a look of perplexity on her face.

"We'll chat again," I said to Kayla. I walked away.

Back at work, I changed then finished up a few matters, and then Brian and I went home. Since I'd found out about my brother, I retreated to my room after work for fifteen minutes of scheduled gushing. I don't think Brian understood my need for privacy, but he gave me time and space. Brian created his own force of emotion, love was the best word for it, but I needed to grieve and process, acts I didn't feel the need to share. At times, I wondered if it was too much emotional effort to have Brian in my life right now, yet I didn't want him out of my life either.

The next day was Tea and Crumpets. Glenda was giddy with excitement; Melanie was concerned with the pile of work she was getting from two attorneys and Brian. Glenda announced each visitor, who was led to a table covered with plates of goodies, along with tea, coffee, and brochures about the law firm. I kept our website running on my laptop. Gus shook everyone's hand, as Brian and I showed off my engagement ring. Gus, Melanie, and I tried to work, but we kept getting called out to the lobby for the next visitor. By five o'clock, we were annoyed, but had committed ourselves to stay till 7:00 p.m. By six o'clock, we'd greeted most of the courthouse staff of Kimball and Cheyenne Counties. Even Judge Shelton stopped by. By seven, we started calling our hostess, Glenda, the Good Witch of the North. We needed to go home and eat something other than delicious, sugary pastries. Back at home, Brian hugged Patty when she gave him a steak. We'd gone punchy, and we still had another day of the ordeal.

Friday after school, Kayla stopped by. I showed her my office. I even let her spin around in my chair. Glenda treated her with grandmotherly kindness, for she knew any young person connected to me was a child client of some family tragedy. Meanwhile, Patty and four of her Lakota friends arrived. I chatted with them for a few minutes. They were pleased that I had convinced the owner of the Whiteclay liquor store to accept only restitution to minimize bad publicity for him. We drifted back out to the lobby where Beulah was chatting with Johnny Two Rivers. Even Blaine and Dane made a brief appearance before retreating back to Custer's. Paul Ritter stopped by and looked pleased that Kayla was in my company. Eldon Strumple and James arrived, followed by Big Joe and Maggie McCready. I greeted Harold and Marva Gush then Beulah pulled me aside. She nodded to the Lakota women and Jackson, who stood nearby, then looked back at me.

"I know you. You got some darkness on you besides losing your pa."

"Just the truth," I said, trying to give her something to chew on without telling her anything. "And dealing with it."

"Heh. You ain't gonna say much, or maybe you did. Guess I'll wait."

I reached out and squeezed her skinny arms.

"Woman, you should eat some pastries, or you'll be blowing away in the wind like Mary Poppins. Go on now."

She shuffled off. Jackson was grinning and nodding his head. He must know his Disney movies. Patty began the story of Bear Lake Beulah, as I sought out Kayla and Paul. Brian was entertaining Johnny and James with a story, probably about football. Bill stood in the doorway, reading the new engraved plates outside the front doors. Despite being mad at my father, I had his name placed first on the new Docket Law Firm gold plate with 1952-2010 beside his name. My name was listed second, then Mark Gustafson. A gold plate on the other door stated: Brian Culhane, C.P.A., Taxation and Accounting Services. Then a thought struck me—I wouldn't always be named Docket. Brian agreed to a long engagement, especially after Bill gave us a lecture on the errors of marrying too quickly. He ran off the names of several such fools, which included himself twice, my parents, numerous movie stars, and Earl Ferdy, the local butcher.

As seven o'clock drew near, it occurred to me that Kathy Whitfield had not visited, despite a personal invitation. I was actually pleased I didn't need to deal with her. Stan Spurlock, another local attorney, who was busy snarfing down one of the Good Witch's butter cream pastries, told me Zach took a job at a law firm in Lincoln. I was pleased he landed on his feet, though I hoped I'd never see him or Lindsey again. I'd also heard that Zane, the older brother of Zach, dubbed "In-Zane" by Derek for enlisting in the Army during a war, had come home last week after his discharge.

After the last guest left, I reflected on the goodwill I felt from all the visitors. This was a community of good-hearted, salt of the earth people, and I was pleased they wanted to remind me of their respect for my father.

Once we finished the clean-up, Bill decided we should go to the Cowpoke for supper and dancing. The Lakota clan agreed to stay, and we even persuaded James to come with us. Big Joe made a point of welcoming James by buying him a beer. Lew came in a few minutes later, though he stopped dead still when he saw the Lakotas.

I came and took him by the arm.

"Them's Indians," he said.

"So what?"

"I'm scared of 'em."

"You watch too many old movies. C'mon."

We filled ourselves with burgers, fries, and salads to counter the excess coffee and sugar in our systems. After we finished eating, the juke box started and we began to dance. The shorter Jackson was actually a better dance partner for me than Brian. Though while we were dancing, a sense of foreboding began to grow.

"Danger is near," I said to Jackson.

He nodded and we went back to the table. I couldn't tell where the threat came from. I spotted one of the Lakota women moving in toward Brian, her dance partner, as a slow song started. I cut in then told him of my concern. Then I saw him—Salt sat in a dark corner by himself drinking whiskey, glowering at James. I pulled Brian over to James, who stood talking to Carlos Hernandez. James agreed to leave immediately with the Lakotas.

Meanwhile, Salt approached Lew, who was sitting at the end of our table. Salt's nose was crooked and it sported a red bump just below the level of his eyes. I had really nailed him. I couldn't hear what was said, but Salt shoved Lew off his chair and onto the floor. I grabbed Brian's cell phone from his back pocket and called Bo, the deputy. Salt then approached James and tried to provoke him. James turned away as Salt found himself sandwiched between Brian and Bill with Big Joe and

200

Carlos standing nearby. Bill attempted to calm Salt and give James time to get away. Salt tried to slug Bill, but Big Joe grabbed his fist. Johnny ordered Salt to leave.

Big Joe said, "Yeah, or we'll let Megan beat you up again."

The room burst into laughter.

Salt hissed in anger, spit flying out of his mouth. Carlos and Big Joe escorted Salt to the door where Bo stood. Salt yanked the door open and stomped through the doorway, with Bo on his heels. The rest of our group left soon afterward.

We persuaded the Lakotas to stay the night; Jackson would sleep over at the Wilson house, while the three women would sleep in open beds at my house. We watched Young Frankenstein before bed and Tootsie in the morning before they left. Comedy was universal.

That evening before Jackson left for the Wilson house, he quizzed me in the kitchen about the things I heard and felt. I answered him with honesty.

"You are The Woman Who Feels," he said.

Patty later told me that the moniker became my name on the reservation and that I was regarded as an unusually spiritual white woman. Soon, I received requests for wills from Lakotas on the rez and from Sioux residents in Nebraska for their divorces and related family messes. They probably thought that spirituality would help me deal with their legal issues.

Chapter 22

Sunday afternoon, Bill woke me from a nap. He led me down to the driveway where two horses awaited us. My old saddle sat atop a chestnut mare, while Bill rode a piebald mustang.

"I borrowed these from Big Joe. Get on, if you think you remember how to ride."

I approached the mare and stroked her neck. She was a beauty, though graying around the nostrils. Bill untied the horses from the drainpipe and I slid into the saddle with ease. Though I suspected this was Bill's prelude to a discussion, I cleared my head and enjoyed our gallop across the east pasture. Ah, it felt good to ride again. The mare was responsive to my every movement. I slowed when I noticed Bill had done so. Oh, shit, here it comes. Yet, he became tongue-tied when he tried to talk. So I asked a few questions first.

"What is it about that blue and yellow quilt in the guest room that does something to me?"

"You had that at your house in Omaha. But you were always taking it off your bed and wrapping Scott in it. Your mom put a futon on the floor for Scott to lie on so he wouldn't be in his wheelchair all the time. You'd wrap him up and snuggle in next to him like you were trying to warm him up. Then you'd coo or hum in his ear. He'd smile and wiggle. You knew something was wrong...he just had nothin' upstairs and his poor skinny body was so limp. I think you were trying to fix him. You couldn't say his name so you called him 'Totty'."

I didn't say anything, but I was wailing inside. Poor Scott. Poor Totty.

"There's a key on my father's key ring that I can't figure out what it goes to."

"A key. Could be my old house key. I'll take a look at it. If it's gold, that's probably what it is."

"Did they divorce?"

"Yeah, but not till a couple of years after they split."

"Did she every remarry?"

"No. You see, she was lovely, but Scott is such a burden, most men wouldn't take on that kind of responsibility."

"What about beige luggage?"

"Hmm. Oh, I had some old Samsonite luggage. Did you see it when my house collapsed? It was in the bedroom closet."

"Yeah, I think I did. Still…"

"And you could have remembered it from when I came to visit your house in Omaha. Do you remember anything from that time?"

"No…well, maybe just the quilt and the luggage. And yet…why don't I recall my mother or Scott? I've never even seen a photo of him."

"I probably had a picture, but it got lost or damaged in the tornado. I had a picture of your folks right before your dad took you away."

"I might have found that one."

"Oh."

We rode in silence for a few minutes. We passed several heifers chewing their cud, looking stupid and lucky to never experience the problems of humans. To the distant northeast, I could see the Eldritch house, grayed from peeling paint.

"Your dad paid for the funeral and a nice headstone."

"I still think it's incredible that he didn't go to the funeral. How heartless."

"He planned to, we bought two tickets, but then he collapsed. I thought it was just the prospect of him confronting the situation. 'Course now I wonder if he didn't

204

have something related to the heart attack. It makes me sick that I missed that warning."

"It still doesn't make sense to me that the three of you kept this from me."

"It's all about getting stuck in the lie...lies, I guess. Liz knew you were strong, so she let you go with your dad to save Scott from an institution."

"Sort of a Sophie's Choice dilemma then...choose one or the other of us. But why didn't she ever contact me?"

"Frank forbid her. He never wanted you to know that your mom let you go. Now this is something you would never know, but when your dad was a teen he found out that our mom was cheating on my dad. She stopped, and my folks recovered, but Frank never did. He talked to me about it in front of her just to make my mom suffer more. I think it broke his heart. And you're wrong about him being heartless... he loved you so much, more than anybody."

"That doesn't make me feel better."

"It comes down to this—your dad was unforgiving."

"He was mad at his mother."

"Oh, that's just the start. He was mad at Liz for not being the woman he thought she was—remember I said they always fought, but then married fast anyway. But he was probably harshest on himself...and I wouldn't have understood all this if he hadn't told me later that night after you said you had that other job offer. He never forgave himself for abandoning his son, his wife, and for separating you from your brother...then telling you that your mother was dead. He'd set himself up for a lifetime of lies. He was a smart man, but he couldn't figure out how to undo the damage without losing you. He even made Liz take back her maiden name so you couldn't find her."

"How much did she sell that for?"

"That's not fair, Megan. It busted her heart into a million pieces."

"Okay, so how does he keep you trapped in this lie? You've deceived me as much as he ever did. And he even apologized to me."

He hung his head, and his horse began to wander. For a moment, he alarmed me.

"Bill!"

"Yeah."

"Get down off the horse before you fall off." I dismounted in the middle of his northernmost pasture. "C'mon!"

He slid down the side of his horse to his knees. I let go of my horse's reins, she wandered a few feet away and started eating grass, as did Bill's horse. I yanked the reins from his clenched fist and knelt next to him.

Old cowboys don't cry, but they can gasp for air and form moisture in their tear ducts. He cleared his throat.

"Your parents separated. I had always been envious, jealous of him for finding Liz. She and I...when they were living apart...we had an affair."

I sat down hard in the grass. No voice in the wind ever gave me this clue.

"Your dad found out. He never forgave me. I never forgave myself for helping to break them up. Then we found out she was pregnant. Oh, Lord. What a mess. Of course, he held that over my head all these years. He wouldn't let me be with Liz and Scott. I'd have brought them here. But he threatened to tell you and Cindy then Kyle when he came of age. Then I lost them anyway. So he threatened to tell Sally when we married. So...like him, I chose you. It's all been a series of guilt trips. He was gonna do and say anything to keep you. He knew he'd never marry again. He discovered what a vengeful bastard he was."

I sat in stunned silence.

"We were both afraid of losing you. Till recently, you and I were closer than I ever was to my son."

The wind was strong, but there were no voices— nothing could have cut its way through my muddled and

206

overwhelmed brain. A thought made me jerk. Bill looked me in the eyes for the first time since we started talking.

"Bill, are you my father?"

He laughed and lay back on the grass. "Oh, hon, I wish. But the timing was wrong."

After a few minutes, I said, "You know, you really screwed up. Don't you see? I would have backed you up if it meant being reunited with my mother and brother. Yeah, I would have left my father and lived down the street with you, my mother, and Scott."

"There's no way I could have known that. And think about this—remember how fast that tornado was on us? Now maybe I can scoop up Scott and get him down the basement steps, but you or your mom wouldn't have made it down those stairs in time. And Scott was always skinny, but he was a big enough man to give me trouble getting down those steps. We could have fallen. And if we did get down there, could we all have survived the collapse?"

"Oh, now you're getting ridiculous trying to justify your part in this mess. You're taxing the boundaries of foresight."

"Now you're talking like a attorney."

"Well, I am. But don't blame my father's profession for the way he was. No, that was all him."

We watched the horses wander to a new patch of grass. Because I was in a cow pasture, I checked the ground before I lay down.

"So, what are you going to do?" he asked.

"You mean…do I forgive the three of you?"

"Yeah, and do you plan to stop pushing Brian away? I've been watching you. He's ready to be by your side. I called and asked him if he was coming over today and he said you had told him to stay away."

"Oh, I did not say that. I just said I wanted some time to myself."

"Well, you're making him sweat a bit, so what he hears may not be what you say."

"I don't want to lose him."

"Then don't mess up your love life because of family screw-ups."

"Advice duly noted."

"So are you going to forgive me?"

"I'll think about it."

"Do you think you'll forgive your mother and go see her? I hope you do forgive her—for you and for me. If you do, then I can go see her and figure things out."

I turned to look at him.

"I've loved her since the first time I met her," he said. "And I love her still."

I resolved not to mess up my relationship with Brian. I called him that afternoon and invited him over for a picnic. He agreed, but I sensed something negative. I packed up some leftover fried chicken and potato salad and four beers in a cooler and stocked our picnic basket. I took him to the creek and we exchanged small talk and began to eat.

"So, what did you learn from your uncle?"

"Can't talk about it now, or I won't be able to finish," and I did want to finish that drumstick.

So once again, he waited—a gesture not lost on me. I quickly finished then downed four Rolaids.

"First, I want to apologize for putting you off earlier," I said. "It's like I've been holding my breath for this last bit of info, this last piece in the puzzle. And it's all been so much, too much at times."

"And I'm the too much part."

"For a while. But I can come up for air now, and I hope you'll forgive me."

He looked down at the low creek water as it passed by us. That was just enough time to launch an offensive. I crawled to him across the blanket we'd brought. I knew he loved me, I knew I possessed something he liked, and it bolstered my confidence. I straddled one of his legs and brought my face inches from his, beer breath and all. I gave him a power kiss and unbuttoned his jeans. I didn't always know if I could win a case, but I knew I would win this one.

Later, we drank our second beer as we lay naked on the blanket. The advantage in being in nowhere land is that you're unlikely to be found there. However, I did keep an eye out for James, who favored this area. Our naked bodies would scare him away from this area forever. I got dressed and Brian followed my lead. Then I told him about my conversation with Uncle Bill.

"Bloody hell, I didn't see that coming with your uncle," he said.

"Neither did I. And you've been watching Harry Potter."

"Monty Python. But anyway, what do you plan to do?"

"I don't know. I'm scared shitless to see her—though it's got to be far worse for her. I mean, think about it...they separated twins. I assume...I hope my brother missed me when I was gone."

"It sounds like the torment just continues for you. Are you sure you want that? Your mother is free to live her life."

"And live thinking I hate her?"

"Am I not enough?"

That struck me as an incredibly selfish and arrogant remark. No, I couldn't say that he was. I stared at him.

"If I had come around when your mom was dying, would you have left your duties as a son to be with me?"

"That's different."

"In some ways."

I sensed we had entered into hostile territory. Despite my occupation, I didn't like to argue, especially regarding personal matters. Sometimes it's better to step back. I packed up the picnic items in a deliberate, leisurely way so that he didn't think I was in a huff. I wanted to give him time to reconsider, but he just stared out at the creek. He scooted off the blanket so I could fold it for carrying. Everything was ready to go. I picked up the cooler, basket, and blanket. A gust of wind caught me and held me in my spot. No, I would not be comforted, but thanks anyway, Beverly.

"Sometimes, I think I've never recovered from losing her," he said. "Her death changed me. I don't know how anyone ever recovers from that kind of loss."

"But you've put a time limit on my grief. And now, you think I can't and shouldn't even try to deal with the knowledge that I have a mother who lives? I'll tell you what is maybe enough right now—the fact that I lost the brother I once loved. In truth, I lost him twice. Shouldn't I be allowed to grieve him? Or my father? Should I ignore him too so that I can spend carefree time with you?"

"It's just that I either see you at work where you're this woman of steel or you're at home crying into your pillow."

"Oh, so you've figured out that I'm in a crisis? Which death was your first clue? Sorry if I don't fawn over you like your football fans."

That was hardly stepping back; my attempt at reconciliation changed to anger over his self-importance. He'd said the death of his mother made him grow up. Perhaps glory days in Husker Nation had permanently altered his self-image. Most men of my age suffered from over-sensitive, fragile egos. It was a shock to discover my fiancé, a man I thought strong, was inflicted with the same weakness. Maybe he was too much, or too little, to handle right now.

I walked back to the house. Brian drove home.

Chapter 23

Brian stayed in Sidney the next two days. In the meantime, I met with Paul Ritter regarding his divorce. The counseling sessions I encouraged weren't going well. I certainly would have preferred to see the family mend than to earn a full fee for a divorce. Through Paul, I set up an appointment with Kayla for the next afternoon. I picked her up after school and brought her home. I showed her photos of Bill's house after the tornado and gave her a tour of my house.

"What's that room?" she asked.

I opened the door. "This is my father's study."

"Was. Now it's yours, right?"

"Yeah, it is. Oh, someday I'll make it my own. I don't really need it. I don't need a house this big. Anyway, let me show you where we hang out."

After I led her to the family room and the basement where we hid during the tornado, I grabbed a couple of bottled waters and took her out into the hills. With trouble, she labored to the top of Big Leo. I was encouraged that she persisted, despite her lack of conditioning. Kids were such wimps these days. I told her stories of the games we played as a kid. She told me about her friends and the activities they did for fun. Beverly was quiet, she knew I was working.

"Parents have their own stuff to deal with," I began. "Kids think the world is about them, but that's only partly true. Our parents deal with things we can't always understand. How well do we really know them? People fall in love, and sometimes they fall out of love, and that doesn't have anything to do with us kids."

"'Us kids'?"

"Sure, my family was a mess. And your parents are struggling, but it doesn't mean their feelings for you have changed. They're probably the same. Do you think your folks love you less?"

"I guess not."

"So what do we do about our messy families? Do we fall apart? Do we become all screwed up and flunk out of school or start drinking or whatever and then blame it on our parents? Do we mess up all our relationships and blame those on our parents too?"

"What did you do?"

I smiled at her as the wind lashed at us. She knew why I gave her a ponytail holder.

"I'm still doing. I'm dealing with things later in life than you. I guess we find a way to tolerate, forgive, be brave, and just tough it out. How you do those things is up to you."

Later that evening, after Patty left and Uncle Bill drove over to Big Joe's for beer and baseball, I sat behind my father's desk in his study, a phone book under my feet. Maybe Bill would make me a carpeted footstool like the one in the kitchen he made for me. Strange, but he was the one I most softened to after Sunday's revelations.

My parents were another matter. My father, the bully—the unforgiving, insecure son of a bitch who tore me away from the twin I had loved. He turned out to be crueler and colder than I could have guessed. And my mother— what a wimp. She let me go, she let my father separate me from my brother, and then she sold her name. How much did she sell me for? Perhaps a lump sum for starters then $3000 a month after that? How was I to forgive them? And me—how do I forgive myself? In the womb, I fought for and won the battle for health and cognition. I should have been allowed to help in raising Scott as my penance. But we were torn apart. The thought ripped at my guts.

I stood up then swept my arms across the desk till I had knocked every last item onto the floor. With the fancy desk set on the floor, I added the contents of each side drawer till I built a hefty pile. If I had been outside, I would have set a match to it. Instead, I took a large trash bag from the laundry room and filled it with the few remaining remnants of him. Then I grabbed his wallet off the counter and shoved it behind some bowls in the kitchen. The ring of keys reminded me of the hidden box, which I retrieved and added to the trash bag. I put the two keys—the desk key and the basement cabinet key in the top drawer with the recent bank statements, the gas and water bill, and insurance records. My respite from rage, along with my burst of common sense in retaining the financial records, cooled my violence. I thought about my speech to Kayla up on Big Leo. It's much easier to spew good advice than to live it.

Totty, the suffering innocent—the child-boy-man from the well, trapped in a warped body with a deficient brain. He had been the source of my yearning all these years. Maybe his was the only voice I really heard. It had been the only one I couldn't control. It was one of my earliest memories of this place. It confused me when it changed, and stopped when I didn't want it to. I felt the pain of his death. He suffered in death as he had in life, my poor palsied brother. I felt my blood pressure rise to the point that blood pounded in my ears.

Then an awareness of danger alarmed me, sending a chill up my back. I walked around the house, wondering what else could possibly happen. Yet the sensation persisted, so I grabbed a steak knife from the kitchen drawer.

A few minutes after I roamed through the main level, I heard a crash. It sounded like broken glass. I dashed down the hall to the front of the house where I heard incoherent shouting. I ducked down and slid my cell phone from my back pocket and dialed the police. A warm breeze wafted through the hall. I peered around the corner and saw that something had been thrown through our living room window, big enough to smash two panes. By shining my cell phone light into the room I could see that it was the mangled copy of Lonesome Dove. Pounding on the front door started. Now that the voice was closer, I could hear that Salt was calling me a whorey bitch or something like that. At least he didn't call me an elf. Bo finally answered the phone.

"Bo," I whispered as I backed down the hallway. "This is Megan. Get over here. Salt is trying to break down my front door."

I knew he couldn't, for not long after the Sidney locksmiths installed the deadbolts on the law office, I persuaded my dad to let them put in floor and deadbolts here.

"Yes, I'm sure it's him. Just get over here." I hung up then dashed to check the back door. I stayed low because of all the windows as I scurried to the back door. Locked, good. If he came in, it would be through a window—where I planned to meet him. The pounding continued—it shook the house. He must be drunk. The pounding stopped. Silence.

Then a blast ripped through a window. I froze. Now it was my heart that was pounding. The bastard had a gun. Though I didn't plan to investigate, he'd probably fired into the study where I'd left the light on. I called the State Patrol as I crawled to the mud room and put on my sneakers and a black hoodie. Now he was smashing the window glass in the study. Then I heard the sound of another gun blast, farther away.

James!

Yelling started. A closer shotgun fired. I ran to the family room window. A dark figure ran out the Wilson back door and charged into the dark backyard. James stopped behind his backyard oak. He looked to be reloading. That's right—he said he only had one shell in the gun. Salt was charging through the house, flipping on lights. The illuminated house showed the shadow of James. He hadn't gotten completely around the back of the tree. Run!

Salt pushed through the back door and fired at James, who fired back. Neither man could shoot worth a damn. The

214

men exchanged fire again. When Salt ran back into the house, James took off for Rufus, as I knew he would. I grabbed a roll of black electrician's tape and covered the reflective patches on the back of my running shoes. Salt ran after him, he was faster than I thought he'd be. I called Uncle Bill, but had to leave a message. I turned off my phone and shoved it in my back pocket as I ran out the front door and around the house then headed north. Once I saw that both men had crested Rufus, I cut west to get closer to James.

They would run out of ammunition, but at least I had the knife in the other back pocket. I sweated under the black hoodie, but I wanted to stay as dark as the moonless night. Once over Rufus, I saw the light of a flashlight. Salt must have grabbed the flashlight James always kept by the back door. He caught James in a beam of light. Shit! But then the light jerked and fell to the ground. Salt couldn't fire and hold the flashlight at the same time. James would keep running to make himself a difficult target to hit. Salt recovered the light and started after him. I ran to where I thought James would go—he'd want to lead Salt over the roughest land. Soon enough, Salt stumbled and fell, cursing. It wouldn't be hard to know the location of the old drunk. A shot rang out. James must have fired on Salt, when the flashlight was still. Salt wailed, but I saw the light rise in the air and move toward the sound of the shot.

Salt ran till he had to work his way through some of the westernmost of the Seven Dwarfs then he slowed. I kept alongside him and behind James. I didn't really want to become a target, but I wanted to help James. I began to fill my hoodie pockets with rocks. Salt fell again. If James fell, he did it without cursing. He led Salt through more of the scarred, pock-marked terrain.

Then I was ahead of Salt. The flashlight started my way. I dropped to the ground, head toward Salt, with my face in the buffalo grass and my hands underneath me. The light swept over me twice. My heart thudded so hard against my chest I wondered if I could be heard. Then the light moved back north. I got up and ran. James appeared in the light for an instant. Salt yelled something, but it was lost in the wind.

The men came upon an open area. Suddenly, Salt stopped. I saw the light lowered to the ground. It moved till it found James. A shot rang out and James fell. I sprinted to him. Salt rose then ran toward his prey. He fell again, losing control of the flashlight which pointed east. I reached James.

"James, where are you hit?"

"Got me with the buckshot in a hundred places."

"Where's the rifle?"

"Here," he strained, "I can reach it. Got to load it again. That bastard isn't givin' me time."

Salt rose and was searched for James, sweeping the light too far north. But it gave James time to reload.

"Two shots left. My arm is torn up. Can you shoot?"

"I could shoot a BB gun when I was ten."

"Here, put the gun into your shoulder, hold your breath and shoot that bastard."

From the ground, I watched the flashlight move our way. I shoved the gun into my shoulder and took a breath. My hand sweated on the hot barrel. I aimed at the body holding the flashlight, and then pulled the trigger. He fell, unleashing a stream of profanities. As he struggled, I helped James to his feet.

"We got to get you to Pooper's Canyon. It's just a few yards."

The yelling continued as we neared the ditch. James slid down the four foot drop and groaned. I handed him the gun. Salt had recovered the flashlight and probably his gun.

"Here, take the gun. I'll try to lead him off. If he comes for you, kill the bastard."

"Wait!" yelled James.

No, I wasn't going to take the gun like he wanted me to. I turned and ran north. The flashlight covered the ground to the south, searching for us. He aimed the light north and

216

found me in the light. I just kept running hard. I could tell he was up and moving. Damn, I only sprayed him with some pellets. I climbed over the edge of the ditch and started hurling rocks at Salt. I once had a decent infielder's arm, so one finally hit him. I crept along the floor of the gully till it got too shallow. I jumped out and took off in a sprint. After thirty yards, I slowed briefly to cross over a series of rocky ridges, and then took off again. Surely, I could run a drunk into the ground then circle back to James.

It took Salt a few minutes to find me, but he was following. He fell often. I turned northeast to avoid the jagged area that ran along the northern end of the ditch. It directed me back closer to him, but I'd created enough distance that he would waste his shot if he fired at me. He did try a couple of times, but never came close. Although I was frightened, I told myself to keep thinking and running. I was now so far north that the ground wasn't as familiar. The light caught me, so I darted right then dropped to the ground. The light flashed above me and I jumped to my feet. I cut back left with a destination in mind.

Then, it happened. I stepped into a creature's hole and fell, my left ankle screaming in pain. I couldn't stay there, the light would find me. I began to crawl westward. The light even found me once, though he didn't recognize that the black form in the grass was me. I knew it was close, though I couldn't see it. Then my hand found only air as my face smashed to the ground. Thanks, Miss Gulch.

Now I needed to let him find me. I stood, mostly on one foot, trembling with pain and fear, as I waited for a crazy drunk with a gun to locate me. The moments piled up, and I began to totter, my heart hammering in my chest. My guts felt icky with churning acid.

As soon as the light hit me, I jumped to the right then found the edge and scrambled over. The drop was almost double my height. Of course, I hit my left ankle more times than I could count. I let out a silent wail. I checked and found that the knife was still in my pocket. I began to search around me. I found a good-sized chunk of dirt that felt substantial. I began to hear his breathing as he chugged closer. What drove this man? He couldn't have been very drunk to have come all this way. No, I was dealing with a lunatic with a shotgun. I had a knife and a dirt clod.

Flattening myself against the wall of the dry creek bed, I waited. Fear welled up inside me and stuck in my throat. My ankle throbbed. It wasn't as frightening to be able to run, to do something. Now I had to wait. The beam from the light shone across the ditch. If he stopped and saw the gulch he could search until he found me. Then I'd be dead. His breathing, his heavy footsteps grew louder till I thought he was on top of me. Then man, gun, and flashlight tumbled headlong into the ditch.

"Ahh-oommph!"

The flashlight ended up on the other side of his body, illuminating his silhouette. He started to roll to his side. I scrambled to my knees then plunged the knife into his abdomen.

"Arrrgh!"

Damn, this crazy bastard was hard to finish. I scooted back from him. He rolled around, probably looking for the gun. He struggled to rise up. Gathering my good leg under me, I launched myself upward, long enough to slam the dirt chunk down onto his head. He fell forward, knocking me down hard, driving my shoulder onto the ground as the barrel of the gun hit my head. I writhed from the excruciating pain in my left shoulder. He didn't move. I felt for and found the shotgun, then pushed myself out of his reach. I listened, but no longer heard his panting. My ankle and shoulder screamed.

For several minutes, I lay on my back, sucking air. I needed to be found. I pulled my cell phone out of my back pocket—the face was smashed in. I must have shoved it in my pocket backward in my haste. It wouldn't turn on. Shit. I

218

wasn't sure if Salt was dead or unconscious. To help them find me, I decided to fire the shotgun, but first I would make sure I didn't need to fire it into Salt. I shifted my body and crawled near to him. I found his arm—the wrist had no pulse. Blood rolled down my temple and onto my chin. I used my hood to wipe away the blood that wouldn't stop. I planted the gun into the ground, held it steady with my right hip, angled it north, and then fired into the air. I waited. I hoped to hear voices, but didn't.

I crawled past the body toward the flashlight, shoving his legs out of the way. I needed to put it up on the ground and point it south toward my rescuers. But the effort it would take would be immense. I groaned and rested. Then with one good arm and one good leg, I dragged myself along, inch by inch, searching until I found a foothold. After I placed the flashlight into my hood, I hoisted myself to a standing position against the gulch wall. By using my head to balance my body tight to the wall, I let go long enough to pull the flashlight from my hood and set it above the level of the gully. I tried to hop down to the ditch floor, but I couldn't keep from landing on my left foot. I let out a wail as I twisted and landed on my back.

Black.

When I stirred, I discovered my head had struck a rock, opening another gash. The stars blurred then cleared then blurred again. Black. A light came, I heard speaking. I felt the blood oozing down my neck and face. Beverly. Hands moved me. I rose on a board, flashing lights. Red and blue. Flashing. Blurring. Flashing. No more stars. Bumpy. Going fast now. Head hurts, ankle hurts, shoulder hurts. Black. Going on wheels. Too bright. Stab in arm. I see tubes. I sleep, but moving, more moving on wheels. A pillow. I try to sleep. A sharp light hits my eyes, back and forth. I want to hurt this person. I want to sleep. I don't want to talk. Lots of people in room. Go away. Terrible pain in leg. Black.

I awakened. Hospital. I was safe. It was dark outside the metal blinds. Uncle Bill came to my side and said something.

"Wha? Uh. How is James?"

"Shot up with buckshot, but okay. He came by before Derek took him home."

"Uh, huh. Good. What time is it?"

"About two in the morning."

"Really? You should go home. I just want to sleep."

"I will pretty soon. Here talk to Brian, he's been waiting. I'll be back in a few minutes."

His face was before me. But I didn't want to deal with him. My head was swimming.

"How come you didn't call me for help?" Brian asked once Uncle Bill left.

"I need to sleep." I shut my eyes hoping he'd go away and thinking it was an interesting question from someone who'd been sulking for two days. "So selfish." Oh, no, I said that out loud. Did I really think that? I felt the bed move, so I knew he backed away. I suddenly felt very sad. I wanted his face to come back, but he was more than my heart and wits could handle now. I kept my eyes shut. I did sleep.

The nurses pestered me all night. I dreamt about a dark woman and a rock that spouted blood. I awakened then became aware of people in my room, so I shut my eyes again to think. I survived. James survived. I was a beat up mess— my arm was in a sling, my head was bandaged, my ankle was wrapped and elevated. But I survived. Thank you, God.

I killed a man.

I remembered the fear. I lacked remorse for the death of that crazy son of a bitch. Him or me—that's how it was. He meant to kill me then go back for James. I could recall the night vividly until the end, but thinking about it made me tired.

Emotions welled up inside me. I felt tears roll down my cheeks, but I kept my eyes shut and my body still. The dark woman—her image kept coming back to me. I wanted to feel Brian's arms around me. I wished I could be riding on a horse next to Uncle Bill right now, without hearing any secrets, without the injuries, without the knowledge that I killed someone.

The dark woman. I was supposed to be deciding whether to go to her. She came to me. I wasn't ready. I kept my eyes shut. I needed to think, but my mind felt blurry. Maybe this was something I couldn't think through. Did I want my mother or not?

Then the door burst open. I opened my eyes.

"Lemme see her," said Beulah, as she shuffled near.

I smiled at her. Others rose from their chairs.

"Heh! Nobody's gonna call you an elf anymore. No, ma'am. You gave that S-O-B a lobotomy. Yeah, you did. The world's a better place."

"My body's not," I said, wondering if that made sense.

"I see you're a bit beat up."

"Miss Gulch helped with that."

"Heh! Heh! You battled the Wicked Witch of the West, too? Don't worry, hon. You'll get your senses back."

I felt I'd done more than wander off the yellow brick road. Beulah looked over to the dark woman. For the first time, I did also.

"You gotta be a relative."

The dark woman nodded. "She needs to rest."

I needed to do more than that. Beulah's presence forced me to think. Beyond the question of forgiveness, I needed to keep secrets—exposing my story meant shame on my father, my uncle, and my mother. Lord, help me. I didn't want to do that. Would I? I shut my eyes. Secrets.

Chapter 24

After Beulah left, I held my mother in my eyes—she was a beautiful woman, slight and dark.

"I know who you are," I said. "I would like to wait till we get home to talk. You must have gotten up early to drive here."

"I left about ten-thirty," she said.

I turned to Uncle Bill. "You called her then?"

"No," he said. "I called while they were resetting your leg, er, high ankle...about midnight, but she was already on the road."

"Then how did you know to come?"

My mother walked to my bedside. "Do you, of all people, need to ask?"

The door swung open. Beulah must have told people I was awake. James squeezed my hand. He had bandages on his right side—neck and arm, and he rested his weight on a cane. He nervously pursed his lips. I smiled at Derek, Vonny, and Patty.

"You saved my life," he said.

"You saved mine. Salt would have come through one of those windows and shot me down if you hadn't shot at him. We helped each other."

People kept coming into the room. My mother backed away. Beulah pushed close. I nodded to Gus, who stood next to Carlos Hernandez and Eldon Strumple. I spotted Kayla and her parents in the back. I waved to Kayla. I was surprised to see Sheila. Glenda and Melanie slipped into the room before the door closed. I began to feel self-conscious—I touched my hair and felt the caked blood and mud.

Uncle Bill told the visitors that I had a concussion, a broken collarbone, and a broken left ankle.

"Megan, hon, tell us what happened and why you ran halfway to Canada," said Beulah.

I saw that Police Chief Dobbs and a State Patrol Officer stood at the foot of my bed. Some woman with a tape recorder pushed in next to Beulah. A man stood next to her, prepping his camera. I shook my head. Brian got in front of the scrawny cameraman.

"I'll just hold that for you, sir," Brian said. He yanked the camera out of the man's hands.

I told the story of last night, omitting the name Pooper's Canyon, while emphasizing the role of James, and later, Miss Gulch. I winked at Beulah, who grinned. Then I answered a few questions. By then, I was tired and hungry.

But James spoke up. "I should've been able to end it. I had a clear shot out there when we were running to hide in the darkness, but I missed."

"I missed him, too," I said. "But it's tough running then stopping and trying to shoot while you're breathing hard. Salt got lucky once, even then he only got you with buckshot."

James smiled at me. "You were better at chucking those rocks. You hit him in the head." He squeezed my hand again.

My head began to throb. "I need breakfast and drugs."

Brian started clearing the room. He even gave Chief Dobbs a shove.

"I'll see you all at Custer's," I said.

I waved over Uncle Bill and told him who to keep in the room. Brian closed the door.

I directed my gaze to my mother. "These are the important people in my life. A motley bunch, I know." I then introduced Brian, Patty, James, Derek, and Vonny. "This is my mother, Liz Simon."

My mother quickly nodded to them then looked at me. I knew this was hell for her. An awkward silence fell over us. Then Brian came to the rescue.

"We've met. We drank about ten cups of coffee together," he said.

"You two stayed all night?" I asked my mother, "Wait, I know you did. I dreamt about you all night."

"She had to check on you every other breath," Brian said. "She was worse than the nurses."

"At least I didn't wake you. I thought you were gonna punch that redheaded nurse if she woke you again."

Laughter filled the room. I smiled.

"Um…about the arrival of my mother…let's keep that confidential for now," I said.

What were we going to say?

A nurse came in and gave me pills to swallow. I ate some breakfast while the Wilsons chatted together. My mother stood by her chair. I beckoned to Brian. I was in the hospital, the right place to heal. I knew to start now.

Brian leaned in close to me. "I'm sorry. I was wrong to—"

I stopped him by putting my hand on his lips.

"I don't want to go back there," I said. "We were both wrong and both right." I took a swig of orange juice to improve my nasty breath, and then I kissed him. "I love you. Stay close."

I barely made it through my scrambled eggs before sleep overcame me.

Late in the afternoon, the doctors decided I was stable enough to be released. A nurse would be sent to visit me twice a day, starting with a visit that evening.

I was happy to be home, though the travel left me wiped out. Brian carried me upstairs to my bed, which looked so welcoming.

"I missed you," I said to my pillow.

When I awoke, a wheelchair was parked next to my bed. At first, I thought mostly about my pain, now difficulties of my situation became clear. Once I was further along in my recovery, I could hop on one leg to the bathroom, but the fogginess of my brain prevented me from wanting to jump anywhere, even to conclusions. A single crutch was set against the wall. In time, I could use it. Patty walked in to put away some laundry. With her assistance, I learned how to maneuver into the wheelchair and then onto the toilet. This was going to be tough. I wondered how long it would be before I could go back to work. As requested, Patty went to get my mother and Uncle Bill.

"We need to settle some things," I said to my mother. "Like who you are."

She looked down, but nodded.

"I was hoping I could be free of the secrets that have eaten away at me, but I think we're stuck. I mean…how can I say you're my mother when everyone around here thinks you died? If we come clean, it just starts the gossip and the questions…and I don't feel up to that. And it's not their business anyway. Even if you left today, people would be asking me who you were."

"So, what do we say?" asked Uncle Bill.

"I think we need to make you an aunt."

My mother nodded, but I saw that the tears had started to roll down her face. I wanted them to stop. She was still the mother who let me go; so, avoiding the complications of her story was partly a selfish desire.

"I insist on this," I said. "And I hope you can stay for a bit, but that will just make problems more likely. I'm still mad at my father, but I don't want town gossip to disparage him."

I waited for my mother to speak. But she appeared unable to.

"Uncle Bill, did you or my father ever mention my mother's name out here?"

226

"No, in fact, we made sure that we never said it."

"I think it's still possible. So, you can't be my mother and you can't be Liz—ever again. Not here."

I wished she would stop crying. Finally, she did.

"My given name is Elizabeth. When I was little, my siblings called me Beth. One of my brothers still does."

Beth. I have another uncle. There was much to learn about my mother's family; but for now, I was intent on eliminating the mysteries in western Nebraska.

"Then you're my Aunt Beth, if anyone asks. But I'll call you Beth."

She nodded. I figured we accomplished enough for one day. I wanted to lie down before Patty brought up my supper. Uncle Bill and Beth rose when I snuggled back into my pillow.

"You can stop the $3000 monthly benefit," said my mother. "It was meant for Scott's care. Your father did make me a co-beneficiary of a life insurance policy."

"I'm glad he did that," I said.

She left the room.

"Are you sure you needed to take away her name and disclaim her?" asked Uncle Bill.

"Yeah. You'll see."

Now I had made two momentous choices—to protect my father and disown my mother in a public sense. I had been a victim of their deceit, now I had ratified it. To do otherwise exposed my father, my uncle, and my mother to disgrace that would spread through western Nebraska. I had hurt my mother's feelings, but spared her from scorn. She gave birth to me, but she was Scott's mother—other people had filled her role during my life. Uncle Bill thought I was being cruel, but he needed to be patient. Wasn't it Shakespeare who said: "What wound did ever heal but by degrees?" We were just getting started.

The next morning, I awoke to find my mother was sitting in my bedroom chair. She helped me to the bathroom. It felt very natural for her to assist me. No matter how old you are, it's nice to have your mommy around when you're sick or injured—at least that's what Patty said to me last night. Back in my bed, she helped me prop up my pillows so I could sit up in bed. She went back to the chair.

"That first day, I didn't think we were going to make it. Scottie cried all day and so did I. It was so hard…I can't begin to tell you."

I knew she would start to work on me. It was natural for her to try.

"He couldn't say your name—or any words—so he called you Mem. Mem-mem-mem, he would say and you would go to your Totty."

Mem. She was doing a good job. Mem.

"At a craft store, I found a big cloth doll with dark eyes and hair with a big smile. He started calling it 'Mem-mem.' He kept it for years. I had to hire another then another made for him."

"I was replaced by a doll?"

"And cousins. When you were around, he didn't want anyone else. After you left, he and I got closer. That was the only good thing."

"That's a big thing."

She nodded. Then she smiled. "I used to scrunch my eyes and say to you 'I squeeze you with my eyes.' And you would giggle. He never had a clue what was going on, but when you laughed, he laughed. He would fight off naps till you fell asleep. Then you figured it out and faked sleep so he would sleep when it wasn't your nap time. Then you and I could play."

"What did we play?"

"Oh, dolls or we'd look at books. You'd hear the story from me then tell it to him, just like you were reading it out of the book."

228

My eyes stung with tears. Too good.

"Did Scott ever relate to my father—or vice versa?"

"It was like they looked right past each other. Your dad tried early on, but Scottie cried whenever he held him. But he did that often. Your dad just didn't understand. Scottie slept a lot and was often irritable when awake. Then he had the feeding tube and the trach tube. It was all too much for your dad."

"My father could be a very cold man. We didn't always get on."

"Bill kept me posted, weekly almost. He'd even tell me your arguments, sometimes line for line. I saw quite a few softball and basketball games when you came east to Lincoln or Omaha. I knew you were doing all right."

"My father was a good man—outside of his cruel dealings with his immediate family. He protected the Wilsons, the Hispanic families, did tons of pro bono work. He fought for the underdog and protected people from the bullying of the local police chief."

"I know all that," she said.

"Well, do you know that I never would have accepted the route you took? I never would have let a child go. I would have negotiated a way to keep us close."

Tears streamed down her face, dripping from her cheeks onto her blouse. My throat swelled with emotion.

"But I'm not you. When will you understand that?"

Maybe never, a thought I kept to myself. We quietly simmered in our emotions for a few minutes. We turned to the knocking on my door.

"I have your breakfast," Patty said as she opened the door. She looked from my face to my mother's, and then started to back out.

"No, wait. I need that." I smiled at her. "These pills make me loopy if I don't have some food, and I need both."

My mother set up the card table we left in my room for food trays. Patty set it down.

"I can take care of her," said my mother. "Patty, I love your Pawpaw bread, and thank you for taking care of my girl all these years."

Patty nodded, started crying then rushed from the room. Overflowing emotions must be infectious. I downed my pain pills then started after the scrambled eggs.

"Have you eaten?" I asked, trying to soften our exchange.

She nodded.

"When I'm better, I'll take you out to Rufus."

"Who's that?"

"The hill and the area beyond the backyard—the playground of my youth and the scene of a shootout."

"Okay. By the way, that Brian is a nice young man. Granted we met under unusual circumstances."

"Unusual circumstances—lots of that going around. You do know he's my fiancé? My father set that up."

It was the first time I'd heard her laugh. It made me smile.

Did God kept me alive just so I could meet my mother? Really, God, you're going to need to lead me along, because I don't know where I'm to go with this.

Chapter 25

I spent the next couple of days in a fog. Yet, I was aware of an unspoken contest to care for me. Patty knew me well, but she hadn't taken care of me since I sprained my ankle one summer playing basketball; and then briefly after a house fell on me. For a former linebacker and defensive back known for his hard hits, Brian was amazingly gentle—I would have found it sensuous if I wasn't so groggy and in pain. My mother was in her own league. After twenty-three years of caring for a desperately handicapped person, she knew what I needed before I did. Uncle Bill just stared at me in bewilderment, as if he deemed my injuries and the precipitating event to be inconceivable.

Once I weaned myself from the pain pills, my brain began to clear. The nasty nightmares that always ended with a shotgun blast began to abate. I hated the wheelchair; instead, I hopped or used the crutch. I discovered I could scoot down the front staircase on my butt, step by step. I didn't like being waited on; and I liked even less waiting for someone to wait on me. I kept in touch with Gus, who was pulling double duty at work. I hoped to resume work the next Monday.

That afternoon, Brian came home from work with two boxes. They turned out to be his and her Glock handguns his dad had bought for us.

"Does he think I plan to continue shooting at people?" I asked.

"Well, you do have a knack for trouble. My dad said that if there are mad men running around, we should be prepared," said Brian. "He also bought some lessons for us. If we have them, I guess we ought to know how to fire them."

"I thought we'd need to register for guns."

"We do. These are just the boxes. They're in my dad's name now, so we'll need to get them registered in our names then we can have them after we're cleared."

Uncle Bill admired the pictures of the guns on the boxes. "And when you have full use of your limbs, I'm taking you for rifle lessons. I've seen James out in the field shooting at tin cans."

I didn't try to argue, though I thought too many people had guns. Yet, if I could have shot well, I could have spared both James and myself a lot of suffering. However, I doubted I'd ever need the reason to use a gun again. Still, I would carry through on the lessons.

That evening, Beulah brought over a crate of root beer as a gift for "riddin' the town of its crazy man."

She looked me over, as I sat on the family room sofa with my leg propped up. She was waiting on me.

Finally, I said, "I found out recently that I had a twin. He died. Scott was his name. It had been weighing on me. And it explains why I always had a strange yearning."

"That ain't so strange," she said. "I had me a twin. We could finish each other's sentences. Our phone bills were terrible—she lived in Michigan—till we got email. When Alice died six years ago, I felt like I had this big hole in me."

A hole, yeah.

"I'd like to keep this between us."

"Gotcha. Otherwise, people just start askin' questions. Gets annoyin' at times." She examined the boxes. "Glock forty-two. Always scared of 'em. Preferred a big dog. But Buddy's been gone awhile now. I like your uncle's dog. Maybe I should get me one of those Labs."

"Traddles is a good dog," I said.

"Hey, who's that purty dark lady?"

"My Aunt Beth."

"Arab?"

"Full-blooded Arab Christian."

"Does she ride?"

"Ah… I don't think so. She's from Omaha."

Uncle Bill joined us.

"Too bad…atop a big white stallion she'd look like an Arabian Queen."

I laughed.

"That's the trouble with this place—there's nobody who looks mysterious and exotic, 'cept when Vonny comes to town—and that's only when you're in a crisis."

Uncle Bill sat down in his recliner. "We should talk about Lew."

"I've been wondering how he's been," I said.

"He's embarrassed to see you. He's just sick over the fact that his brother tried to kill you and James. And then he found out you paid for the burial and sent over your pastor for it."

Beulah stared at me for a few moments. It would be the news at Custer's.

"I've seen Lew," said Beulah. "He's stayin' in the old Dewitt house."

Bill nodded. "He won't go back home. So he's been staying at Brian's room on Benson Street."

"Really? I didn't know."

"Brian probably told you, but you were loopy for a few days. Thursday you ate supper twice."

Beulah cackled.

"Well, I'm off that stuff. But what do we do about Lew? A guy like him needs help…as in some good advice. Uncle Bill, think of some."

"He doesn't want to ranch anymore. My hands have been tending his herd. I bet he sells it. He should be a carpenter."

"Can he make a living off that?" I asked.

"He's a natural. He can get some work driving around the county, doing work this summer. He's been doing stuff at my house. He did most of the repairs to my barn last summer. The winter might be a problem."

"He should pick up some classes at the community college in Sidney during the winter. That would probably help him get indoor work. And what about selling his house?"

"You haven't seen it. The county would condemn it. Might as well bull-doze it."

"You Dockets are like fairy godmothers," said Beulah. "Plannin' people's lives for 'em."

"And Megan is helping James redecorate."

"Uh, huh. So, missy, what's your advice for an old lady?"

"Better shoes."

"Heh! I like these."

"But those flip-flops don't have any support and your arches have fallen."

"Heh, heh. Tellin' an old lady what to do. My arches were never up. Yeah, you're right, but that don't mean I'll do it. Best be goin' now."

"Thanks for the root beer," I said as she shuffled out of the room with a wave.

Uncle Bill and I chuckled. Beulah always waved like Queen Elizabeth. I knew it was coming, but I laughed every time.

On Saturday, Uncle Bill and Brian carried me out to the shady side of Rufus to have an afternoon picnic with my mother. I tended to think of her as my mother, though I needed to train my brain to think of her as Aunt Beth. I pointed out to her the important areas, such as the Seven Dwarfs and Big Leo. I described the key locations of the attack.

"This was once my playground. It became a weapon that helped me kill a man."

"That was self-defense. I bet your pastor would agree. Have you thought of talking to him or her? Might be a good idea."

"He'll tell me that as a Christian, I should be feeling remorseful. Mostly, I just feel shock. But yes, I should talk to him. In fact, he called the house, but I avoided talking to people while I was doped up. I didn't want to sound like a babbling idiot. I'm quite vain in some ways."

"You're not frou-frou, but you have nice clothes. Your desire for respect outweighs most other feelings. I'd like to see you in court some time."

I was supposed to be angry with this woman. But she was likable, and she had me pegged.

Beth gave me a shot of hand sanitizer—something Patty never would have thought of sending. We ate for a while in silence.

"Megan, you were right about the name and the relationship. I'll never forget how your friends at the hospital looked at me. I don't want to be known in town as the mother who parted with you."

"My gang know the reasons. And they are trustworthy."

She nodded, but hesitated. "I would like to date your uncle. That would put me more into your life than you might want. So you need to agree to it."

"Uncle Bill said he's loved you ever since he met you. I would never stand in the way of something like that. And yes, I want you in my life... I'm still working through some things... I'll admit to that."

She nodded. "He really said that?"

"He thinks I'm disowning you, but it's one reason for the name and relationship change. I just couldn't say anything at the time... I didn't know how you felt about him."

I turned to feel the wind and hear Beverly. She was urging kindness.

"This is where I heard you and Scott. I don't know why I could."

"You hear someone now."

"Yes, Beverly, Mrs. Wilson. She likes to calm me, just like she did when she was alive."

Once I had questioned my emotional balance, now I felt validated. I needed some connection to hear and feel. But I did sense things; I felt things.

"You knew I was in trouble," I said.

"I never sensed things like you do. But I did feel alarmed by you—twice. The first was in late April when you woke me up. I thought you were terribly ill, as in dying. But then I checked on Scottie... I realized it was him not you. He'd been having problems... heart and lungs."

"My. God, that hurt. I did think I was dying. Then it just stopped. I ran out here, but I didn't hear him anymore. I only heard your wailing. I was so confused."

"Then I knew you were in trouble when you ran out here, trying to help James. You made me jump out of my chair."

"I did think I could die. Then I bashed my brains against a rock and I stopped thinking."

"I was on the road by then."

We drank our root beers in silence for a few minutes.

"Why do you think we can—whatever it is—feel? Is this some Syrian thing?" I asked.

"Oh, I doubt that. Nobody in the family is like you."

"Patty has been calling Jackson—we told you about all that with the Lakotas. Jackson says the need to love heightened my senses. Then he quoted a chief...let's see how that went... 'My friends, how desperately do we need to be loved and to love.'"

"Yes, we need both. Now with Scottie gone, I feel lost. Since his death, everything has seemed so easy. I don't know what to do with myself without the demands of taking care of him. It's as if that's all I knew. Yes, I have a job, but that's nothing in comparison."

"What do you do?" I asked.

"I work in the registrar's office at Creighton. I saw you every day for seven school years, except for that semester in

236

Europe. I had access to your class schedules, so I always knew when you'd be going to lunch. Mostly, I just peeked out a window, sometimes I sat on a bench at a distance."

"Most days before lunch I had this eerie feeling. I got so I'd pop Rolaids before I left for the sandwich bar or the cafeteria. I often had trouble eating." I grinned. "You did that."

"I suppose I did. And your uncle sent me photos through the years. I went to both your Creighton graduations. I even sneaked into your Law School Hooding at Joslyn."

"A bunch of purple plumage. It was hot."

She reached into the picnic basket and pulled out an envelope. She handed it to me. Leaning on my right arm, I fumbled with it. She took out several photos and handed them to me. I looked at the first one and lay back onto the blanket.

The first photo featured Scott as an adult, sitting in his wheelchair, the feeding tube visible as it emerged underneath his shirt. He was smiling. It was difficult to guess his age, though he no longer had the tracheotomy tube. I couldn't determine his height, but he didn't look big. With his head braced by a padded headrest, he leaned to one side, his body limp, except for his hands, which were clenched in fists.

"When is this?"

"About a year ago."

"Was he in pain?"

"No, his meds controlled that."

His hair and eyes were dark like mine. Emotion churned in my guts. I looked at the next photo. It was a young Totty, with Mem sitting behind him on a blanket, holding him up. His smile was bigger than mine. I dropped the photo and gushed. I guess I was overdue. I wrapped my good arm over my face. I felt the need to hide the emotions my mother had dealt with all her life. I fought with the lion while she tended the wounded lamb. I couldn't stop the tears. Her cheek touched mine as she thrust a napkin into my hand. I pulled her in tight. After fifty days, I regained control. She tried to take the rest of the photos away, but I pulled them back. Better to face it now. Why put off anguish? I viewed photos of us together or alone and sometimes with my mom—never with my father. I set down the last picture as my mom shoved a small tumbler into my hand. She poured the contents of a flask into my glass and hers.

"I guess if I'm going to fit in, I better learn to drink bourbon."

I sniffed and took a big swallow. She took a smaller one.

"And I do love to read Dickens, though I confess I haven't read Barnaby Rudge or Martin Chuzzlewit."

I smiled and wiped my eyes. "You might still be in the club—but only if you can answer one question. Which book featured Dick Swiveller?"

She thought for a moment then said, "The Old Curiosity Shop."

"You're in. But you don't really need to drink bourbon. Like James, I often drink brandy in the winter."

"Do you like wine?" she asked.

"Yeah. A red, like a Merlot or a Cabernet Sauvignon. A Pinot Noir is a bit too wimpy."

"And wimpy is a big problem for you."

I smiled. "Yeah, like you. I'm engaged to a former linebacker and you want to date a cowboy. I don't know who could be more masculine, maybe a Navy SEAL."

She smiled. "You look tired. We better call for your transportation."

I was tired, but mostly I felt the heaviness of loss. She dialed her cell phone while I took another look at the photos. I needed to go to his grave. It was the very least I could do.

"I don't think Patty likes me," she said as she snapped shut her phone.

"My father was her hero. She's suffering now that the best man she's ever known has fallen off his pedestal. And

238

she's accustomed to tending to me. Make conversation about Wounded Knee or ask about Jackson… that should help."

"She looks up to Jackson."

"Definitely, but she told me he's been married twice, so he's not perfect."

Uncle Bill and Brian were somber when they picked us up. Back at the house, we understood why. My uncle handed me a packet of anonymous letters sent from the Sidney hospital. It took a few lines for me to understand. These were letters of gratitude from the recipients of my father's organs. My mom read one then plopped down hard in a chair. Patty sat in one of chairs with her head in her hands. Kidneys, liver, spleen, pancreas, eyes.

A glass of bourbon appeared before my swimming eyes. Mom and I took big swigs. Brian managed a peaked look, despite having a tan. Uncle Bill was pouring the bourbon, but his face was flushed red. I called James— might as well spread the emotion far and wide. Brian put his hand on my shoulder and his cheek against mine. His touch, his presence comforted me. He didn't try to say anything— he knew better than to talk when there was nothing to say. But I planned to tell Beulah so she could spread the solemn, uplifting news.

My father lived neglecting two lives, but with his death he saved four others.

Chapter 26

I worked my way up to a full day at the firm. In time, I graduated to a walking boot. Later, after a bit of therapy, I was restored to full strength. During the late summer, Brian began taking riding lessons from Uncle Bill. Meanwhile, my mother commuted back and forth from Omaha. I bought her a record player and returned her albums from the attic. James found a golden Labrador-German Shepherd mix, and named him Barnaby. Brian and I came to an agreement that I would stop working at the law firm on Saturdays, except before an early week trial, or in Brian's case, during the tax season push. Consequently, we repaired and redecorated the study and added a second desk. I still worked on Saturdays, just at home. It also became a good day to visit the kids in my divorce and custody cases, and to call upon my injured clients.

In September, Uncle Bill, Brian, and I went to a stable near Kimball and purchased two hardy quarter horses—a black stallion for me and a tall palomino for Brian. We had made arrangements to stable the horses at the McCready ranch until we finished preparations at Uncle Bill's barn. When we got home, the first thing I insisted on was to take the horses to the hills. I took the lead and guided the horses around each of the five Seven Dwarfs, over to Raccoon Creek, around Big Leo and even into the rougher land near Miss Gulch. If these horses were to be ours, they needed to handle the rough land, the bit of Wild West in my life. Of course, we gave them many opportunities to charge across the smoother grassland paths, the preference of humans and horses alike. We rejected horse names like Blackie and Goldie as prosaic. Although we faced no threats from orcs or goblins, we stole from J.R.R. Tolkien by naming my horse Gondor and Brian's steed Rohan.

Later that month, Bill moved into his house. I bought him a new recliner as a house-warming gift. Uncle Bill and Brian hauled my father's old recliner over to the Benson Street apartment for Lew, who was now renting the entire lower level of the house. Patty brought him food and taught him some basic cooking skills. One Saturday, he joined us at the Cowpoke, where he met Beth. She made him twitchier than I'd ever seen him. He and I had a few awkward moments together, with the entire tavern looking on. So, I asked him to dance. It was our version of smoking a peace pipe. He was a better dancer than I expected. I had wondered how he could be a good carpenter when he was so herky-jerky—he must need to have a set pattern for his body and mind to follow.

In October, we made the big trip. Uncle Bill, Beth, Brian, and I traveled to Omaha in the Shark to meet the Simon clan. Beth had been telling stories about her family all summer. I devised a flow chart to keep track of the major players in the big event, one that made my palms sweat from North Platte to Omaha. I'd been around Brian's large family, but this was different, this caused my guts to roil. I packed a huge bottle of Rolaids for a two-day trip.

Except for a ramp in the garage, my mother's house bore little evidence of my brother, apart from pictures of him on the mantle. Surprisingly, there were as many pictures of me as there were of him. I hadn't been forgotten. The tidy ranch house possessed one curiosity—a bedroom door that was never opened. I imagined items pertaining to Scott were stored there. Otherwise, the house belonged to the category of older middle-class houses the suburbs had passed by in its westward expansion. My mother and Scott had moved to this house in Millard, an area southwest of Omaha, eighteen years ago to take advantage of their special education services.

Brian carried in our luggage and deposited it in a guest bedroom, whereas my uncle and mother would shack up in her room. That was strange. Brian kept urging me on to get dressed, for I was dawdling. I smoothed out the few wrinkles in my khakis and laid out my black cashmere sweater. What would they think of me? I was to meet so many people tonight—aunts, uncles, first, second, and third cousins. A few had come from both coasts to meet me. I managed to dress even as cowardice started in my brain and dropped with a thud into my feet. I hoped my tongue wouldn't go to lead, my legs certainly had.

Finally, my mother came in. Only she could appreciate my trauma.

"Megan, I know this is tough, but remember they've always known. It wasn't like me barging into your life. I faced the family lies, and hoped you would still accept me. Your family here knows you were the victim. They've been mad at me all these years. But in their eyes, you're the long lost cousin and niece. Plus, you're the fat cat attorney who killed a lunatic to save yourself. They're gonna love ya. So, just put one foot in front of the other, that's right."

She led me out of the room. I felt like that sheep in the hospital, now on my way to face more trauma.

We were a few minutes late, but I was assured that was okay. We parked in the street near a two-story rector's house, for my Uncle Peter was a Methodist pastor. I ran through the names in my head. Brian held my hand tight. But what did he know? He would be the big-time football player. I had to be—I didn't know what. But I was walking up the driveway, I took deep breaths.

"Oh, by the way," said my mother, "they know about the Aunt Beth thing."

I halted. Shit. I wasn't blameless.

"But hon, I told them it was a plan we all decided on. So it's okay."

Brian placed his hand in the center of my back and gently then more firmly pushed. My legs got going again. Then we were on the porch, then in the house, and then I was in the hugs of my aunts and uncles and cousins. The house reverberated with chatter and laughter. There was a crowd of people in every room in the modest house. Some of my family were tall, some were short, they all had dark hair, though one older cousin didn't get the dark genes are dominant memo—he sported thinning light brown hair. Many possessed the more European skin tone like me, and then there were my uncles, Peter and Paul, and a few cousins who looked like they could've just jumped off a camel. Then I met my aunts, Stephanie and Sophie, who also had the olive skin of Phoenicians. The Simon spouses all possessed a light-skinned European look.

I clenched Brian's hand until we moved to the next room and into a new round of hugs. I grabbed his hand again until a flock of little cousins came to meet us. They were blunt—they referred to me as the "stolen girl," Brian as the "big football player," and Uncle Bill as the "old cowboy." Just as they started with the questions, we were called to dinner. I was delighted to see grilled burgers and hot dogs. I've eaten some Mediterranean food and liked it, but I didn't like hummus. The sight of ketchup and mustard pleased me.

This large group of people laughing and telling stories was mine. In a strange way, it was both traumatizing and pleasing. I engaged in pleasant conversation—the two glasses of Merlot helped. After dinner, while Brian was telling football stories, my aunts and four cousins cornered me and asked for my version of the attack. They said it had made the newspaper in town. I obliged them.

Overwhelmed by the extensive socializing, I was pleased when Uncle Bill suggested it was time to leave. From the look on my mother's face, I could tell she found the evening nearly as exhausting as I did. Plans were made to meet for breakfast before we all would go to the Methodist church to hear my uncle preach.

And I survived it all. I appreciated the support my long lost family gave me. And it was nice to just be me, not the Pocket Docket or the shelf elf. I looked forward to going home—where I belonged. But we had one important stop before we headed west—my brother's grave.

The hilly, multi-acre cemetery was full of winding roads and massive oak, spruce, and maple trees. We parked about a quarter mile in. My mother walked past two rows then paused at a plot. She took the metal vase from the ground and filled it at a nearby pump with water for the flowers she brought. Then I saw it. Scott's granite tombstone was in the exact same style as my father's—right down to the copper color, shape, and font for the letters. A chill ran up my spine. Uncle Bill's jaw slackened.

I slipped a photo out of my purse of him and me as toddlers. Tears dripped off my chin onto my top. For me, time had frozen—I had no appreciation of the trials my mom endured in raising him, nor did I truly understand or accept the action and inaction of my parents. He was my Totty and I was his Mem. He probably never understood why I left his side. I hoped he simply forgot me. In an instant, I knew why I could no longer hear him—he was at peace.

My situation was more complicated—or was it? My father deprived me of a childhood with my mother and separated me from a beloved brother. But I wasn't my father—I was tougher and more loving than him; I wasn't my mother—I was braver and more resolute than her. I would never understand their predicament nor appreciate the full extent of their guilt. But I did know the anger festering inside me harbored sin that blackened by soul.

The truth smacked me so hard I collapsed backwards in the grass. Simple, complete forgiveness was required. I often asked God to forgive my sins, but I hadn't forgiven my mom and dad. God never set demands on the guilty, so neither should I. Seventy times seven. On my own I couldn't do it, but God told me I could then gave me the strength. So I repented and believed and wept with joy. He restored my soul. Scars healed, unconditional love became possible. Forgiveness set me free.